MINDY FORD

PUBLISHED BY FIDELI PUBLISHING, INC.

ISBN: 978-1-60414-943-2

Contributing Editor — Sara Jo Butler
Editing — Karen Ford, Charles Mink, and Robin Surface

For information, please contact
Fideli Publishing, Inc.:
info@fidelipublishing.com
www.FideliPublishing.com

For Karen Ford

My mother, my teacher, my best friend
No one has ever believed in me more.

Special thanks to...

Darren Shell—

My mentor. You were such an inspiration to finally give me hope in shooting for the stars. I would not have pursued this life long dream without you.

Robin Surface—

You made my book come to life and you made my dream come true. Thank you for all of your hard work.

Kaina Makua—

You are a Godsend! Without your help I would have had to change the book drastically.- Mahalo

Karen Ford & Sara Jo Butler—

You are the heart and soul that kept me motivated. All of your hard work has paid off. Thank you for helping me keep my head in the game.

Charles Mink—

Thank you for all of your hard work and patience.

Thank you to all that helped:

Catrina Barnes	Mark Mondello
Leigh Caraway	Michael Mook
Jennifer Dolly	Desireé Page
Karen Dutridge	Denise Pierson
Katie Encalado	Patty Porten Shell
Carey Fornal	Jim Sherman
Becca Hill	Chad Stone
Brande Kahalewai	Sidney Strunk
Angel & Andy Kusmits	Selina Swartz
Paul Markwood	Jolene Wolfenbarger
Taylor Mink	Rachel Workman

Mahalo,
Mindy

Prologue

*D*evan didn't understand why she had to go to dinner with her parents. She didn't even remember this kid they were talking about. She was six years old when they first met and she was 12 now. She told her parents she had better things to do than entertain some dumb boy. However, she realized that no amount of arguing or eye rolling was going to get her out of this one.

Devan and her parents walked into the diner, and her father was greeted with a hug from a tall man who said, "Chris, you look the same, my man!"

Devan saw this man's face all the time in the picture on her dad's desk in his study. It showed her dad, his platoon and Mr. Iakona. Her dad and Mr. Iakona were standing side by side, circled in bright yellow marker.

"This is our little Devan," her dad said and pushed her forward.

Mr. Iakona hugged her and said, "Aloha, Devan! I'm sure you don't remember me. I'm your dad's old Army buddy, Nāhoa, and this is my wife, Cassandra.

"You're in my dad's Army picture, Mr. Iakona," she said and smiled.

"That's right. This is my son, Kale Kai. Do you remember him?" Mr. Iakona said and pushed his son toward her. He was a good-looking kid who was a bit taller than her. He had dark hair, green eyes and sun-kissed skin like his father.

"Hey," she said politely.

"Kale this is Devan Montgomery, and Elaine, her mother, and Chris, her father." Mr. Iakona said, introducing them.

"Isn't Devan a boy's name?" he asked in a snarky tone.

"Isn't Kale a lettuce?"

"Actually, it means *man*," he fired back, arms folded across his chest.

"Oh yeah? Well my mom puts you in her smoothie every morning," Devan countered.

Kale rolled his eyes, "Whatever, *Monty.*"

"What did you just call me?"

Kale grinned, "I think I'll call you Monty from now on. Ha! It still sounds like a boy's name."

"Yeah, whatever, Lettuce Head."

Chapter 1

Hawaii 1994

It was the summer of 1994. I'd just turned 16 and little did I know I was about to embark on a struggle that would last the rest of my life...

"Oh, my god! Mom, how many times do we have to change planes?" Devan grumbled.

Her mom, equally exhausted, replied, "Calm down, Devan! It's a long way to go. We only have to change planes one more time."

Devan was beyond annoyed and fired back, "Seriously? We left yesterday at 7 a.m., and it's now 10 p.m.! Ugh!"

"Okay, okay!" her mom said and sighed, "So, there were a few layovers. Look at it this way, it's only 4 a.m. Hawaiian time. The total trip takes about 17 hours. We're almost there."

Devan rolled her eyes. She was excited to see Hawaii, but she hated all the traveling. *I am so not looking forward to palling around with that Lettuce Head kid! I miss James!* Even though she'd just seen her boyfriend yesterday, she knew she'd miss him because she was going to be stuck in Hawaii for a whole month!

The Iakonas met Devan's family in the hotel lobby for breakfast at 8:30 a.m. the next day. She'd had only two hours of sleep and was still groggy and jetlagged. She threw her dark golden hair into a messy bun and pulled on an old oversized sweatshirt, jean shorts, and flip-flops.

"Hey! How was the flight?" Mrs. Iakona asked with a warm smile as they entered the restaurant.

"You mean flights, plural?" Devan muttered under her breath.

"Aloha, Devan. I didn't see you back there. What a lovely young woman you've become," Mr. Iakona commented.

That was creepy, Devan thought.

Her dad pushed her forward, to the point she almost stumbled. Mr. Iakona grabbed her and hugged her.

"Where's Kale Kai?" her mother asked, looking around.

"He's actually working here at the hotel. How else do you think we got your rooms so cheap?" Mr. Iakona joked.

Yes! she thought. *I won't have to deal with that jerk if he has to work.*

After breakfast she excused herself so she could check out the resort. It was beautiful. There were coconut palms everywhere, as well as small pools, big pools, lagoons, water slides, and the crystal blue Pacific off in the distance. "Hey, Mom, can I walk out to that beach right there?" Devan asked, and pointed in the direction of a few cabanas on the shoreline.

"Sure," her mom replied.

The salty scent of the ocean mixed with the chlorine scent of the pools, the sand and the fragrant native flowers intoxicated her. To say it was beautiful was an understatement. The walk to the beach seemed like it took forever because of all the resort's amenities, but she finally saw an arrow-shaped sign that said: "Beach Straight Ahead."

She headed down the last set of stone steps, and then it happened. Her left flip-flop broke and she tripped on the second to last step. "Damn it!" she exclaimed, as she was stopped mid-fall by something hard.

"Whoa, you okay?" the guy who'd caught her asked. He steadied her and helped her down the final step onto the sand, with Devan's face smashed against his warm chest the whole time.

That was his chest I hit? she realized in awe as she looked up. He smelled of sunscreen, coconut and lime, the scents swirling all around her. "I'm so sorry! My stupid shoe broke and—"

He leaned down to get a closer look at her. "But you're okay?"

"Uh, yes," she stammered. "Thank you. I'm sorry to have, uh fallen for— on you. I mean *on* you." *Smooth, Devan. Could that have been more embarrassing?*

He chuckled. "Here, why don't you sit down over here for minute." He reached for a cabana chair and offered it to her.

Devan sat down, while trying to get a good look at her beautiful rescuer. The sun was too bright to see his features clearly, but she could tell he was gorgeous. He had to be at least 6'3," and anywhere from 16 to 20 years old. He had bronze skin and dark brown hair that was shorter on the sides and back and slightly longer on top. He seemed muscular, but wasn't built like a gym-rat. *Definitely not bad.*

He reached for another chair and sat down next to her.

Devan finally spoke up and said, "I really am sorry for interrupting your swim."

"Well, I wish I'd been swimming; but I'm working. Plus, to interrupt me swimming, I think I'd have to have been in the water." He laughed and gave her a quick wink.

She was so embarrassed. "Oh, duh! Sorry," she said and blushed, which made him smile. *Wow, that's some smile!* "So, am I interrupting your work?"

"Not really. I'm a lifeguard at the resort, and technically I don't start guarding until 10. They have us 'teens' clean up the beach before we start our shifts. Low men on the totem pole and all," he said, and laughed.

"That sucks," she said turning up her nose.

"Not today. The beach is pretty clean and I got to rescue a beautiful girl."

Devan stood up then, embarrassed. "Well, I'll let you get back to it." She turned to walk away, paused, then turned back to face him. "Thank you again for rescuing me." She gave him a shy smile and turned to walk away.

"Hey, wait. Come on back and sit with me for a while. I have another 30 minutes before I have to go back to work up to my lagoon."

She paused before asking, "Are you sure?"

He grinned at her. "Yeah, and you're welcome."

I could stare at his smile and chest all day! James who? She was so lost in her daze she didn't even hear him talking to her.

"Hey, you there?"

When she didn't respond immediately, he laughed.

"Huh?" she shook the fog from her brain, "Oh, I'm sorry. What?"

Kale asked again, "I haven't seen you here. Did you just get in?"

"Yes," she answered quickly.

"How long are you here for?"

"A while," she said and shrugged.

He smiled again, "A while, huh?"

Still somewhat lost in her thoughts, Devan replied with a simple, "Yeah." She couldn't wipe the stupid smile off her face.

He reached out his hand and said, "By the way, I'm Kai."

She shook his hand and said, "I'm Dee."

"Nice to meet you, Dee. Where are you from?"

"Ohio. You?"

"Hawaii," he said and laughed.

Devan blushed again. "Oh, right. Duh!" *Oh, my God, quit being stupid Devan! Use your brain!*

"Actually that was a good question. A lot of the people who work here are from the mainland."

"So how old are you, Kai?"

"I'm 19. How old are you?"

She thought quickly. "Eighteen — I'm 18." Devan didn't want to lose his interest if she was too young. *Why ruin a good thing by being too young, right?*

They talked for a while longer and Kai offered to walk Devan back up to the resort.

"Well, I have to go guard some lives now."

"Thanks again."

"Anytime," he said, as he bent down to kiss her cheek. The scents of the sunscreen, coconuts and lime hit her again.

"Aloha, Dee."

"Aloha, Kai."

Kai took several steps in the direction of the pool, then stopped. "Hey!" he called back to her, "if you're free tonight, meet me at the luau. It's at six."

"Okay," she answered with a smile.

Kai turned and jogged off toward the pool.

Devan stood there and watched him disappear up the hill. *Did that really just happen?* "He totally makes 17-hours on a plane worth it!" she said aloud for the birds to hear. With a smile on her face, she walked away to lose herself in the sun and sand.

Chapter 2

The Iakonas were already seated at the table when Devan sat down beside her mother. Just then, another person joined them.

"Kale, how nice to see you, son," her dad said and shook the young man's hand.

"Ugh," she groaned searching the crowd looking for Kai.

"Kale's here Devan. Say hello," her mother said and elbowed her.

"Hi," she said as she reached across the table to shake his hand without looking. She was still looking across the sea of faces for Kai. Because she wasn't paying the slightest bit of attention, her extended hand managed to knock over a glass of water. Ice-cold water ran off the table and landed in her lap. "Damn it!" she shrieked.

"Devan Marie! Language!" her mother warned.

Devan blushed. "Sorry!" She pushed back her chair and stood up from the table to go dry off.

"Kale will show you where the outside restrooms are, sweetheart," Mr. Iakona said.

Devan tried to wave him off. "It's okay, I'm sure I can find my way." She didn't want to deal with him and this embarrassing situation.

Kale stood and said, "No, it's fine. I'll take you." He moved to help her and their eyes locked.

"You?" they said in unison.

"What's going on, guys?" Mrs. Iakona asked.

"Nothing, um ... we'll be right back." Kale took Devan by the arm and led her toward the restrooms.

"You said your name was Dee!"

Devan fired back, "Um, it's a nickname, stupid. *You* said *your* name was Kai!"

"It's my middle name! I can't tell girls my name is Kale the first time I meet them. I don't need them thinking my parents named me after a leafy green vegetable," he replied with a sinister grin.

With her hand on her hip, she said "Yeah? Well you said you were 19—"

"And *you* said you were *18!*" Kale folded his arms and jerked his head to the side, "Restroom's right there. I'll wait for you."

"Don't bother! I'll be just *fine!*" Devan barked at him, and walked away in a huff.

Kale snickered as she walked away. Devan's sundress was white and the neon pink bikini she was wearing under it was *extremely* visible thanks to the water.

"What are you laughing at?" she snarled.

"Oh, nothing. I'm just admiring your bright pink panties," he said and chuckled again.

"Jerk, it's a bikini!" *He's such an ass! Ugh, and to think I was supposed to have a date with this guy. No way that's happening now!*

Devan had been in the restroom for a good five minutes, before Kale decided to knock on the door. "What's taking so long? We're going to miss dinner!"

"I told you not to wait," she hissed.

"Come on, let's go!"

"I can't! I'm still wet."

"It will dry. Let's go!"

"Why, so everyone can see my pink butt? Kai...Kale — whatever the hell your name is — I don't think so!"

He laughed. "Come on, I'll give you my shirt. It's long enough to cover you."

"Um, no," Devan said rolling her eyes. "You ever hear of 'no shoes, no shirt, no service'?"

"Devan, it's fine, I swear. I have a tank on under my shirt. A boy scout is always prepared," he said and laughed again.

"*You* weren't a boy scout," she said as she walked out.

He took a nice long look at her. *She's beautiful. She looks a lot different than I remember. Her hair's long now, and her eyes seem a lighter shade of blue than before. The thick glasses she used to wear probably hid them last time I saw her.*

He unbuttoned his shirt and gave it to her. She shoved her arms into the sleeves and Kale smiled. "See, I told you it was long enough. It looks like a dress on you."

She wasn't listening. Instead she was checking out his broad shoulders and muscular arms.

"Are you ready to go back and eat?"

"Huh?" she snapped her head up and met his eyes. "Oh, yeah. Thank you — for the shirt I mean."

After dinner, Devan and her family headed back to their hotel room. After they got there, Devan sat on the bed thinking maybe Kale wasn't as bad as she first thought. *He's definitely not bad to look at, that's for damn sure!* Just as she thought this, her mom sat down on the bed beside her. "My goodness, Kale has grown into a very nice-looking young man. Hasn't he?" she asked and smiled.

Devan rolled her eyes but agreed without saying it.

"It was kind of him to give you his shirt. Don't you think?"

Devan couldn't help but smile. She could still smell the lingering scent of Nautica around the shirt's collar, "Yeah, it was."

As soon as her mom walked away, Devan pulled the shirt closer to her nose, closed her eyes and breathed in his scent.

After washing her face and removing her contacts, she climbed into bed and inhaled Kale's scent from the shirt one more time before she closed her eyes.

The next morning, Devan woke to a loud pounding on her hotel room door. She rubbed the sleep out of her eyes and looked around for her glasses. When she got to the door, she looked through the peephole.

"Come on, Devan, open the door! I just saw your eyeball in the peephole, and I can hear you breathing," Kale said and laughed.

"Hold on," she said quickly taking her glasses off.

She unlocked the door and Kale walked in carrying a tray filled with mouthwatering pastries and fresh fruit.

"Hungry?" he asked as he set the tray on the table in front of her.

She squinted to see what was there, and grabbed a croissant. She took a bite and exclaimed, "Oh, my god! This is the best thing I've ever tasted!"

Kale smiled. "They're baked fresh from scratch every morning."

This is giving me a food-gasm! It practically melts in my mouth. With a mouth full of croissant Devan asked suspiciously, "Wait! Why are you here?"

He grabbed a doughnut off the tray and said, "Your parents are at my house helping my parents pack. They wanted to let you sleep in, so they told me to come get you and show you around the island."

At that moment Devan squealed in embarrassment. She just remembered she was still in his shirt. She dropped the croissant, and stumbled around looking for her bag.

"Are you drunk? What are you doing?" he asked.

"No, I'm not drunk! I don't have my contacts in," which was true, but wasn't the reason she was acting so crazy.

Just before the bathroom door slammed shut, Kale yelled, "Make sure to put a suit on underneath your clothes!"

She cracked open the door. "What?"

From where he was sitting he could see her reflection in the mirror. "Um ... bathing suit," he said trying to catch a peek of something interesting.

"Bathing suit?" she asked and gave him a confused look.

He couldn't see much from this angle, but it was enough. Kale shouted, "Put one on."

"Okay," she said and shut the bathroom door, disappointing him.

Kale held open the passenger side door of his Jeep for Devan and helped her in.

He got in the driver's side, and asked with a smirk, "Are you ready?"

"I think so," she replied.

He winked at her and they sped off.

Devan lost herself in the beauty of the island. She watched the tall grasses dance as they flew by the hills along the winding road. She admired the coconut trees and could smell the salty air from the Pacific. They drove for about 20 minutes before Kale pulled off onto an unmarked road.

"Where are we going?" she questioned.

"You'll see," he said mysteriously and winked again.

Kale parked the Jeep and Devan looked around. *Well, this is nothing special.*

"From here, we walk," he said, interrupting her thoughts.

It wasn't a long walk, but the path was rocky. He stopped near a large moss covered boulder, pulled his shirt off and handed her a pair of water shoes. "Get undressed. We're going in."

"In where?" She still didn't see anything but rocks, and the ocean was quite a ways off in the distance.

"Come on," he said, and walked away.

"I don't see anything," she almost whined.

"You will."

The two of them rounded a corner and the view that came into sight was the most beautiful thing she'd ever seen. "Here's Ole Blue. Well, that's what I call it. Its real name is Nani Mau Loa. In English that means forever beautiful," he said.

"I can see why."

"The water here is cooler than the ocean but it's not cold. Most tourists don't know about this little gem," he said proudly.

They slipped into the water. It was a little chilly for her liking, but she didn't care. The water was crystal clear, and she could see little fish swimming around them. "This is *so* awesome!"

"You wanna see something even better?" He took her by the hand and led her into what appeared to be a small cave. It was dark, but she could see a blue light in the distance.

When they reached the light she saw it was coming from a small opening in the roof of the cave. The sun beamed down onto the blue water and created a gorgeous glow. She couldn't find words to describe how beautiful it truly was. The blue glow touched everything around her — even Kale, who was smiling at her.

"See why I call it Ole Blue?" he asked.

At that moment his smile was all she could see. *I could stare at him all day. He really is a piece of work. His green eyes...*

She felt herself moving closer to him. He looked down at her lips and she looked up at his. His hand emerged from the water and barely touched her cheek as he moved a strand of her hair away from her face. Her lips were begging to be kissed.

"Sorry, that's been bothering me," he said, as their eyes met and time stood still.

"*Next!*" he shouted, and took her by the hand again.

I could've sworn he was going to kiss me, but no. It was the perfect place — romantic and beautiful! The perfect moment! Just...Ugh! Well, he ruined that, she thought as he dragged her to their next adventure.

Chapter 3

"We're going cliff jumping!" Kale shouted.

"Excuse me? " Devan couldn't hide the shocked look on her face.

Kale pulled the old black Jeep into a small parking lot, parked and got out. Devan didn't move from her seat and just stared at him as he walked around the front of the Jeep to her door. He reached across her lap to unbuckle her seat belt.

"Yeah, no offense, Kale, but I think I'll sit this one out."

He didn't give her a chance to argue, and practically dragged her to the cliffs. She heard screaming and giggling off in the distance as they rounded the final corner in the path.

Kale took Devan's hand and said, "Look! It's safe! See that kid over there?"

"Yeah?" she said, hesitantly.

"He is my neighbor's nephew —he's seven. Are you going to let a seven year old be cooler than you?" he asked with a smirk.

Devan watch as the child jumped from the cliff like he'd been doing it his whole life.

"The natives have been coming here for years, and only one person ever died."

"Yeah, until today! You're trying to *kill* me!"

Kale took her by her shoulders and leaned down to look into her eyes, "You're safe with me. Okay? We'll jump together."

With no warning Kale dropped his hand to hers and ran to the edge of the cliff and jumped! They plunged feet first into the crystal blue water, holding hands the whole way down.

"See?" he said when they surfaced. "You're always safe with me."

Devan was smiling so big it hurt her face, "That was awesome! Let's do it again!"

Kale helped her out of the water and they walked back up to the top of the cliffs.

"This time I'm going on my own," she said to him with a smile.

He raised an eyebrow. "Ladies first!"

Devan ran and jumped. When she surfaced, Kale yelled down to her, "How was it this time?"

"Incredible!"

Just then, someone ran passed Kale and jumped from the cliff's edge. *"No!"* he yelled, but it was too late. The teenaged boy landed on top of Devan, kicking her in the back of the head in the process and forcing her deep under water.

Devan was sent spiraling downward, and she couldn't tell up from down. She struggled to reach the surface as Kale jumped from the cliff and began searching for her.

Shit! Where is she? He saw something shimmer in the water. Devan's ankle bracelet had caught the light just enough for Kale to see it.

When he brought her to the surface, she was unconscious and she wasn't breathing.

He swam her to shore and carried her a few steps before laying her down in the rough sand and immediately began CPR. "One, two, three, four, five," he counted as he pumped her chest.

"Breathe, Devan!" he yelled as he pinched her nose closed, tilted her head back and blew air into her lungs. Nothing. "Shit, Devan, *breathe!*"

He continued CPR and got no results. He felt for a pulse. It was weak, but it was there. "Come on Devan! One... two..."

Devan began coughing up water and Kale turned her on her side. She slowly opened her eyes and looked at him. "Oh, thank God!" he cried, resting his head on her arm.

"I don't want to *ever* do that again," she choked out.

He chuckled, both out of fear and relief. "Yeah, I don't think you're going to be a champion cliff diver now."

Devan put her hand on his chest. His heart was beating so hard she thought it might burst. "Thank you."

He laughed nervously then asked, "For what? Letting you get hurt after I just said you were safe with me?"

"I *was* safe with you —just not on my own. It's okay, though. You saved me," she said, looking up at him with eyes full of sincerity and trust. "Maybe we shouldn't tell my mom about this."

Kale laughed with a little more ease. "Yeah, maybe we shouldn't!"

I shouldn't have let her jump on her own, Kale chastised himself. *I can't stand the thought of losing her. Wow! Where'd that come from?*

◈◈◈

"It went through — we got the house!" Nāhoa, Kale's father exclaimed.

"That's great! Now you don't have to rent," Devan's mother said.

"This calls for a celebration! Where's the champagne?"

"I'll get it," Kale said.

He walked back into the dining room and started to twist the cork.

"No, I got it, son," Nāhoa said, reaching for the bottle.

"So, I guess we're going to be neighbors," Kale said and smacked Devan on the back.

"Huh?"

"The Iakonas bought the Price's house," her mother told her.

"You mean the house right next door?"

"Yep!" Kale said with a smile.

Devan wasn't sure exactly what to think about this latest development, but she sure did like the idea of having some alone time with Kale.

"This is really great Nāhoa! Hey, do you play football?" Devan's father asked Kale.

Nāhoa laughed. "Does he play football? Have you looked at my son? He takes after his Mākua kāne!" he chuckled. "Yes, he plays football."

"Father," Kale whispered in Devan's ear.

"What?"

"Mākua kāne is 'father' in Hawaiian," Kale explained.

"That's great!" her mother said. "When we get home, Devan will introduce you to James. Practice has already started, but I bet he can still get you on the team."

Devan screamed in her head, *Oh, my God — James! I completely forgot about him! I haven't thought about him since I laid eyes on Kale.*

"Sounds great," Kale agreed. "Who's James?"

Devan's father, Chris, started to explain, but Devan abruptly cut him off. "My friend. Uh ... he's my friend," she stammered.

Devan's father didn't take the hint and continued, "Oh, stop being bashful, sweetheart. He's her boyfriend *and* captain of the football team. Got one hell of an arm, too."

Kale raised an eyebrow at her.

Well this is just shit-tastic! How am I going to get out of this one? Lie! Yep, I'll lie long enough to get Kale on the team and I'll figure out the rest later. "No, Dad! James and I ... we broke up. We're friends *only* now."

"Well, I'm excited to meet this James. I'm sure it will be interesting," Kale said while raising his eyebrow again and cocking his head at her.

Great, he doesn't believe me.

"He's a really good kid. He's a senior and a little arrogant, but he treated my daughter well. Why'd you break up?"

Is this really happening? Oh, my God, Dad! Will you leave it alone already?" "Because, Dad, uh ... he decided football was more important than me." *There is a fair amount of truth to that, and James is extremely arrogant.* The more she thought about James, the more she realized she didn't even like him anymore.

James the Terrible

Devan and her family hadn't been in their home a full 20 minutes before the phone started ringing.

"Hello?" Devan said into the receiver.

"Oh, my God — *finally!* I knew you were getting home today but didn't know when. I've been calling for hours!"

"Kristy, take a breath, please! What's up?" Kristy was one of her best friends. She loved her dearly, but the girl was hyper and extremely dramatic.

Kristy took a deep breath and said, "Okay...um, I don't know how to say this other than to just say it. James cheated on you with Ashli Carmichael! Like, I saw them with my own two eyes — *saw them!*"

"Wait. What?" exclaimed Devan.

"James cheated—" Kristy began.

"Kristy! No, wait." Devan sighed. "I heard what you said. I thought she was my best friend! That slut!"

"Um, no. Okay, no! *I'm* your best friend, and *yes*, she is a *slut!*"

Hold on, Devan thought, *boyfriend problem solved!*

Just then, the doorbell rang.

"Devan, you have company," she heard her mom call from downstairs. Devan looked out her bedroom window and saw James standing at the front door. *Oh, Christ! He's standing on the front porch with a bouquet of white roses 30 seconds after I find out he cheated on me!* Movement caught her attention and she looked beyond James to see the Iakonas rented van and their moving truck pulling into their new driveway. *Shit! Boyfriend problem not solved!*

Devan cringed and said, "Sorry, Kristy, I gotta go!" and hung up the phone without giving her a chance to say goodbye.

She ran downstairs, opened the front door and stepped onto the porch. James handed her the roses and kissed her cheek, "I missed you, babe! Can I come in?"

Devan pushed him toward the garage, where they could talk in private.

James leaned in and tried to kiss her, but Devan took a step back and dodged the kiss.

"What's wrong, babe?" he asked with a furrowed brow.

Her hands on her hips she hissed, "Is there anything you'd like to tell me, *babe?*"

"Yeah, I missed you and I love you," James answered as he leaned in for another attempt at a kiss.

Devan side-stepped that one too and continued, "That's funny! Is that what you said to *Ashli?*"

"What're you talking about?"

"Well, let's see. Did you tell *Ashli* how much you missed me and how much you loved me while you were shoving your tongue down her throat?" Devan gritted her teeth as she waited for his answer.

"You were gone for a whole month, that's like 35 days!" James bellowed and threw his arms up in defeat.

Devan rolled her eyes and shoved the roses into his chest. "James, you can take these and shove them up your—"

"Hey, you must be James," Kale said as he towered over the feuding couple. Devan hadn't seen Kale walk up and jumped in surprise at the sound of his voice.

"And you are?" James questioned.

While Kale was built like a Greek god and had a good six inches on him, James was less than impressed. Then again he was the type who thought he was God's gift to the world.

"I'm Kale, the boy next door," he said with a snicker.

"You expect me to believe you're a *boy?*" James asked mockingly.

"Uh yeah, man. I just turned 17." Kale nodded his head to the right, "My folks and I are moving in next door. So, anyway, I hear you play football."

Oh, Lord, here it comes, Devan thought, shaking her head. *The monster is about to be unleashed.*

"Play?" James scoffed, "You hear I *play* football? Son, I don't *play* football. I eat, I drink, I sleep, and I *breathe* football! I'm the *captain* of the Erie Central Tigers! Grrr!"

Devan tried to keep from laughing and thought, *Did he really just growl and flex? Well, that's embarrassing.*

"Okay, man," Kale chuckled. *This guy's an idiot. How does a 5'10", medium built guy make captain of the team?*

"So, anyway ... I'm pretty good at sports. Any chance you could get me a tryout?"

James circled Kale and looked him up and down like he was some kind of show horse. "Yeah, we could use someone like you on the team. Offense or defense?"

"Both," Kale answered proudly.

"Okay, yeah. Have Dee drop you off at the field tomorrow at 10 a.m."

"Thanks," Kale said and walked away.

"So, Dee, will you bring him by tomorrow or what?"

"Sure," she said rolling her eyes.

"Awesome, see ya tomorrow," James said and gave her a sloppy wet kiss.

Devan screamed, "Ew, *gross!* Hey, you can take these and shove them up your ass!" she screamed at him, shaking the flowers.

James stood by his open car door and calmly said, "Nah, babe, they're for you! You're my GF and don't go forgetting it." Then he had the nerve to wink at her.

"I am *nothing* to you!" Devan screamed and threw the flowers at his car as he backed out of the driveway.

"And there are *not* 35 days in a month, *dumbass!*" she yelled, and then turned around to head back to the house. Instead, she smacked right into Kale's chest.

Kale! Ugh! Bumping into him is like running into a brick wall, but dammit he smells so good. That crisp, clean and intriguing scent of Nautica just does something to me.

"Oh, sorry!" he apologized while steadying her with one hand on each of her shoulders. "I didn't mean for you to run into me." He smiled and said, "So, James, your um boyfriend, sure seems cool."

She gritted her teeth for the second time that day and thought, *God he is such a smart ass!* "He's *not* my boyfriend!"

Kale turned and headed toward his yard. "Maybe you should tell him that," he called over his shoulder.

"Damn it! I did!" Devan huffed.

Chapter 4

Funny Man Kale, July 1994

Kale and Devan pulled into the parking lot next to the practice field the next morning. "Well, here we are," she said as they walked toward the field. "I hope you're as good as your dad said. I'll wait for you over here."

Devan turned and walked over to the bleachers. Kale started to run onto the field, then changed his mind. Instead, he turned to face her and jogged backwards so he could talk to her.

With a smile he said, "I'm not good, I'm grrreat."

That smile kills me! She rolled her eyes and said, "Whatever!"

James greeted Kale with a high five. "Sup, bro?"

"Hey, where do I gear up?" Kale asked.

"Over there, and then the coach wants to meet you."

Devan watched Kale's every move as he got ready, then continued to stare as the coach spoke to him. When he ran out onto the field, he moved like a panther — sleek and agile. *Damn, he's sexy!*

Coach Davis blew his whistle and hollered, "All right, listen up. This is Kale Iakona. He's from the Aloha state. For the more academically challenged players among you, that's Hawaii. He wants to try out for the team, and he asks that you not hold back. I think we should have a quick scrimmage. Kale and James, pick your teams."

"Coach, James has an unfair advantage over the new guy. You want to give him a fair shot, right?"

The coach patted the kid on the back. "Good point, Pete. You pick their teams." Pete Monahan was a sophomore like Devan and Kristy. He was about 6'1" with a medium build and blond hair. He was fast and accurate — definitely one of the better players on the team, and Kristy had a huge crush on him.

Teams were picked. "Shirts and skins!" Coach said pointing to the separate teams.

As Kale started taking off his shirt, Devan was mesmerized just like the time in Hawaii. *It's like he's moving in slow motion — that chest, those abs, those arms…they just don't make 17 year olds like that around here. I wish I could rewind that and play it about a million times.* Devan was deep in the moment and didn't notice her friend sitting down next to her.

"Who is *that* marvelous wonder?" Kristy asked, her tongue practically hanging out of her mouth.

"*That* is Kale Iakona," Devan answered with a sigh.

"No way!" Kristy exclaimed, "*The* Kale? The guy you were stuck with for a month?"

"Yep, and now he's my next door neighbor," Devan said and smiled.

Kristy shoved Devan's shoulder, "You lucky bitch!"

Devan laughed. *I am lucky,* she thought as she watched Kale's team kick butt. She couldn't wait to tell Kristy everything, but right now she wanted to enjoy the scenery. Apparently, Kristy did too.

"So, maybe tomorrow you can invite me and him over to your pool and introduce us?" Kristy elbowed Devan.

"What about Pee-eet?" Devan said his name as though it had two syllables.

"Yeah, yeah, invite him, too," Kristy replied, no longer paying attention because a fight was about to break out between Kale and James.

"Jesus, man! You about broke my arm when you tackled me!" James yelled at him.

Kale helped him up and apologized. James was irritated with the new guy, and he had no problem letting his arrogant side out.

"Hey, coach. I have an idea. Let's see if K-man here can throw." James popped off as he threw the ball like a big shot. It landed near the 30-yard line.

Coach threw another ball to Kale and he caught it easily. Kale positioned his fingers along the ball's laces, pulled his arm back and fired.

"Forty-five yards, Coach," Pete said, impressed.

Coach was impressed as well. "Damn, that kid has a good arm," he said to the offensive coordinator and quarterback coach.

"What're your stats?" Coach asked, knowing they'd be decent.

"Six-four, 235," Kale answered.

"You work out?"

"Every day, sir — bench 250."

Devan couldn't believe her ears. She looked at Kristy with amazement, "That's like 110 pounds more than me."

Kristy nodded. She couldn't believe it either. "That's *hot!*"

"What else can you do, Hawaii?" the coach asked, intrigued.

Devan thought this was a good sign. If Coach gave a kid a nickname this fast, it had to mean he was a shoe-in for the team.

"I can run, kick, and tackle, as you have seen," Kale replied, as James rolled his eyes.

"What all did you do in Hawaii?" the Offensive Coordinator asked.

"Swimming, volleyball, wrestling, football, and I was a lifeguard."

James snickered, "Oh yeah? Save anyone, asshole?"

Kale turned to face James, "Yeah, a few people. Your girlfriend was one of them — had to give her mouth to mouth, too."

The rest of the team began to laugh and give James a hard time. Kristy's mouth dropped open and she looked at Devan, who didn't say a word. She didn't have to — she'd turned a lovely shade of crimson.

James threw a punch aimed at Kale's jaw, but Kale caught his fist. Looking James in the eye, he said, "Hey, man, I was just doing my job. No harm done." He looked over, made eye contact with Devan in the bleachers, and winked.

Coach stepped between the guys and said, "All right, boys, if you can't get along you'll be running laps 'til you puke." Then, he slapped Kale on the back and said, "Welcome to the team, Hawaii."

Pete and Kale became pretty good friends over the next few weeks. They were together at practice, workouts and even got in trouble together. Like the day Pete found an old mask and thought it would be hilarious to frighten Devan. The boys thought it would be funny to pop up in her bathroom window wearing the mask. She'd just turned on the radio and stepped into the shower after helping the Iakonas move.

"Okay, Pete, hold the ladder," Kale ordered with a whisper as he looked in the window. He couldn't believe his eyes. Devan was dancing in the shower — well it looked more like a strip tease to his hormonal teenage mind! The shower curtain was frosted, so he was only able to make out her silhouette, but he could tell that she was shaking her hips and tracing her hand up her wet body and across her breasts. The rest he left to his imagination.

"Hey, do you at least see some side boob?" Pete asked.

"Shhhh," Kale said, waving at him to be quiet.

Devan continued singing and started running a red washcloth up her legs in a suggestive manner.

"Dude are you gonna scare her or not?" Pete whispered loudly.

"Shut up, Pete!" Kale hissed.

Devan thought she heard something and froze. She slowly turned her head toward the window and let out a blood-curdling scream. Kale was so startled that he lost his footing, and he, Pete and the ladder ended up on the ground.

"Dude! What the hell was that?" Pete asked rubbing his arm.

Kale stood up and was trying to brush the freshly cut grass off his shirt when he felt a hard slap on his right cheek. "Ouch!"

"Ouch!" Pete exclaimed a second later.

Devan stood there with her hair wrapped in a towel and another towel wrapped around her dripping wet body. "You two are *assholes!* I hope you liked what you saw!" she yelled at them and then stormed back around to the front of the house.

"Oh, I did," Kale muttered as he watched those long legs stomp off.

There were only a few weeks left before school started. The Iakonas were over at the Montgomery's for a small cookout and they were trying to plan a last-minute trip.

"What about the lake in Tennessee?" Chris suggested.

"That's a great idea! It's been a few years since we've been there. If I remember right, they have all different size cabins. I'm pretty sure they have one that would sleep six," Devan's mom, Elaine, said enthusiastically.

Devan was sunning herself and acting like she wasn't listening to the conversation. She had her earphones on but had them turned off so she could eavesdrop.

"What all is there to do at the lake?" Cassandra, Kale's mom, asked.

"Well we could rent a cabin and a boat for the week. We can ski, tube, and they probably have WaveRunners this year, too."

"Oh, that does sound fun." Cassandra smiled.

"It's no Hawaii, but it'll be great. The kids will love it, and Nāhoa and I can go fishing. I can show him what it's like to fish in fresh water," Chris said happily.

Devan smiled and thought, *This could be fun.*

Cold water suddenly dripped onto her leg. "What the—" she said just as Kale dumped a large bucket of ice on her and ran. Devan threw a handful of ice at him and then chased after him.

"Think they can get along for a whole week?" Elaine asked, half seriously.

"I think anything is possible," Cassandra said and laughed.

Chapter 5

The Lake, August 1994

Their families were having a great time at the lake. Kale and Devan's relationship had become slightly more flirtatious, but Kale was still mischievous.

One day, as Devan walked by him, he pulled one of the strings holding her bikini top on. She squealed and managed to cover herself without flashing anyone.

Another time, Devan was lying on the dock, getting a tan. She'd fallen asleep on her stomach and Kale thought it would be a good idea to get a pair of scissors and cut the strings to her bikini top.

He also replaced her hair detangling spray with SunIn, which turned her hair white blonde like it was when she was a little girl. He was actually quite pleased with himself on that one because she looked even hotter as a platinum blonde.

Kale wasn't the only troublemaker though. Devan quietly slipped into the water while Kale was fishing from the dock. She tugged on his fishing line a few times and made him think he'd caught a big one! Instead, when he reeled it in, there was one of his brand new Nike high tops hooked through the laces. Needless to say, Kale was disappointed and pretty mad.

She also took a few of the worms out of his bait box and put them in the swimming trunks he was going to wear that day. The two were walking down the hill from the cabin to get into the boat when he felt something odd in his shorts.

"Ugh, what is that?" he asked as he dug at his shorts trying to not look too obvious. Something was going on down there and he did not like it. Devan began laughing hysterically at Kale as he danced around grabbing at his shorts.

Kale ran into the water where no one could see him and pulled his shorts off to have a better look at was going on. *"Devan!"* he yelled and threw a worm at her.

Devan's laughter quickly turned to shrieks. "Ew, ew, ew! It's in my hair!" she screamed, combing anxiously through her hair with her fingers.

"What is going on?" Chris asked, confused.

"Dad, Kale threw a worm in my hair!"

"Kale Kai!" Nāhoa scolded his son.

"Well, she put them in my shorts! See?" he said throwing the trunks onto the dock at his dad's feet.

Devan raced over, grabbed his shorts and ran up the hill, laughing. "They're mine now!" she yelled over her shoulder. Kale ran out of the water and across the sand chasing her back up the hill toward the cabin, all the while trying to keep his man parts covered.

Kale's dad shook his head, "Why didn't he just ask for a towel?"

Devan screamed when she saw him coming after her and threw the shorts at him. He caught them with his free hand and stopped to slide them on.

She kept running and tried desperately to dodge him, but Kale was too quick for her. He caught up to her easily and picked her up, threw her over his shoulder while she screamed and kicked with all her might, and then threw her in the lake. She came up sputtering water and laughing.

Their parents laughed as they watched the horseplay. "Cassandra, if I'm not mistaken, I think they like each other," Elaine said.

"I think you're right, Elaine."

The practical jokes on that trip stopped after Nāhoa and Chris ended up with blue teeth. Kale and Devan both had the brilliant idea to put a little bit of blue food coloring on what they thought were each other's toothbrushes. Because the bristles were already a light blue they thought no one would notice until it was too late.

Needless to say, their fathers weren't too happy with them, but their mothers got a kick out of it and laughed every time the men flashed their blue teeth.

There were a few sweet moments during the trip as well. Kale's dad gave him permission to rent a WaveRunner, and he came back to the cabin and threw Devan her ski vest.

"Come on, Monty, let's grab some waves!" She was surprised, because she thought for sure he was going solo.

He was a gentleman a few times too — helping her in and out of the boat, carrying her stuff for her and just being a generally nice guy. Kale was nothing like James and she found that refreshing.

One evening after the dinner dishes had been washed, dried and put away, Kale and Devan were sitting on the front stoop watching the lightening-ing bugs.

"So, what are you going to be when you grow up?" Kale asked out of the blue.

"When I grow up—" she started. After a brief pause she continued, "I'm going to be a screenwriter."

"Wow. That's not what I expected at all."

"What did you expect?"

Kale raised his arm up slowly while pretending to yawn and rested his wrist on her shoulder. She looked at his hand then back at his face and laughed, "Smooth move, Ex-Lax!"

He ignored her comment and looked down into her eyes, "I thought you'd be a weather girl."

She burst out laughing and elbowed him in the ribs, "Do I really seem that shallow?"

"What makes you think weather girls are shallow?" he asked, feigning offense.

Devan smiled up at him and scooted just a little closer. "Well, what are *you* going to be?"

Kale dropped the smile and put on his serious face. "Well, if you're going to be a famous writer and get rich, I guess I'll marry you and be a professional trophy husband!" He gave her a quick peck on her cheek and stood up. He leaned down and reached for her hands and helped her to her feet.

"Nah! You aren't gonna mooch off this chick!"

Kale got serious again, "I'm just kidding. I don't exactly know what I want to do yet."

Devan looked up at his long dark eyelashes and full lips. She moved closer to him. "Well, you could always..." she said as she stood on her tip toes so she could be closer to his face, while he lowered his head toward hers at the same time. He looked like he had every intention of kissing her when the cabin door suddenly opened.

"Oh! It's just you guys. I thought I heard a noise," Cassandra said and she closed the door.

Kale and Devan sheepishly turned away from each other.

Thanks for the buzz kill, mom.

The next day didn't go quite as Devan planned. She'd decided to make Kale jealous by making some new guy friends.

Kale wanted to go diving and was hoping she'd like to tag along, but he couldn't find her anywhere. With dive masks in hand, he headed down to the marina. He found her hanging out with some guys in the parking lot, strutting her stuff.

One of the guys picked her up and set her on his motorcycle. Kale thought the dude had to be at least 21 — too old to be flirting with Devan. He walked over to the group of men to introduce himself, and Devan rolled her eyes at his approach.

"Hey, man, check this guy out. He's an overgrown Cherokee or something!" the guy in a sleeveless t-shirt said.

"This your boyfriend, sweet cheeks?" the guy she was flirting with asked.

"No," Kale answered for her, "more like her *big* brother."

Well that pisses me off! Devan thought. *Here I am trying to get more attention from him — the jealous kind — and he plays the overly protective brother card. What the hell?*

The object of Devan's flirtations continued, "Well, Tonto, your little sister has agreed to go on a ride with me. That okay with you?"

Kale smirked and replied, "Actually no. You see, she's only 16, and I'm guessing you're a bit older than that. Also, I'm Hawaiian not some fictitious Native American."

The man stepped quickly away from Devan, saying, "Oh, darlin', shame on you. You said you were 19."

"Thanks a lot!" she said getting off of the bike and giving Kale a shove as she walked by. "I wanted to go for a ride!"

"Oh, baby, I'll give you a ride. Why don't you climb up on this?" one of the other guys said while grabbing his crotch.

The guy Devan had been flirting with flicked his cigarette at his friend, "What the hell is wrong with you man?"

"What? She's hot! Come here, little girl!" he catcalled.

Kale turned around and walked over to the jerk, completely towering over him. "That's my sister you're talking about!" Kale growled.

The man backed away and said, "Sorry, man. Jackass ain't got no manners. Sorry we messed with her." Then he pulled his friend away by his shirt.

"If you see her again, don't talk to her," Kale ordered and then followed Devan back to the cabin.

He jogged a little to catch up to her. "What in the hell were you thinking, Monty?"

"Just making new friends," she said and shrugged.

"Those guys are the kind of friends your parents warned you about!"

"Piss off, Kale!" *I refuse to talk to him the rest of the day.*

When she got back to the cabin, Devan joined her father at the table with a bowl of fruit. Chris folded the newspaper he'd just finished reading and said, "It's supposed to rain later today. Why don't you kids go ahead and take the boat out for a little bit before it hits. Just make sure to put gas in it and don't ski or tube because you don't have an observer. If it starts to cloud up and look like it's going to storm, head on back."

"I don't wanna go," Devan told her dad petulantly.

"Devan, just go with him. I know he wants to go and he's not allowed to go out on the boat alone."

"But Dad," she whined.

"No buts, just go."

They went down to the docks and got into the rental boat. Kale pulled it out of the slip and cruised slowly through the no-wake zone, then out of the cove onto the open lake. "Where ya wanna go, Slick?"

"I don't care," she huffed, pouting.

Kale drove around a bit, exploring the shoreline before stopping the boat. "Do you want to swim or anything?"

Devan rolled her eyes, "Well, since we're out here, I guess I want to ski." She took her shorts and shirt off, put on her Connlley ski vest and zipped it up. Then, she put on her gloves.

"Your dad said no skiing or tubing. I'm not going to be able to watch for boats and make sure you don't fall on your ass at the same time."

"I don't care what he said. There are no other boats around and it's not like I don't know what I am doing." She jumped in the water to end the conversation.

He didn't want to argue, so Kale grabbed her ski and sent it gliding across the water to her. He unrolled the rope into the water and hooked it onto the boat. She put on her ski and positioned it so the tip was in the middle of the "v" in the rope.

"Pull the slack out!" she yelled. "Okay, hit it!" she yelled with a nod. Kale pushed the throttle down and looked back. As she steadied herself, he backed off the throttle to a more even speed. He enjoyed watching her jump the wake and skim over the smooth water. But, he liked watching her a little too much, and wasn't paying attention.

When he turned around, there were larger wakes heading toward them. "Shit!" It was too late. The boat started bouncing and soon Devan was bouncing on the ski. The last wake was a doozy and she fell face first into the water. He sped up, turned the boat around and then put it in neutral and coasted close to her.

"What the hell was that, Iakona?" she hissed.

Kale turned off the boat. "I didn't do it on purpose! I told you I couldn't watch you and other boats at the same time." He pulled her ski from the water and tried to help her up the ladder and onto the platform.

"Don't touch me! I don't need your help!" she snapped as she climbed up the ladder into the boat. She unzipped her ski vest, letting it fall to the floor.

Kale quietly pulled in the ski rope, trying to avoid her wrath.

"Where the hell is my towel?"

Kale rolled his eyes. "You didn't bring one," he said, and threw her his.

"I don't want your damn towel, Hawaii!" she barked.

"Why are you acting like such a bitch?"

The rain began to fall as Devan stood to confront him.

"Just sit down!" he shouted. "We have to go."

The rain was coming down in sheets. At the speed their boat was skimming across the water, it felt like hail pelting their skin. Kale threw the towel at her again. "Use it!"

Devan obeyed this time. She didn't want to admit it, but it did help.

Suddenly, the boat stopped. Kale looked both frustrated and confused. "What the—" He put the boat in neutral and turned the key off and back on again. The motor sputtered, then nothing. "Damn it!"

"What?" she hissed.

Kale threw his arms up in defeat, "We're out of gas."

"Dad told you to get gas," she said giving him a cold stare.

"No, he told *us* to get gas."

"Well, what are *you* going to do, Hawaii? Can't *rescue* us now, can you?"

"Is that what this is about? Yesterday with those guys?"

"Hmpf!" was her only response.

"Jesus, Devan! Our dads would've kicked my ass if I hadn't gotten you out of there."

Devan glared at him. "I didn't *need* rescued, asshole!"

"Maybe you didn't think so, but I'm a little more educated about how guys think than you are."

Devan's temper ignited and she stood up. Throwing the drenched towel down, she got in his face and poked his chest with her finger, "Stop rescuing me! I'm not as stupid as you think when it comes to boys." She was so cold and angry that she was shaking.

"Really?" he asked taking a step closer to her.

"Yes!" she spat at him.

Kale grabbed her head and pulled it back so he could reach her lips. She was stunned and initially tried to push him away, but that urge quickly faded as she began to return his fiery kiss.

Her hands found their way from his chest to the back of his neck, deepening the kiss.

With his fingers tangled in her hair, he pulled away. "No, you don't! You had no idea I was going to do that," he said angrily.

"Oh, so you're into incest?"

"What?"

With her hands on her hips she sassed, "You told those guys I was your *little sister.*"

He rolled his eyes and said in his best hillbilly imitation, "Yep, if I had a sister I'd kiss her just like that. Mmm-hmm."

"Well, your *sister* would be disappointed in your kiss — if that's what you want to call it," she said sarcastically and laughed.

"You think you can do better?"

"Oh, I *know* I can," she said with a devilish grin.

She shoved him down onto the driver's seat and straddled his lap. She grabbed the back of his neck and tangled her hands in his hair, pulling him to her. She touched her warm lips to his and gave him the best kiss he'd ever had. He put his arms around her waist and pulled her in even closer. His powerful arms engulfed her as his lips began searching hers for more.

A horn blew and Devan jumped off his lap, startled. Another boat from the resort had pulled alongside. "You kids need a tow?"

"Um, yeah. We ran out of gas." Kale said.

"You been out here since this started?"

"Yes, sir."

The man tossed a towrope to Kale and he tied it to the boat's bow.

"You kids are probably freezing. Let's get you back to the dock."

Devan and Kale exchanged glances. They weren't so cold anymore.

They headed back to the cabin after getting the boat taken care of. Neither said a word. The steady rain let up after a few hours, and Kale and Devan stayed on opposite sides of the cabin for the remainder of the day. Devan lost herself in a book and Kale played chess with his father.

After dinner, Kale asked Devan if she'd like to go for a walk. The rain had cooled the night air, so she pulled on a hooded sweatshirt before meeting him on the porch. They walked down the crushed shale path to the water's edge to watch the sunset. Kale sat down on a large flat rock and patted the spot next to him, asking her to join him.

As she sat down, Kale said nervously, "So, I guess we need to talk."

"Go ahead," she said and turned her body so she could still see the setting sun.

"I actually don't know what to say," he said shyly.

She looked up into his green eyes. They were just dark enough she could see the sun's reflection in them. The sunset was gorgeous — the pinks, purples, and oranges reflected in the dark waters of the lake — and she could see it all in his eyes.

"Then don't talk," Devan said and kissed him gently. His eyes were closed when she opened hers, so she closed her eyes again and continued kissing him.

They could hear fireworks going off. They opened their eyes and saw the sparks cascading down before fizzling out in the lake.

She pulled away from him and said, "Let's go watch." They walked to the docks near their cabin and sat next to a willow tree that hung over the edge of the water.

Chris stepped out onto the deck and handed Elaine a glass of wine. "Are the kids back?"

Elaine and Cassandra looked at each other and smiled. They'd been sitting on the deck watching the show — both of them.

Cassandra spoke up first, "Yeah, they're down by the tree."

Chris looked down the hill where Cassandra pointed and watched Kale take his jacket off and put it over his daughter's shoulders, leaving his arm around her.

"Oh, good, they're finally getting along," he said and walked away. The women giggled.

Kale leaned closer, "I want to kiss you, but I think we're being watched."

Devan glanced back at the deck and said, "I don't care," and kissed him lightly on the lips. Their eyes met and they both smiled.

Chapter 6

School/Fall 1994

Things changed quite a bit when they got home from the lake. There were no more romantic gestures or stolen kisses. Kale resumed football practice and Devan started working at a diner in the next town over. They didn't even see each other again until the first day of school.

Devan grabbed an apple and a piece of toast and walked out the front door. She opened the driver's side door of her car just as James pulled up, blocking her exit. "Ugh!" she groaned and threw her bag into the backseat.

"What're you doing, babe? Get in my car."

Devan clenched her fists. "Will you please stop calling me *babe*?"

"But you're my GF," he said while unbuckling his seatbelt and getting out of his car.

Kale had stepped onto his front porch in time see what was going on. He walked over to Devan's car and said, "Hey, Captain James!"

James rolled his eyes at Kale and said, "Ugh! Why are you here, sasquatch?"

"I'm the boy next door. Remember? Your *GF* here is giving me a ride to school."

"I am?"

"Yep." Kale winked.

Oh, let the awkwardness begin, Devan thought with a sigh. "I guess I am. James, you need to get out of my driveway *and* out of my life."

Kale shut Devan's door after she got in, and walked around to the passenger side. He opened the door, looked at James, and waved him off like an annoying fly. "You can leave now."

"This isn't over Devan Marie!" James shouted and sped off.

Kale laughed as he got in the car. He shut his door and looked at Devan while buckling his seatbelt. "I just hate a lover's quarrel this early in the morning."

"Shut up, Lettuce Head!" Devan hissed. She didn't say another word on the way to school.

Once at school, Kale was the star of the gossip mill. Devan could hear the girls whispering about him as they walked through the hallway. "He's *so* cute." "Did you see his arms?" "Oh my god, he's hot!" And on and on and on.

Devan was pulling her books out of her locker when James grabbed her around the waist and kissed her cheek.

"Damn it, James! Stay away from me!" she yelled as she pulled away.

James laughed and walked away, "Nope. Remember you're *my* gal."

Where's Kale when I need him? That morning wasn't the first time James had harassed her. He'd walked by her in the gym and smacked her behind, too. She didn't see him at lunch and thought maybe she was safe, until she felt a hand on her left shoulder.

Devan spun around and punched Kale right in the mouth. Her hands flew to her mouth in shock. "Oh, my god, Kale! Are you okay?"

She handed him the compact mirror from her bag so he could check out the damage. "So, that wasn't intended for me?" he asked as he looked in the mirror.

"I am *so* sorry! I thought you were James. He keeps messing with—"

"Miss Montgomery! That is unacceptable behavior and you both need to come with me," a short curly haired teacher said and grabbed Devan's arm.

"Ma'am it was an accident, she didn't—" Kale tried to explain.

"I don't know who you are mister— Mister?"

"Iakona, Kale Iakona," he said extending his hand.

"Ah, yes, the exchange student from Hawaii."

Kale snickered. "Um, ma'am, you do know Hawaii became part of the United States back in 1959, right?"

"So, think you're smart, huh? That's fine. *Both* of you can sit in detention."

The teacher took them to her classroom and wrote out the detention slips. "I'll be seeing you both after school."

"Yes, ma'am," they said in unison and walked out of her classroom.

"What's her problem?" Kale asked.

"She needs a boyfriend." They both laughed.

After the final bell rang at 2:45, Kale went to his locker. He found Devan waiting for him there, along with five other girls. He was surprised to see them all there. "Good afternoon, ladies," he said with a nod.

One girl pushed Devan completely out of the way so she could speak to him first. "Hi, Kale. Remember me? We're in health class together." She flipped her long hair over her shoulder and it almost hit Devan in the face.

Devan raised her fist, but Kale grabbed it and acted like he was resting his arm on the girl's shoulder. "Denise, right?" he asked.

"Desireé," the girl corrected him, "but you can call me *desire*."

"Okay, Desireé."

"I wanted to know if you'd give me a ride home?"

A girl Devan had never seen before interrupted Kale's answer, "No, he's going to give *me* a ride home!"

Pretty soon the girls were arguing and yelling at each other. Devan grabbed Kale's arm and led him to detention before they got into any more trouble.

"Aw, come on! That could've been really interesting," he protested.

The pair sat down in the classroom and a few of the girls followed them in. "So, who are you taking home?" Desireé demanded.

"No one, you morons!" Devan said.

Desireé stepped closer to Devan and said snottily, "He can speak for himself, heifer!"

"Okay, there's no need for name-calling," Kale said and shrugged. "I can't take anyone home because I rode with Devan."

Desireé rolled her eyes and the girls began to whine and pout as they walked away.

"That was easy, Kale," Devan said and laughed.

"Actually it was."

Devan reached into her bag and took out her notebook, "Like you didn't find those girls attractive."

"Oh, I'm not saying that."

Devan blushed and felt a twinge of jealousy, "Okay?"

"It's just that I'm not interested," he said with a wink.

The teacher walked into the room and everyone went silent. The next 45 minutes dragged on forever.

Devan worked on her geometry homework, while Kale doodled pictures of surfboards and palm trees on his spiral notebook cover. Devan stole a sideways glance at his work. *He's actually a pretty decent artist.*

The teacher announced time was up and she released everyone from her classroom. Just outside the door, James grabbed Devan around the waist.

"Hey, babe! Detention on the first day? Really?"

"That's it, I'm done!" she said through clenched teeth. She threw her bag on the floor and spun around out of his grasp. She took a step towards him, but Kale came to his rescue. He stuck his long arm between the two and pushed Devan away. "Okay. Look, James, you have to leave Devan alone, man."

"Really? Do you know who you're talking to?" James asked arrogantly and dropped his bag and keys, ready for a fight.

"Yeah, you're Captain of the football team, you eat, drink, sleep, and breathe football...grr. I get it," Kale said and sighed.

James tilted his head and flashed a Cheshire grin, "That's right, son, which means I could kick you off my team right this second if I wanted. So, how 'bout you step back and let me handle my girl."

"Dude, she's not your girl. Okay? I'm just trying to be nice here."

"She *is* my girl and I'll do with her what I want," James boasted. He grabbed Devan's arm, intending to pull her down the hallway.

"I don't belong to anyone!" she yelled, trying to shake him off. His grip was starting to hurt her elbow, so she stomped at his toes to make him let go.

"Not cool," Kale said, grabbing James by the shoulders and squeezing hard.

James grimaced. "You don't know when to leave things alone, do you?" He dropped Devan's arm and turned to swing at Kale, who ducked and tackled James into the lockers.

"Jesus, man, I think you fractured my shoulder or something," James whined.

"You better never touch her again. Do you hear me?" Kale yelled, and then let go of his shoulders and stepped back.

Devan was shocked and stood there wide-eyed. She'd never seen Kale get mad like that.

Kale picked up Devan's books and took her by the hand. As they walked away, James declared, "You're off the team, ass wipe!"

"We'll see!" Kale yelled back, as he watched James slide down to the floor rubbing his shoulder.

Kale didn't realize he was still holding her hand as they walked to Devan's car until he reached for his door handle. He dropped her hand and Devan blushed a little as she walked around to her side of the car. They put their bags in the backseat, climbed in and buckled up.

She didn't start the car right away. She stared straight ahead and said, "Thank you for dealing with James."

"No problem. The thought of you getting back with him makes my blood boil."

She wasn't expecting him to say that and turned to look at him, waiting for him to say more.

"What?" he shrugged. "I just don't like the guy."

"Yeah, me either."

She turned the key, put the car in gear and drove home. The radio playing softly was the only sound interrupting the silence.

Were you thinking he'd actually like you and you'd have a fairy tale romance? Sure, dream on.

After the first week of school, Kale started driving himself in his mom's car. Devan missed that little bit of time they'd spent together each day. They were both too busy to see each other otherwise. Kale was a star player on the football team and she was always working, even volunteering for extra shifts.

She was saving up for a summer writing program at the local community college.

Even with her work schedule, she'd been able to go to two of Kale's games with Kristy. When he spotted her in the bleachers, he waved. She smiled and waved back.

I've missed that smile, he mused. *I think I'll go have a late breakfast at her restaurant in the morning. I don't have practice and I can sleep in a little bit.*

The next morning Kale woke up and headed to the diner. Sandy, the hostess, greeted him at the door and asked where he'd like to be seated.

"Wherever Devan is, please," he replied.

Sandy led him to a row of empty booths. He sat down and opened his menu. Sandy stepped into the kitchen and yelled, "Hey, Devan-girl! You just had a tall drink o' water sit down in your section. Asked for you, too! Go get him!" she encouraged, practically drooling.

"Oh, no," Devan said when she saw Kale sitting in her section.

"What's wrong, darlin'? I can take care of him if you want, know what I mean?" Sandy winked and started coughing her smoker's cough.

"No, I'm fine. Go get yourself some water. I got him." Devan smiled and casually walked over to his booth and sat down. "To what do I owe this honor?"

"Hey, you," he said. "I- uh- was hungry?"

She laughed. "Is that a question or—"

"No, I mean I *am* hungry, and I wanted to see you. We never see each other anymore and I guess I miss you a little bit."

Devan couldn't believe he'd just admitted he missed her. "Just a little bit?" she asked, giving him a hard time.

"Yeah." He laughed. "I can't pick on Pete the way I pick on you. It's just not as much fun."

She gave his shoulder a shove, "Awe, poor baby."

"Admit it, Monty, you miss me, too."

"I suppose," she agreed. "Maybe that's why I went to your game last night when I got off work."

"Thank you for that," he said, smiling.

I'm gonna melt into the seat. Why, oh why, does he have to be so damn gorgeous? "Well, you'd better place an order so I don't get in trouble."

"Okay. I'll take coffee with cream, six eggs and a steak medium rare ... hmm, and hash browns with honey mustard on the side, please," he said, handing her the menu.

"Six eggs? How do you want them?" she asked.

"Sunny side up!"

She flashed him a smile. "Okay, I'll be right back with your coffee."

Devan took his ticket to the counter and shouted Kale's order to the cook. She turned to pour his coffee and Sandy joined her. Leaning with her back on the counter and facing Kale, Sandy asked her, "You know that hunk? Oh he is h-o-t!"

"Sandy!" Devan laughed, "He's 17!"

"Oh, shit! No cradle-robbing for me!" Sandy laughed and walked back to a table that needed cleared and wiped down.

Devan brought out Kale's coffee and sat down with him.

"Are you doing anything tonight?" he asked with a smile.

She was lost in his smile when her manager approached. "Hello. Is everything all right here?"

"Yes, sir! Devan is taking very good care of me," Kale replied.

"Well, that's good to know. I'm going to borrow her for just a second," Travis, her good-looking manager, said.

"Hey, Dee, Jessica just called in sick for tonight. I'm going to need you to work. Okay? Maybe you can go home for a few hours at three and come back at six and stay until close?"

"Um, yeah, I guess," she said with disappointment. Not wanting Travis to think she was immature, she straightened her shoulders and smiled. "Sure, I'd be happy to." Devan normally liked Travis. She even had a little crush on him, but right now she hated him.

She glanced at the counter and realized Kale's food was in the window. She went over, set it on a tray and delivered it to him.

"Wow! This looks great!" He sprinkled salt and pepper on his eggs and asked, "So, about tonight. How about we go see a movie or something?"

She frowned and looked down at her food-splattered apron, "I can't. I have to work."

"That sucks," he said and took a bite of his food. "Mmm, that's good stuff!" He tore into his plate like a starved teenager who plays football.

Devan laughed and walked back to the kitchen.

Chapter 7

Homecoming 1994

The boys were at their lockers gathering their things, when Pete said to Kale, "Hey, you know Homecoming's gonna be here in a few weeks. Have you asked Devan yet?"

"What makes you think I'd ask her?"

Pete laughed. "Dude, come on! I'm not as dumb as I look."

"Nah, man. Dev and I are just, you know, friends."

"Well, if you aren't going to ask your *friend*, I will," Pete said with a sly grin. He shut his locker door just as Devan walked by.

"Hey, Dee! Do you—"

She turned around in time to see Kale push Pete into the lockers and take a step toward her. *I don't like the idea of anyone asking her out. What if she said yes?*

Kale finished Pete's sentence, "Um, do you want to be my date for Homecoming?"

Pete doubled over laughing.

"What's so funny?" Kristy asked, walking up behind Pete.

"I just tricked Kale into asking Devan to Homecoming," Pete said, while wiping tears of laughter from his eyes.

"How'd you do that?" she asked.

Pete grinned proudly. "I told him *I* was gonna ask her."

Kristy scrunched her face in confusion, "But you already have a date."

"I know," he said, and kissed her cheek.

"Well?" Kale could hardly stand the suspense of not knowing her answer.

Devan was still trying to make sense of the situation. She tilted her head and looked at him with suspicion, "Why did you push Pete?"

Kale blushed. "Be- because he was going to ask you and you can't go with anyone but me," he said hurriedly.

Devan put her hands on her hips. "Oh really? I don't have a say in the matter?"

"Uh, no. It's not that, I just meant I wanted you to go with me," he stammered. *I don't know what it is, but she's different. Most girls throw themselves at me, but not her. She's special. She keeps me on my toes. She's my friend, sure, but do I want it to be something more?*

"You realize that Pete already asked Kristy a few days ago, right?"

Kale snapped his head around to look back at Pete and scowl. Pete just smiled his car salesman smile.

"So, are you sure you want to go with me?" she asked, interrupting his plan to pulverize Pete's face for tricking him.

"Let me try this again!" Kale said and dropped to his knees. "Will you *please* let me take you to Homecoming? Pretty please?"

They'd attracted an audience by this point, and the theatrics made them laugh.

"Get up you fool!" Devan said, reaching to pull him up and turning red from embarrassment.

He pulled his hands away and hid them behind his back, "Not until you say yes!"

"Well, then I have no choice." She sighed.

"That's right!"

Kale's smile always got her, so she tried desperately to ignore it. She looked down at him and smirked. "Nope," she said flatly and walked around him toward her classroom.

The crowd booed her reply and Kale jumped up and ran after her.

"Come on, Monty! Please?" he begged while giving her his best puppy dog eyes.

She glared at him and made him sweat a little longer before saying, "Fine, I'll be your date."

"Thank you!" he kissed her cheek and ran to his next class.

Devan stood there a moment, laughing, before heading to her English Lit class. *What am I going to do with him?* she wondered, as she hurried down the hall.

◦◦◦ ◦◦◦

The Homecoming dance was on the second Saturday in November. Kale and Pete met the girls at Devan's house, where they took pictures in the backyard. The air was crisp and the trees were dressed in beautiful bright hues of orange, red and yellow, making the perfect backdrop.

Kale and Devan still claimed they were "just friends," while Kristy and Pete had no problem flaunting their relationship status. Pete had officially asked Kristy to be his girlfriend the week before at school. He'd made her a mixed-tape with all of her favorite songs and recorded himself at the end asking her to be his girlfriend. He'd left it along with a note in the front seat of her car. It was cheesy, but Kristy loved it and eagerly said yes.

Things were slightly awkward between Kale and Devan, but not enough that they kept their distance. Sure the first few slow dances were filled with tension, but as the dance progressed they relaxed and enjoyed themselves.

The last song of the night was "Fade into You," by Mazzy Star. Kale took Devan's hand and led her to the dance floor for their final dance. He leaned down and whispered, "I should've told you how beautiful you look. I- I was just nervous, I guess."

She blushed a little and smiled. "Well, Mr. Iakona, you look pretty damn good yourself."

He looked down at himself and said, "I do, don't I?" He grinned and she laughed at him.

He's so silly.

He whispered in her ear again, "I really have missed you."

44

She looked into his eyes and longed for his lips to touch hers like they had at the lake. Kale leaned in for the kill just as Ms. Jenkins walked by. "I see you, Mr. Iakona. Don't try anything funny."

He nodded, and said, "Ma'am, you look lovely tonight."

Ms. Jenkins smacked his arm and giggled. "You're rotten!" She walked away, grinning from ear to ear.

"I hope you know you just made her night," Devan teased. "She's going to go home and have sweet dreams about her handsome little school boy."

Kale couldn't stop staring at Devan. There was just something about her. He couldn't put his finger on it. He just felt the need to protect her, and hug her and kiss her. He wanted to pick her up in his arms and have the perfect ending to their night by riding off into the sunset.

Devan didn't even blink as he looked at her. She studied his beautiful face. *How can a 17-year-old boy be so bewitching?*

Kale leaned down toward her and their lips met. Both were caught off guard by the strong emotions behind the kiss. The song ended, but the sensation didn't.

The following morning, Devan groaned when the alarm clock went off ordering her out of bed. Since beginning work at the diner in late August she'd never asked for a day off or gotten to work late. She was always early for her shift and stayed late to help others if the diner was busy when her shift ended.

That's why she'd been surprised when Travis wouldn't give her the one and only day off she'd asked for. She was more than a little annoyed about it, too.

Once she got to the diner, she put her apron on and greeted her regular Saturday morning customers with her usual smile and a steaming hot cup of coffee. Travis flirted with her, like always.

Before she started spending so much time with Kale, she'd considered going on a date with Travis. She'd even admitted to Kristy that she had a crush on him. That was a thing of the past as soon as Kale came back into the picture. He was the only one she was interested in now.

Kale woke with the sun streaming in his bedroom window. He couldn't stop thinking about Devan's soft, sweet lips on his. Being with her made him happy. He'd never felt this way about a girl before and decided he wanted to do something special for her. He wanted her to understand she was special to him.

Suddenly, Kale realized he had deep feelings for Devan. *That whole "just friends" thing is history. I've gotta make her see me as someone other than the guy who pestered her at the lake.*

He knew Devan was stuck working a double shift that day because one of the other waitresses had a family emergency, so that evening while she was at work Kale put a peach colored rose on her car. The florist had explained that when you need to emphasize the earnestness of your gesture, you send pale peach roses. From that day on, Kale decided he would only give her peach colored roses.

Kale and Devan hadn't been able to talk much since homecoming. He tried to stop by the diner on nights she was working, but football practice took up most of his time. When he wasn't at practice or games, he was studying hard to keep his grades up. Sure, he was a football star and scholarships were certainly a possibility, but a career-ending injury could happen at anytime.

Football season was almost over, but the Tigers had made the playoffs. If they won this game, the team would go to the state championships.

Devan managed to get the day off for Kale's last playoff game. She and Kristy made the two-hour trip to Columbus with the Iakonas and the Montgomerys in the family's van.

The game was amazing! Her favorite part was when James got benched for unsportsmanlike conduct just before halftime. The second string quarterback had been injured in the previous game, so Coach's only option was to sub Kale in as quarterback.

In the final seconds of the game, Kale threw a pass to Pete. Pete caught it and scored the game-winning touchdown! The girls almost lost their voices from cheering so loudly through the intense game.

The parents made their way to the van and let the girls hang back to congratulate their favorite players. Devan was shoved out of the way as Desireé ran passed her.

"Hawaii! My hero!" Desireé cheered as she threw herself at him and kissed him full on the lips.

From where Devan was standing, it looked like he kissed her back. Kristy's jaw dropped and she looked at her best friend. She watched as Devan's facial expression quickly changed from excitement to hurt and then despair. Devan dropped her game program, turned and walked back to the van.

Pete picked Kristy up in a big bear hug. "Great game, baby!" she exclaimed.

"Thanks!" he said and kissed her with his sweaty, mud covered face.

Desireé joined her fellow cheerleaders and Kale walked over to where Pete and Kristy were standing.

"You were phenomenal, man!" Kale said, slapping Pete on the back.

"Couldn't have done it without my boy," he said, returning the slap.

"Too bad Dee wasn't here to see all the action," Pete said.

"Oh, she was here," Kristy said making direct eye contact with Kale. "We drove down with your parents."

"Well, where'd she go?" Pete asked.

Even though Pete asked the question, Kristy put her hands on her hips and narrowed her eyes at Kale. "She suddenly felt ill."

Kale smoothed back his hair with both of his hands. *Game over.*

Devan worked the following day. When their shift ended, Travis asked her out. She didn't hesitate to take him up on his offer.

Kristy told Pete about it, and then Pete told Kale and he went ballistic.

"What the hell, man?" he said throwing anything that was within reach before he threw himself down onto his beanbag chair.

"Maybe she's using the jealousy tactic?" Pete said, trying to calm him down.

"Or maybe she saw Desireé kissing me?" Kale wondered out loud.

Pete looked over at the mound of muscle on the floor, "Huh?"

"After we won the game, right before Kristy walked up to us — I think you were picking up your bag and helmet. Anyway, Desireé attacked me with a full blown make out session."

Pete's mouth dropped open. "Well, did you kiss her back?"

Kale didn't answer.

"What the hell, man? Did you or didn't you kiss her back?" Pete demanded.

Kale shrugged. "Not really?"

"Well, 'not really' isn't a good answer. If she saw you — you're screwed."

Kale put his face in his hands and groaned.

The Tigers lost in the second round of the semifinals, and football was finally over for the year. Kale and Devan avoided each other the best they could until they found themselves in the same movie theater during Christmas vacation.

Pete elbowed Kale and whispered, "Don't look now, dude, but your gal is four rows in front of us."

Kale sighed. "You know, I probably wouldn't have noticed if you hadn't said anything." Kale watched as Travis put his left arm around Devan's shoulder and put his other hand in her lap.

"What's that creep doing?" Kale asked angrily.

Pete leaned over the person in front of him and looked, "Relax, Kujo. He's just getting some popcorn."

Pete handed Kale a napkin, "Here, I think there's some foam coming out of your mouth."

Kale shot Pete a vicious look and Pete laughed.

The movie was halfway over when Kale noticed Travis's hand was back in Devan's lap. He thought for sure there wouldn't be any popcorn left by this time, so he kept watching them. He saw Devan's hand quickly slap Travis's face.

"Bitch!" Travis shouted.

Kale flew over the seats in front of him as he saw Travis return Devan's slap. Kale picked Travis up out of his seat and threw him in the aisle. He towered over the him as he lay on the floor, then punched him, giving Travis a bloody nose.

"You okay, Monty?"

She nodded rubbing her cheek. Although they hadn't fallen, Devan had tears in her eyes.

He looked back at Travis with fury, "You *ever* touch her again, I *will* destroy you."

The theater manager and two ushers ran down the aisle with their flashlights shining. "I'm gonna have to ask you people to leave."

Kale took Devan by the hand as she stood up. He kicked Travis hard in the gut on his way up the aisle. Pete grabbed Kale's coat and met them outside.

"What was that?" Pete asked.

Kale was furious. "He touched her! When she slapped him, he slapped her back! No way was I going to let him get away with that!"

Instead of being grateful, Devan was angry. "How did you— I mean, what the hell? Were you spying on me?"

He wasn't expecting that reaction. "No! God no. Pete and I were—"

"On a man date," Pete interjected.

"A man date? Really, dude?"

Pete shrugged.

"Look, Iakona," she said poking him in the chest, "I can handle my own situations. Okay? Stop, and I do mean *stop* trying to rescue me!" She started walking away.

"Let us at least take you home," Pete called after her.

"I drove. Besides, I don't want to be anywhere near *him!*" she practically spat as she pointed at Kale.

They watched her get into her car and speed off.

"There goes my ride," they heard Travis whine.

Kale was disgusted. "You made a girl drive?"

"I have a moped."

"You're such a loser!" Pete yelled at Travis as he pushed Kale into his car before there was another altercation.

Chapter 8

Spring 1995

Kale didn't think Devan would ever forgive him. But she did. She'd quit her job and football season was over, so they finally had time to just be kids. It took a little time for the awkwardness to fade, but before they knew it, their relationship was back to normal.

They still had strong feelings for each other, but neither did anything about it. The fear of rejection was too much for either of them to overcome.

Over spring break, Kale and his parents went to visit family in Hawaii. Pete's parents were out of town for the weekend, so he decided to have a party. Kristy and Pete had broken up but remained friends, so both she and Devan were invited.

Devan had just finished curling her hair and was putting on her lip-gloss when Kristy got there to catch a ride with Devan.

"Oh, my God. I am *so* excited! Our first big high school party!" Kristy shrieked.

Devan laughed. "I know. I'm excited, too. You know there's gonna be alcohol, right?"

"Uh yeah, but you're driving sooo..." Kristy winked.

"Come on, Kris, please don't drink."

Kristy's shoulders sank, but she gave in. "Okay, fine. It's still really exciting though."

When the two girls arrived at the party, half of the kids were already stumbling drunk.

"I guess we're late," Kristy joked.

"I think you're right!"

"Hey, hey, hey, ladies. So glad you could make it. May I offer you a frosty cold beverage or a jiggle shot?" Pete asked, holding a tray of Jell-O shots.

"Do you have anything non-alcoholic?" Kristy asked.

"Um, we have vodka punch, beer, good old Jack, some kind of frozen thing, but nothing without booze in it."

"That's okay. Any water?"

"Sure, but are you sure you don't want anything tastier?"

"No alcohol for us tonight, Pete. Thanks for the offer, though. Your mom would be proud. You're a mighty fine host," Devan teased him.

"I think we should keep that to ourselves. Mom wouldn't approve of any of this. Oh, hey, I think we've got some of that powdered tea stuff. Want me to make you some of that?"

"Sure," both girls replied.

The girls made their way through the house, talking with friends as they went. The party was starting to get rowdy. Devan saw Desireé hanging all over James and rolled her eyes.

"Hey, Dev! Crazy party, huh? I haven't seen Hawaii. Where's he at?" Ramie asked.

"Oh, he's in Hawaii. He and his parents should be home tomorrow."

"Cool. Hey, would you come to the bathroom with me? Everyone's so crazy, I don't want to go by myself."

Devan set her drink down and walked down the hall with Ramie. She didn't want to leave her alone in the crowd, either. Ramie was a freshman, with beautiful Italian features, and Devan was afraid one of the upper classmen might try to take advantage of her.

They quickly found the bathroom, but of course it was occupied. "I'm sure there's another one around here. Let's find Pete and ask."

Devan led the way back through the masses, and found Pete with Kristy. It looked like they were getting along a little too well to be "just friends." She had to pull the couple apart to get Pete's attention. "Pete, we need to use your other bathroom."

"And another drink it looks like. Follow me. I'll be back, my sweet," Pete said and kissed Kristy on the cheek, making her blush.

Pete made more iced tea for the girls and showed them where the other bathroom was. After using the facilities, they decided it was getting hot and stuffy in the house, so they went out to sit on the back porch.

As soon as she sat down, Devan started feeling a little strange — light headed and sleepy at the same time.

"Ramie? I'm not feeling so good. Can you get Kristy for me?"

"Sure, maybe if you drink the rest of your tea you'll feel better." Ramie handed Devan her cup and left to find Kristy.

Devan chugged the rest of her tea and leaned against the porch rail. Time moved slowly and she felt like an hour had passed before she heard Ramie's voice saying, "I couldn't find Kristy, but James said he'd take you home."

"What? No! Find Kristy or Pete."

Her eyelids felt so heavy she was having a hard time keeping them open. She slumped down on the porch floor, and the next thing she saw was a blurry face peering down at her. "No. Go away, James."

"No, baby, I'll make you feel better." He leaned down and kissed her. She couldn't feel much but she knew something was happening with her shirt.

"No, James! Stop!" She couldn't fight back. He knew that, so he took advantage of it. The next thing she knew she was in the back seat of his car. "What's going on?"

"It's cool, babe. I'm taking you back to my house. My parents are at some lawyer convention this weekend."

She tried moving but she was paralyzed.

"No, just take me home," she slurred.

"Oh, *I am!*"

Kale walked into the party.

"Hey, Hawaii. You made it!" Ramie said, practically jumping into his arms. "Devan said you weren't coming back until tomorrow."

"Yeah, we got home early. So, Devan's here?" he asked looking around.

"Yeah, but she's out back with James. They're kinda busy, if ya know what I mean."

"No, I don't know what you mean."

"You know, they were *getting busy*. Something we could be doing right now."

"Are you drunk, Ramie?"

"Noooo, I's only had a few cups of punch," she said and slapped the drink in Kale's hand.

He sniffed it. "Ramie, this isn't regular punch. Stay put while I find Devan."

He looked everywhere and asked around, but everyone he asked was too drunk to give him a straight answer. Then he saw Pete and Kristy. "Hey, Pete, have you see Devan?"

"Not for a while."

"She left with James a little bit ago," a slurred answer came from somewhere in the crowd.

"Something's wrong. Devan wouldn't go anywhere with James," Kristy said.

"Was she drinking?" Kale asked.

"No, all she had was some iced tea."

"When did you see her last?"

"Like an hour ago maybe."

"Okay. Was James drinking?" he asked Pete.

"Honestly, I don't know."

"Yeah, he was feeling pretty good," Desireé answered from her position slumped in a chair.

"Pete, Kristy, are you sober?"

"Yes,"

"Aren't these hers?" Kale asked holding up a purse and keys.

"Yeah, and she would never leave them," Kristy said, starting to freak out.

"Okay, you guys drive to James's house and see if they're there. I'll go to her house."

James was all over the road, and Devan was sliding around in the backseat. She was becoming more alert and asked, "What is going on?"

"James? James!" He'd passed out, but his foot was still on the gas. She tried to get into the front passenger seat, but she was still really weak and couldn't make it.

"James! Wake up! *Wake up!*"

He nodded his head a few times and grabbed the wheel. "Sorry, babe. I must've dozed off for a second."

"Stop the car!" she screamed. "I want out!"

"No."

"James—" The car hit the railing on the bridge. The impact made James hit his head on the windshield, knocking him out instantly. Devan was thrown into the front seat. Neither had seat belts on.

At least the car has stopped, she thought as she tried to regain her composure so she could get out and get help. It was too late — she could hear brakes screeching. She turned her head and saw the headlights coming right at them. Then, a truck slammed into their car, pushing it over the edge into the creek.

Kale saw a truck stopped in the middle of the road ahead of him and slowed down. He saw a man yelling and stopped his car and got out.

"I tried to stop, man! I did—"

Kale pushed the man out of his way and looked over the edge. There was James's car lying on its side. He could see someone inside. He ran down the hill to the creek, which was about three feet deep. It was possible they could still drown. "Go get help," he yelled up.

It didn't look like much water was getting inside the car, so he wasn't worried about that, but the car was smoking. He saw James through the window, and pounded on it until James opened his eyes. "Unlock the doors!"

James could barely move his hand. "I can't, man. I can't!"

"Is Devan in there with you?"

"Yeah."

Kale looked around then grabbed a large rock. "Cover her face and yours."

"No! You can't hurt my car!"

"Cover your faces!" Kale yelled.

He slammed the rock into the window until it shattered.

"Get me out, man. I can't move."

Kale unlocked the door and opened it. He pulled James out and dropped him on the bank.

"Devan? Devan!" He reached in trying to get to her. She wasn't responding. He got her arm and pulled but she was stuck. He climbed into the car and then everything lit up around him. He saw fire reflected on the windshield. "Come on, Devan. Wake up!"

He felt around. Her right leg was pinned between the seat and the passenger side door. He couldn't get it loose. He didn't want to break it or hurt her, but if he didn't get her out she was going up in flames with the car.

He pulled as hard as he could and felt her leg moving a bit. He gave one final tug and she was free. He got her out of the car and carried her to the bank, where he put her down. The moment her body touched the ground, the car went up in flames.

"My car! My poor car," James wailed, rocking back and forth.

Kale cradled Devan's head in his lap. He watched her chest rise and fall, relieved that she was still breathing. He felt for her pulse, and it seemed strong.

He caressed her hair. "Devan? You're going to be okay. You hear me? You're going to be okay."

Her breathing started to become shallow, so he felt for her pulse again. It was there but wasn't as strong as before. "Devan, wake up!"

He set her head on the ground and hovered over her, positioning himself in case he had to perform CPR.

He rubbed her arms and pleaded, "Stay with me!" He grabbed her hands and bowed his head to pray, *"God, please, please help Devan—I beg of you. Please have her be okay. I need her here with me."*

Devan opened her eyes. She heard a woman's voice and saw a figure in the light. *"Mahalo í ke no kēia lā, wake my child, for love is here and now."*

She felt the warmth of a soft hand on her cheek. The figure had a face. *"Mahalo i ke akua no kēia lā,* you are safe, for love is here and now," the woman whispered in her ear.

"Who are you?" Devan asked.

Her hair was long and dark and she had soft wrinkles around her eyes and mouth. There was something familiar about the kindness in her eyes. She'd seen those eyes before. *"Mahalo i ke akua no kēia lā,"* The figure faded away and Kale's face appeared.

A large gust of wind came out of nowhere, and he felt her hand move, so he opened his eyes. She groaned and opened her eyes a little.

"Don't move," he told her calmly.

She lifted her hand to his face. "Mahalo i ke akua no kēia lā, for love is here and now," she said and closed her eyes.

He felt a shiver run down his back as a tear rolled down his face.

"Is she okay?" James asked.

"I think she will be. No thanks to you," Kale growled and glared at him.

"What did she say?"

"Thank God for this day, for love is here and now."

"See, man, she still loves me."

He reached over and grabbed James by the throat. "If you ever go near her again, I will kill you with my bare hands." He dropped his hand before he did something he'd regret. It wasn't worth it.

Chapter 9

Devan opened her eyes. The room she was in was bright and she could hear machines beeping.

"She's awake!" she heard her mom yell.

"Mom?" She whispered.

"Yes, honey. I'm here. We all are."

Devan looked around the room. Her parents and the Iakonas were there. "What does *Mahalo i ke akua no kēia lā* mean?"

"Devan, where did you hear that?" Mr. Iakona asked.

"I had this strange dream. There was a woman there and she kept repeating those words."

He turned to his wife and then looked back at Devan.

Devan looked closely looked at Kale's dad and realized she knew where she'd seen the woman's eyes before.

"My mother, when Kale was small, would always say that and put a hand on his cheek. It means 'Thank God for this day.' Did she say anything else?"

"Something like love is here..."

"I bet it was for love is here and now. She would say to you and Kale when she babysat you when you were very tiny, '*Mahalo i ke akua no kēia lā*, for love is here and now.'"

"Where's Kale?" Devan asked.

"He's right over there, sleeping. He hasn't left your room since you were admitted," her mother said.

"He even got yelled at by a few nurses," her dad added, and chuckled.

"How long have I been here?" she asked, rubbing her hand near the IV.

"Three days. You were really lucky. No broken bones, just a few bruised ribs, and a sprained ankle. The only thing wrong was you wouldn't wake up," her father said, frowning.

"Kale's been here for three days?"

"He wouldn't leave until he knew you were okay," Nāhoa told her.

"Is there something you aren't telling me?"

The adults all looked at each other. Her dad stepped closer to her bed and said, "They had to pump your stomach. You'd ingested something and you had an allergic reaction. It had already hit your bloodstream, but you're okay now. They think it was benzodiazepine."

"What?"

Her mom got up and whispered in her ear. "It's a drug that can relax your body and make you go to sleep. A lot of people take it for anxiety. They think someone slipped something in your drink at the party."

Devan's stomach turned. *Who would do such a thing?*

Kale yawned and stretched, then saw everyone gathered around Devan's bed. He jumped up and quickly asked, "What's wrong?"

The worry in his eyes disappeared when he saw Devan smiling at him. He smiled back. "You're awake!"

Their parents slowly moved away from the bed, and for a moment Devan forgot anyone else was even there.

"Well, we'll leave you two alone," her dad said, heading for the door.

"Wait, can someone get me a water?"

"I'll get it," Kale said and walked out of the room.

"Mr. Iakona?"

"Yes, Devan," Nāhoa said, and turned around.

"Why did your mother say that to Kale and me?""

Nāhoa walked over closer to her and grabbed her hand.

"Because Devan, she thought you were made for one another. She believed that the magic of the islands made you and Kale twin flames. Each flame is a half a soul, when they are together they are whole."

She didn't know what to say, so she smiled and thanked him as Kale walked back into her room with a glass of water.

"We'll be in the lobby," Kale's dad said, giving Devan's arm a gentle squeeze.

Kale handed her the water and then moved her hair out of her face.

"Thank you," she said and blushed.

"Oh, thank god you're awake!" Kristy shrieked as she and Pete ran in.

"Hey, Pete," Kale said. "Wanna come with me to find some food for Devan? The girls probably want some alone time."

"Sure."

When they were gone, Kristy took a seat and asked, "Do you remember anything?"

"I remember waking up in the car. James was passed out at the wheel, then we hit the rail and stopped. When I looked up, I saw headlights and we got slammed."

"Do you remember anything else?"

"Just a weird dream I had of an older woman. Why?"

"You don't remember *anything* else?"

"No why?"

"Apparently you got roofied at the party. That 4x4 that crashed into you pushed the car over the edge into the water."

"Is James okay?"

"Well, he has a broken clavicle and arm, but you shouldn't care," Kristy said bitterly.

"Maybe not, but I'm glad he's okay. Did you know Kale's been staying here since they brought me in?"

"Yeah, I know. Did *you* know he also saved you and James?"

"He wasn't home from Hawaii yet, how'd he save us?"

"They got home early and he came to the party. When he realized you weren't there, he went looking for you. He knew something was wrong. If he hadn't got there when he did, well you and James would be dead. He pulled you out like 30 seconds before the car blew up."

"It blew up?" Devan's eyes got huge.

"A small explosion, but the car is completely totaled."

Kale and Pete walked in and Devan said, "I need to talk to Kale alone."

"Hey, Pete, she's okay now. Let's go home," Kristy said. "I'll see you tomorrow. Okay?"

"Thanks for coming by, you guys!"

"Glad you're okay now," Pete said with a warm smile as they left.

Kale sat on the edge of the bed and said, "Your choice: Twinkies, fattening yet tasty; Gummy Bears, zero fat but may pull out a filling; or traditional M & M's — chocolate does a body good."

She smiled and reached for his face. "I choose you."

He leaned over and kissed her cheek. "I'm so glad you're okay. I almost lost you."

"How many times are you going to save me?" she asked as her eyes sparkled.

"As many times as you need saved."

"Kiss me," she whispered.

He leaned down and kissed her lightly on her lips.

"No, I mean *really* kiss me."

Kale lifted her head and she looked deep into his eyes. Then she began to cry.

"What's wrong?" he asked with a furrowed brow.

"Nothing."

"Seems like it's something."

"No, nothing's wrong as long as you're here."

He wiped a tear away with his thumb. "I'm not going anywhere."

She pulled him down so their lips met. This time it was much more than a quick kiss. His lips were full and soft against hers. It wasn't passion, it wasn't lust — it was love. She finally felt all the feelings he'd had for her all this time, and he felt hers, too.

He's rescued me not once, not twice, but several times now, she realized. "Can we stop playing games now?" she asked pushing him away.

"Yes, I'm tired of the fighting," he said clearly.

"Fighting?"

"Every time you walk into the room, my eyes only see your beautiful face. Every time you speak, my ears listen. Every time you smile, I smile. Every time you cry, my heart hurts. And every time you're near me, I *fight* to keep my hands to myself. I *fight* the urge to grab you and kiss you. I'm exhausted from *fighting* every feeling I have for you."

"Then stop," she said and grabbed his shirt, pulling him down to kiss her again. And at that moment it was official, they were more than just friends.

ᴏᴏᴇ ᴏᴇᴏ

Over the next few months the four of them were inseparable. Pete and Kristy got back together and everything was as it should be. When they got home from the last day of school, both sets of parents were at the Montgomery's sitting in the living room wearing solemn faces.

"What's wrong?" Devan asked, worried.

"Why don't you two sit down? We have something to tell you," Nāhoa said softly.

They sat down on the empty loveseat.

"We won't be going on vacation together this year."

Well, that's not a big deal. It sucks but no biggie, Devan thought.

"Kale we're going back to Hawaii in a few days."

"Oh, okay. When will we be back?" Kale asked.

His father looked at his mother then back at Kale. "We won't be back for quite a while son. Your Aunt Noelani was in a car accident."

"Did she die?" Kale asked bluntly.

"No, but she's in pretty rough shape. Uncle Russo can't take care of the rentals and farm by himself. As her brother, it's my responsibility to step up."

"But we *are* coming back. Right?" Kale asked.

"Yes, but it won't be until next spring at least," his mother answered.

"So, I'll be graduating in Hawaii, not here?"

"Yes, but you should be able to start college here the following fall if you want to," his father said with a half-smile.

"But the team needs me *this* fall! What about the college scouts?" Kale's frustration kept building.

"I'm sorry, son, but your aunt needs you more than a high school football team does."

Kale nodded and put his chin on Devan's shoulder as she fought back tears.

Chapter 10

School Year 1995/96

In a sense, Kale was glad to be back in Hawaii, where he'd grown up. He had lots of friends here and he got his old football position back. It was no problem for him to adjust to the move. He even got his old lifeguarding job back. The only bad thing was how much he missed Devan.

They wrote to each other a lot, and they talked on the phone once every two weeks, but it wasn't the same.

Devan had a much harder time with it than Kale. She went over every other day and watered Cassandra's plants. Sometimes, she'd spray his room with the little bit of the Nautica he left behind, just to feel like he was near. Then she'd lie on his bed and cry.

She wore his letterman jacket to school every day. School definitely wasn't the same without him. She was a bit reclusive now, and she didn't show much emotion around other people.

Her parents noticed the change and were worried. Even Kristy and Pete noticed. Devan still hung out with them from time to time, but just wasn't herself. Kristy even tried talking to her about it, but got nowhere.

One day when Kristy was at the Montgomery's for dinner, Kale called. Devan took the phone into her room and Kristy followed. There, she saw something she hadn't seen since Kale left — Devan's smile. When they hung up, all expression fell from Devan's face again.

"I get it, Dee," Kristy said and sighed sadly.

"You get what?"

"I understand your pain."

Devan turned around to look at her friend with eyes full of anger and hurt. "So, you know what it's like to have something so awesome, more wonderful than you ever thought it could be, and then have it ripped away?" Tears were starting to form in Devan's eyes.

"Well no, not exactly."

"It's like my heart has been ripped out of my chest and torn to shreds right in front of my face, and then burned to ashes. Then those ashes are rubbed into the gaping hole where my heart used to be."

My God she's dark. At least she's finally showing some emotion, Kristy thought. She went over to her best friend and hugged her. Despite Devan's resistance, she'd finally let someone in.

Kristy felt awful and knew she had to do something. That night, she called Pete and told him what happened. Being the sweet sensitive guy he was, he called his buddy Kale.

"Hey, is there any chance you guys will be coming home to Ohio anytime soon?"

"I was hoping to come at homecoming, but that's not gonna happen," Kale said sadly.

"That sucks." Pete frowned.

"We're going to try for Christmas break now," Kale said, sounding hopeful.

"That would be good."

"Is everything okay?"

"Yeah, man, we all just miss you."

Christmas break 1995

The Iakonas did make it back for Christmas break. With Kale home, Devan was back to normal. Since the Montgomerys really didn't have any family left, they were excited to celebrate the holiday with their 'made family.'

Devan and Kale exchanged gifts. Kale opened his first. It was a necklace made of black and red beads and white puka shells. He hugged her after he put it on. "My favorite colors are black and red. Thank you, Monty. Now open yours." He nudged a small box toward her.

She untied the ribbon and slid it out from under the box, then opened the lid. She pulled up the leather cord of a necklace and felt the smoothness of its charm. "It's beautiful, thank you."

"My aunt taught me how to make it. It's carved from Ox bone."

"You made this?"

"Yeah, and it wasn't easy. One of the cool things she taught me is when you're making something for someone you need to put all your heart and soul into it so the charm will work."

"What is it exactly?"

"It's a Maori twist. It represents the everlasting bond between two people that never fades even if they're far away from each other for a while."

She smiled and asked him to help her put it on. He did, and then turned to face her. Their eyes met and she quickly looked away. "Hey, since they're still eating, want to go over to your house and um... water your mom's plants?" She winked.

"Oh, I already did that this morning," he told her earnestly.

"I bet they're still thirsty," she said winking at him again and grabbing his hand to pull him toward the door.

He raised an eyebrow.

When they got to his house, Kale didn't even get to shut the door all the way before Devan pounced on him. Her kisses were deep and hard, and their passion was reignited instantaneously.

They continued to kiss as they found their way to his bedroom. She pushed him onto the bed and started to unbutton her blouse, revealing a satin push up bra.

He bit his lip nervously as she beamed down at him and unbuttoned his flannel shirt. Her eyes shifted to his toned chest, as she ran her hands over his smooth skin.

He took both of his hands and grasped the back of her head pulling her down to his level. His caresses were soft yet sensual. She loved his hands on her body. He loved her fingers running through his hair.

Things were getting intense when the phone rang, breaking the spell. They heard Kale's mom on the answering machine saying, "Get your butts over here, it's time for dessert."

"Mmm ... I have my dessert right here," she said then slowly licked her lips.

Kale kissed her hard and then moved her off of his body and buttoned his shirt. "If *we* don't go over now, *they* will come here."

She groaned and got herself together.

Too soon Christmas break was over, but Devan didn't go back to her somber ways when Kale left. His letters continued to come every week and the phone calls actually increased in number.

Kale got a football scholarship and would be a University of Hawaii Rainbow Warrior, and Devan kept busy with school. She wrote to him every day and mailed all seven letters at the same time each week.

Iakonas came home to stay the summer after Kale had graduated high school, but Kale stayed in Hawaii with his aunt and uncle so he could play football.

Prom 1997

Things between them slowed down during Devan's senior year. She was studying hard, and Kale was dealing with college and football practice. They still made time for one another, even though the phone calls were short and fewer letters were written. Their commitment to each other remained strong.

"Have you heard from Kale yet?" Kristy asked, while thumbing through a hairstyle magazine.

"Not since he told me he had finals the week of prom. That was almost two months ago. Maybe he's mad at me because he knows I'm disappointed," Devan said sadly.

"I doubt it. He's probably just busy. You *are* still going. Right?"

"No. It's really not a big deal, and it just wouldn't be fun without Kale."

"Devan, it's senior prom. You *have* to go," Kristy pleaded. "We've fantasized about prom since we were in middle school."

"No, I don't *have* to go."

They heard a knock on Kristy's door, but when they opened it no one was there. Instead, they found two oblong boxes with one card. Kristy opened the card and smiled.

"Well?" Devan asked.

"Pete has invited us to the prom."

"Oh, that's a sweet way to ask. You guys will have such a good time."

"No, Dee, one of those boxes is for you."

She untied the ribbon on the box and opened it. There were 11 red roses and 1 peach rose inside, along with a card that read:

"Please, please, please be the other half of my date. I promise you will have a wonderful time.

Love, Pete"

"It's such a sweet gesture. How can I say no?"

The day before prom, Devan stared at herself in the mirror. *I'm sick of my blonde hair. I look like half of the preps at school. I need a change, and I know exactly what I'm going to do.*

That evening Kristy came over to drop her dress off for the following day. Devan was just getting out of the shower when she got there. She unwrapped the towel covering her hair, and Kristy said, "Oh-my-God! What did you do?"

"You don't like it?" Devan asked as she started combing her fingers through her thick dark hair.

"I mean, I don't know. I- ugh ... it's *black* Devan ... Jet black."

"Yep, it was time for a change."

"That's a *big* change."

The girls had only 30 minutes before Pete was supposed to pick them up. They were putting final touches on their makeup and making sure their hair was perfect. "I have to admit, Devan, I didn't think the black was going to work, but you look like you were born with it. I love it."

"Aw, thank you, bestie."

"Well, how do I look?" Kristy asked, fluffing out her dress.

"That green really looks great with your red hair. It's beautiful. You look gorgeous." They hugged.

"It's too bad Hawaii isn't here to see you. We'll take a ton of pictures to send him so he can see what he missed," Kristy promised.

"That's a great idea, let's start now." Devan pulled out a Polaroid camera and snapped some pictures of the two of them.

A short time later, the limo pulled up and Pete and the driver got out. "Your chariot awaits," he said when they answered the door. The driver was huge. He looked like he was taller than Kale. He opened the door and helped Devan in, while Pete helped Kristy.

There's something strange about that driver. He held onto my hand a little longer than was appropriate. Kinda creeped me out. She tried getting a look at his face but he turned his head too quickly.

Well if I'm going to get kidnapped the only description I could give is that he had dark facial hair and a dark ponytail, she thought. *"Ew..."*

"Ladies, I have faux champagne. Peach Orchard sound okay?" Pete asked. He'd gone all out with the limo, the drinks, and the corsages. Kristy's was made up of red rose buds and ferns with green and white ribbons.

Devan's had purple and white orchids with tiny peach rose buds, and dark purple and black ribbons to accentuate her dress.

When they got to the prom, the first two songs the DJ played were fast. Pete danced like a pro, swinging both girls around like they were floating on air. They had so much fun. When things started to slow down, Devan excused herself so Kristy and Pete could have a slow dance.

Someone came and sat next to her on the bleachers. "There's something about this song," she heard a familiar voice say. She looked over and it was the creepy limo driver. "Would you like to dance?" he asked.

Who does this guy think he is? He was paid to drive, not flirt with the clients. "Um, no thanks. I think I'll sit this one out," she said and fake smiled.

He set his hat down and rubbed his goatee. "Come on, I won't bite," he said and grabbed her hand.

She tried pulling away, but his hand was huge. "Excuse me. I said *no*." She looked up at his face and all her anger subsided. "Kale? What are *you* doing here?" She smiled, trying her hardest not to cry.

"Rescuing you from being a wallflower." He got up and led her out onto the dance floor where Mazzy Star's "Fade into You" continued playing. She wrapped her arms around his neck and he held onto her waist.

"I thought you were mad at me. I haven't heard from you in two months."

"I was too busy working a few extra jobs so I could take you to prom."

She gave him a nasty look. "Wait, so this was planned?"

"Yes ma'am, with my buddy Pete's help." He nodded to Pete.

She looked over at Pete and Kristy. Kristy was looking right at her with a surprised smile on her face. Pete winked at Kale.

"That jerk," she said and laughed.

"Hey, now, it was really hard for him to keep such a big secret. I told him I'd kill him if he told Kristy."

"Thank you," she said hugging him tight.

He kissed the top of her head. "I almost didn't recognize you," he said touching her dark hair.

"Well, I didn't recognize you with your beard and longer hair, plus I swear you're even taller than last time I saw you."

"Well, I grew an inch and gained 10 pounds of muscle. I can't look like the boy next door forever, Monty."

She'd missed those green eyes and long eyelashes. And those lips, those plump, pouty, perfect lips. She grabbed his chin and kissed him. His lips were just as soft as she remembered. Being in his strong arms brought on a flood of emotions — safety, passion, love, happiness.

"It killed me not responding to you for two months, but I couldn't ruin my surprise. I did, however, still answer your letters. You'll get them, I promise."

"I missed you *so* much," she said, kissing him again.

"Excuse me, there's no kissing allowed at school functions. Affection leads to fornication," Ms. Jenkins said, tapping Kale on the shoulder. "Mr. Hawaii, hmph, I can't give *you* a detention anymore, but I can certainly give one to Miss Montgomery."

This time Kale actually saw a small but firm smile appear on the woman's face as she walked away. *She's a pretty lady when she smiles. If she'd just loosen up a little she'd be pretty all the time.*

They danced until midnight; it was a magical time. When prom was over, all four of them went back to the Iakona's to watch a movie. Instead of walking over to her house to change, Devan just put on one of Kale's old jerseys and a pair of his boxers.

Halfway through the movie, Pete nudged Kristy and pointed at Devan, who was curled up on the couch with Kale wrapped around her. Both were asleep. Kristy grabbed the camera and said, "They look like angels."

Late the next morning, Devan awoke to the smell of bacon cooking. Kale was still asleep and his arm and leg were wrapped over her like a blanket. She tried getting out from under him just as his mom walked in. She saw Devan struggling and laughed. Then, she yelled as loud as she could, *"You're gonna miss the bus!"*

Kale jumped up so fast that Devan fell on the floor. "I'm up!" he yelled.

"Still works," Cassandra said, laughing hysterically. "I'm sorry, Devan. Are you okay?" she asked helping Devan up. She was laughing so hard tears were streaming down her face.

"Well, I'm glad I could entertain both of you this morning," Kale said before huffily walking to the bathroom.

Devan sat down at the table with Cassandra who asked, "Did you kids have a nice night?"

"Oh, yes, it was — Hold on. You knew about this the whole time?"

His mother nodded.

"Did my parents know?"

"Not until after you left your house. Kale Kai made me swear not to say a word."

"Well, thank you for helping him. It was a great surprise."

Kale came back out of the bathroom and kissed the top of her head and then his mom's. "My two favorite ladies," he said as he went into the kitchen to get the coffee pot and bring it in.

"Devan, do you want to go with us to take Kale back to the airport this afternoon?"

"Yes, she does," Kale said with his mouth full of food.

"Kale," his mom scolded him.

"What? She does." His mouth was even fuller this time.

"Yes, I want to go," Devan said and laughed.

At the airport he said goodbye to his parents and asked Devan to walk him to the gate. "I'll see you in a few short weeks," he said, scooping her into his arms. She wrapped herself around him and they shared a long, intimate kiss that made the stewardess walking by blush.

"We'll finish this later," he promised.

As he walked away, she whispered, "I love you."

Chapter 11

The Lake, 1997

Devan was sunning herself to pass the time, because Kale's plane got in late and his parents were going to be later getting to the lake than they'd planned. She was so excited she could hardly stand it. She'd been thinking about that last kiss since it happened, and it had her all hot and bothered.

She'd almost missed her name being called at graduation because she was daydreaming about it. She would've kept thinking about it right through graduation if Pete hadn't nudged her.

Devan fell asleep in the sun and didn't hear the Iakonas arrive. Being the naughty boy he was, Kale devised an ambush. He had ice-cold water balloons in each hand and was only a few feet away from her when he smelled her coconut shampoo and tanning lotion and was intoxicated by the scent.

Her black hair shimmered in the sunlight, and her hot pink bikini looked like it had been painted on. "I remember that pink suit," he said and laughed to himself.

He threw the first balloon and missed on purpose. A little bit of the water landed on Devan's legs and she sat up. When she did, Kale threw the remaining three — one right after the other, soaking her.

She got up and glared at him as he laughed. "Hmm, think you're smart, don't you?"

He grinned at her, taking a few steps closer.

"Well, Mr. Iakona, you see these?" she asked and pointed to her lips.

"Oh, yeah," he said moving closer.

"You can't have them."

He got a petulant look on his face and said, "That's okay, I don't want 'em anyway."

"Yes you do."

He was getting closer to her. "No, I *really* don't."

She walked right up to him and untied the top of her bikini and let a string fall, exposing just a tiny bit more of her breast than was already visible. "Are you sure?"

"Damn you, Monty!" He wrestled her to the ground and kissed her hard.

"Okay, you two, quit horsing around. Devan, go help your mom. Kale, we need you to get the coolers and take them down to the boat," Chris ordered with a laugh.

"You, me, the willow tree on the other side of the road, after dinner," Kale demanded.

She licked her lips, smacked her behind, and sashayed away. He ran up behind her, locked his arms around her and squeezed, while whispering in her ear. "That ass is mine." He let go and watched her walk back up to the cabin.

A little later, they all took the boat out for the remainder of the day. Kale and Devan both exchanged many meaningful glances during the afternoon. "After dinner" couldn't come fast enough for either of them.

When they got back to the cabin, Cassandra asked the kids to go down to the marina to buy some butter. They decided to take the long way there. When they were out of sight, Devan grabbed Kale's shirt and shoved him against a tree.

"Is there a problem?"

"Yeah, there's a huge problem!" she replied with a serious look on her face.

"What?"

"Your lips aren't on mine." With that she kissed him, and he wrapped his long arms around her tightly. She stopped kissing him and stared into his beautiful green eyes with adoration. "I missed you," she said softly.

"I missed you, too, Monty," he said, adding a sweet peck on her lips.

"Well, I suppose we'd better go get that butter," she said, winking at him.

"Hold on, we aren't going anywhere yet. I need more." He took her hands and put them behind her back and held them there with one hand. With his free hand, he grabbed her ponytail and pulled her head back to the side just enough to expose her neck so he could kiss it.

That did something to her she couldn't explain. Her whole body tingled. She closed her eyes and a tiny moan escaped her throat. He moved his mouth back to hers and she kissed him passionately. She wanted him, and she wanted him *now!*

He pulled away. "Whoa, let's uh, go get that butter before we get in trouble."

She gave him the nastiest look he'd ever seen. "Oh, you *so* can't just do that and then stop!"

Kale laughed and said, "Well, maybe now you'll come back for more," and ran off ahead of her.

"Payback's a bitch, Iakona, and her name is Devan Montgomery!" she yelled after him, trying to catch up.

After dinner the parents decided to take a walk and go check out the new general store. Kale decided to walk with them, but only halfway. He was planning to meet Devan at the willow tree.

Devan stayed behind and showered. By the time Kale got to the tree, Devan was waiting for him with her hair still wet and dripping.

"Hey, pretty lady. My name's Kale," he said and extended his hand slowly.

She giggled. "Not interested." *Oh this is going to be fun.*

"Really? Are you taken?" he asked, getting closer.

"No, I just don't like tall men," she said while turning her nose up at him.

He was doing his best not to laugh. Everyone knew Devan had a height fetish. "Well, do you like short men?" he asked politely.

"No, average is fine."

"Average, huh? Well, I'd like think I'm above average in every way, not just height. Is there anything I could do to change your mind?" He raised an eyebrow.

"Hmm, I guess you could try," she said, looking unimpressed.

He pulled his sleeve up and flexed his bicep. He knew she had a weakness for his physique. She'd never admitted it, but he'd noticed it over the past few years.

She shrugged. "It's okay."

"*Okay?* I work really hard on these." He thought for a moment then had a great idea. He took his shirt off, grabbed her hand and glided it across his chest, knowing that would do the job.

She fought the urge to grab his hard pecs. She could hear them calling her name, but she held her ground. "Yeah, I can tell you work out," she said nonchalantly.

Ooh, she's better at this than I expected. He picked up his shirt to put it back on. "Oh, well you don't need this," she said, snatching the shirt out of his hand and throwing it out of his reach.

He got so close to her there was hardly a breath between them. She could feel the heat radiating off his body, and it made her quiver with anticipation.

He leaned down and moved her hair away from her ear. His lips so close to her neck that she could feel his breath. "You sure you're not interested?" he whispered, breathing more hot air onto her neck.

She whimpered as he ran his massive hand down her arm, then slipped it under her shirt, just brushing her breast. His hand continued its upward trek as he reached up through the shirt to caress her neck. Then he slid his hand back down, lightly brushing her breast again. His hand left her shirt and came up under her chin. He lifted her face and looked into her eyes with intensity.

"It's too bad, really, because your lips look perfect enough to kiss," he said seductively.

I'm done playing! Devan stood on her tiptoes to reach him and put her left hand on his shoulder, while pulling the band holding his hair. Once free, his dark brown curls cascaded over his shoulders.

She ran her hands through his thick hair, untangling strands here and there while kissing him deeply. Her erotic touch sent a never-ending shiver down his spine — straight to his nether region.

He growled with anticipation of what was to come. With his muscular arms holding her, he walked into the woods where they were completely out of view, without missing a single stroke of her tongue as it wrapped around his.

He laid her down gently on the cushion of grass and positioned himself above her. Holding himself up with his arms he looked into her inviting blue eyes.

"Isn't this Kale's?" they heard his mother ask.

"I think so, that kid just leaves his things everywhere," his father replied.

Kale didn't move a muscle. Devan was so worried they'd get caught that she contracted a bad case of giggles.

"Shhhhh!" He covered her mouth with his hand until the parents were nowhere to be seen. When he released her, she was still laughing.

"Devan Marie, that is *not* funny. We almost got caught!"

"I know, it was frightening," she managed to say before laughing uncontrollably.

"Devan, *stop* laughing!" He got off her and helped her up.

When they opened the door to the cabin, Kale's father threw his shirt at him.

"Oh, thanks, the wind must have blown it away."

Devan lost it all over again.

The next day Devan made plans to meet an old friend she'd met at the lake several years ago. The Iakonas and Montgomerys went out on the boat all day, and Kale stayed home with a headache.

Devan's visit ended early because her friend was called in to work. When she got back to the cabin, she walked into her bedroom and saw rose petals all over her bed, along with a card and a single rose. The card read:

"If there was only one thing I could have in the entire world it would be you.

Love,

Kale."

She breathed in the sweet scent of the rose. It was a truly romantic gesture. She walked by his room and saw he was asleep. She quietly walked in, trying not to wake him.

She crawled into bed with him, snuggled up behind him, and put her hand on his hip. He quickly put his hand on top of hers. *He's awake!*

He moved her hand to his bare chest. His heart was beating fast. She could feel her own heart rate rise to match his. She scooted closer to sniff his soft hair. *How does this guy always smell so good?* She was starting to believe Nautica leaked out of his pores.

She kissed the back of his neck and said, "Thank you for the rose and the card."

He got up off of the bed and pulled something out from underneath it. It was a full box of roses. He selected one and pulled the petals off one by one, dropping them along her body. He didn't say a thing. When he finished with that rose, he did the same with another.

Then, he lay down next to her again. She started to say something, but he shushed her with his finger. He put his lips softly on hers, and slowly pulled her shirt up and over her head.

He grabbed another rose from the box and put the bud on her slightly parted lips. Slowly he moved it down her neck, then between her breasts and on down to her navel. The petals felt like satin against her skin.

He moved the rose back to her lips and started the process all over again, but this time he followed the rose with his lips. When he got to her navel he stopped and unbuttoned and unzipped her shorts, slowly pulling them off.

Now she was lying on his bed wearing nothing but pink cotton panties and a matching bra. He took another rose out of the box and pulled the petals off, again letting them drop all over her body. He put the empty stem down and took off his shorts, leaving him wearing only his boxer briefs.

His body is a work of art. It's like he's a tall drink of water and I'm dying of thirst.

He took in her beauty — her perfectly shaped breasts that rose when she inhaled, her long toned legs, her slender neck — paying attention to every detail.

Lying down next to her with a rose in his hand, he glided it across her legs. She grasped his hand and pulled the rose out of it, then turned on her side to face him. She moved his hand to her thigh, and slid it up to her hip where she left it. He moved it to her behind, pushing her into him.

The thing she'd been waiting for was finally happening. *I want this to be perfect, not just for me but for Kale too. What if I do something wrong?*

He put his mouth on hers, and his passionate yet forceful kiss melted her fears. He didn't stop there. He moved on to her neck, where his soft kisses electrified her body.

Kale lowered his hand and slipped a finger over the band of her panties, pulling them down. She leaned back against the mattress and pulled him on top of her. She could feel him throbbing against her.

She couldn't fight the raging hunger for him to be inside of her. She reached down to pull off his boxers, but he stopped her.

"Wait," he reached in the drawer beside the bed and pulled out a foil wrapper. "Are you sure about this?" he asked softly.

She nodded her head. "Please," she begged.

"I don't want to hurt you," he said fumbling with the package.

She gave him a moment to get situated and said, "You won't."

He was gentle, but that just made his love making more amazing. *Not that I have anything to compare it to.* After a few minutes, instinct took over and they both surrendered to the moment.

A little while later, they cleaned up the room and made the bed so there would be no evidence of what they'd done. They decided to go ahead and put dinner in the oven, thinking their parents would be back soon. While it was cooking, they played UNO, and tried not to look suspicious.

After dinner, Kale and Devan walked down to the marina. "Hey, are there any cool places we could explore?" he asked the guy behind the counter. The man picked up a map and started circling different areas and explaining how to get there. Devan walked up behind Kale and put her arms around him, and the guy glanced at her and then back at Kale.

"My favorite place is over here," he pointed and circled. "There's a pretty cool waterfall and it's pretty secluded," he said with a wink.

"Hmm," Kale said, nodding. He shook the guy's hand and thanked him. He had a plan!

Chapter 12

On the way back from the Marina, they stopped at the willow tree and Kale took her hands in his. "After we go skiing in the morning, I was thinking about renting another boat for the day — just for us. We can pack a cooler and check out some of the places that guy was showing us."

"I like that idea. Remind me to bring my camera," she said eagerly.

He looked into her eyes and realized how glad he was to be here with her. He kept a picture of her on his desk at school and looked at it often. *Seeing her in person is so much better! Man, I hate to leave again so soon, but I'm going to make the most of this time we have together.*

She wrapped her arms around him and hugged him tight. *I wish I was brave enough to tell him I love him. There's no better feeling than being here in his strong arms. I feel so safe.*

He kissed the top of her head and asked, "Can I have a kiss before we go back?"

"You don't have to ask, Kale Kai. You *never* have to ask for that."

He leaned down and brushed his lips against hers. "Can I keep you?"

Her smile and long amorous kiss answered his question.

The next day when they went down to rent the boat, the same guy was working the rental desk. He was in his late 20s, and six feet tall with a thin frame. "Hey, Stretch, I forgot to tell you something. We've started having special events on Friday nights. This Friday it's a corn roast and a local band's gonna be playing. I'm sure there'll be dancing, too. You and your girl ought to check it out."

"Thanks, I think I will."

"Don't forget to go to the waterfall when you're out today," he said and winked.

Kale and Devan checked out a few of the places on the map before going to the waterfall. When they got there, Kale pulled the boat up on shore and tied it to a tree. He took the cooler out of the boat, while Devan grabbed a quilt and a couple of towels.

They couldn't see the waterfall from where they were, but they could hear it off in the distance. They walked around the edge of the island and found large slate stones with water cascading over them and down into the lake. Mature oak and maple trees shaded the entire area, making it even more secluded. Myrtle decorated the ground and the effect was breathtaking. The mist that encircled the area completed the enchanting atmosphere.

Kale set the cooler down and hopped in the water, while Devan spread out the quilt. When she was finished, she slowly walked into the water. She was shivering by the time she reached the falls.

"Cold?" Kale asked, laughing.

"It's just a tad bit nippy in here," she said through chattering teeth.

"Come here, I'll warm you up."

He wrapped her in his arms and she ran her fingers through his hair. He loved it when she did that. It was a complete turn on. He kissed her, catching her a little off guard.

He held her tighter, and Devan pulled his hair back and moved her mouth to his chiseled jaw. The stubble tickled her lips, so she moved down to his neck. He moaned and untied her bikini top, throwing it onto to ground near the water. Her bare breasts against his warm, hard chest excited both of them even more.

With his lips still pressed to hers, he carried her to the shore and gently laid her on the quilt. His kisses were deep and tender. His lips moved to her jaw and she instinctively tilted her head so he could have better access to her neck.

Her pulse quickened as his lips brushed along her earlobe and down her neck. Kale was holding her close, but she could never be close enough to him.

When Kale put his warm hand on her breast, a small gasp escaped her lips. He traced his fingertips down her taut stomach and untied her bikini bottoms.

He groaned low in his throat as Devan's hands explored the solid wall of his chest, then his mouth moved over hers and took possession. She slid her hands into his hair, tangling her fingers in the dark silky curls.

He pulled away and asked, "Do you have any idea what it does to me when you run your fingers through my hair?"

"Is it bad?"

"It could be if I can't control myself," he said slyly.

"So you like it." She smirked back at him.

"Um, no. I love it."

She pulled on his hair just enough that he could feel it without it being painful. He groaned and removed his shorts, throwing them somewhere in the myrtle. She pulled on his hair again, and he said, "Be careful little girl, you don't know what you're asking for."

She knew exactly what she was doing. She was no longer innocent, so why bother acting like it. She needed to feel him inside her once again. "Oh, I know," she said and looked deep into his eyes as she pulled a curl again. He growled, and she thought she saw his eyes shift from light jade to a dark forest green.

He nudged her thighs open with his knee and positioned himself above her. Her hands quickly moved to his tight butt, pulling him down on top of her. She raised her hips and encouraged him to thrust. With his mouth on hers, he slowly pushed himself further inside, trying not to hurt her.

Her tongue wrapped itself around his, turning his sensual kiss into something much more erotic. Her hands moved to his head, and with a yank of his hair, she pulled his lips off hers and slid her mouth to his thick neck. When he felt her teeth on his skin, something inside him snapped.

He grabbed her hair and pulled her head away from his neck, his pupils fully dilated. He had an almost sinister look on his face as he buried himself to the hilt. She gasped at the pain and ecstasy. He continued, getting slightly rougher with each thrust.

Oh-my-god! She bucked her hips against his, meeting his thrusts over and over again, as their coupling increased in speed.

He was panting and dripping sweat from his brow. She buried her nails in his biceps, as her back arched and she let out a scream as waves of pleasure overtook her.

When they finally stopped, Kale crashed down on top of her.

"That was amazing," she sighed breathlessly.

He turned over on his side, and she noticed his eyes were back to normal. *Hmmm, that's different.* "Wanna go again?" she asked, raising an eyebrow.

His chest was heaving, and he was still out of breath. "Oh my God, woman, let me breathe first." He fell onto his back and grabbed Devan's hand and put it on his chest over his heart. "Do you feel that?"

She could feel his heart pounding. She turned over to face him and lightly brushed her lips against his.

"Oh my god!" he jerked up in a panic.

"What's wrong?"

"We got caught up in the moment, and I didn't use—"

"It's okay, Kale. I'm on the pill. I have been for some time."

He sighed in relief, then said, "That's not always effective though."

"Relax, even if it wasn't, it's the wrong time of the month," she replied, while starting to climb on top of him. "Are you ready to go again now?"

The six of them spent all day out on the boat the following day. When they got back, they decided to eat at the marina's cafe. They sat beside the boat rental guy and Kale asked, "Hey, man, you never go home do you?"

"This *is* my home," he said, and chuckled. "Hey, you guys comin' tomorrow?"

"What's tomorrow?" Devan asked.

"A corn roast," the guy said, and smiled.

"Well, that sounds like fun," Elaine chimed in.

"It's a good time for all ages," the rental guy said, tapping Kale on the shoulder as he walked away.

The next day, they went out in the boat for a few hours, then came back and packed so they'd be ready to leave in the morning. Kale didn't have the heart to tell Devan his parents were taking him straight to the airport the next morning.

They went to the corn roast and enjoyed the dinner, and the band was amazing. A slow song came on and a few people got up and danced, so Kale pulled Devan out of her seat to join them.

Devan knew that her time with Kale was slowly disappearing, and she was starting to get depressed.

"Hey," he whispered in her ear, "I didn't want to tell you this until the last minute so it wouldn't ruin our time together. I'm not going home with you guys. I'm going straight back to school."

"I figured you would."

"I'm sorry."

She didn't really want to look in his eyes right now, because she'd probably cry. So, she just held on to him tight and rested her head on his chest. She stayed that way until the next song started.

She looked up and Kale was smiling down on her.

"Are you kidding me?"

The band was doing a cover of Mazzy Star's "Fade Into You." The words didn't really fit, but this song had become an integral part of their relationship, and it would forever haunt them both.

Chapter 13

College 1999

Kale and Devan didn't see each other again for two years after their magical time at the lake. They were both so busy with school that they even studied or practiced during breaks.

Kale changed his major to architect his sophomore year, which added two more years of school for him that he was trying to get down to one. He still played for the Rainbow Warriors, which also kept him busy.

Devan was always preoccupied with school. Creative writing wasn't as easy as she'd thought it would be. She almost gave up on college completely the summer after her freshman year, but her parents talked her out of it.

Kale and Devan wrote to each other once in a while, and every few months they'd have a quick phone conversation, but that was it.

One day the phone rang, and when Devan answered it, Kale said, "Monty, I looked at the schedule and we play University of Colorado on November 2nd."

"Here?"

"Yes! We'll be in town for three days and two nights."

"Oh, wow!"

"They're really strict about what we do with our time and try to keep us focused on the game, but I really want to see you."

"Yeah, I wanna see you, too."

"Don't plan anything for that weekend. I'll figure it out."

"Okay, I'm all yours."

"God, I hope so. I gotta go. I'll call you before we leave."

"Sounds good."

"And, Monty, I really miss you. I can't wait to see you."

"I miss you, too."

"Take care."

"Back at you."

Back at you? What was I thinking? I wasn't. I'm too nervous. He's coming to the school that's only 30-minutes way! She looked at her calendar and then in the mirror. *I've got three months to fix myself up. I've got to do something with my hair, and I'm too pale and flabby. I've got a lot of work to do!*

A few days later the phone rang and it was Kale again.

"You'll be getting something in the mail from me in seven to 10 days. If you don't get it by then call me. And Monty—"

"Yeah?"

"You're mine!" *(click)*

He hung up? "What the hell?" she said out loud.

She got the package in the mail a week later. It contained a ticket to the game, a Warriors sweatshirt, Kale's jersey, and two envelopes. The first one contained a letter from him explaining what he had planned. The second had a receipt for a hotel room. His letter explained that the easiest way for him to see her was for her to stay in the same hotel as the team, so he'd reserved a room on the same floor they'd be staying on.

She was so excited that she almost forgot she had a tanning appointment and a meeting with her trainer afterward. *I've got two and a half months to get myself ready to impress Kale.*

Kale called again two weeks before the game. "Aloha, Monty."

"Aloha, Kale."

"Are you ready for my visit?"

"Yep."

"Okay, good. I'll leave a note at the hotel desk for you the night before the game so you'll know what time I'm going to meet you in your room."

"Okay. Do you want me to bring anything?"

"The only thing I want is you." *(click)*

He hung up again. Really?

The day before the game, Devan went to the salon and had her nails done and her hair recolored. After that, she went out and got a new outfit and some new makeup.

When she looked in the mirror before leaving to check in at the hotel, she was happy with her look for the night. Her long black hair was smoothed down, yet curled under on the ends, and parted on the side. Her new makeup made her eyes pop and her skin had a healthy glow.

She'd lost the 10 pounds she'd gained since she'd last seen Kale and her muscles now had some tone. She looked great in the skinny jeans and the long crocheted gray sweater that showed her slinky black camisole. She topped the look off with long black boots that reached her knees.

When she headed back to her hotel room after checking in, she saw a large group of guys standing in the hallway. She heard one of them say, "I bet I can get with the next girl who walks by."

"Whatever, dude. I never see you with any women."

"Just watch."

Devan scooted past the group, trying to get to her room. She was stunned when she was grabbed and locked in an embrace that included someone's lips plastered to hers. When she realized it was Kale, she reciprocated.

There was laughter and clapping, and when they finished their kiss, he introduced her. "Warriors, this is my girlfriend, Devan. She's the reason why you never see me with any other girls."

He let her go and turned to one of his teammates. "Devan, this is Kahuna Ho ókano. He and I grew up in the same neighborhood."

A large Samoan picked her up and swung her around while hugging her. "I've heard so much about you. Please call me Kuna." He had a sweet chubby face, and his brown eyes had long eyelashes that made him look a few years younger than he actually was. He was also huge. He looked like a giant adorable child.

"But they just said they didn't know you had a girlfriend," she said, turning to Kale.

"*They* didn't know, but I tell Kuna everything."

She gulped, *Everything?* She hoped she was only imagining Kuna's eyes roaming all over her.

"Did you get the note?" Kale asked, distracting her uncomfortable thoughts.

"Yeah."

A man she assumed was the coach walked up to them. "Miss, I'm sorry to interrupt, but my boys need their sleep. We've got a big game tomorrow. You can see them after we win the game."

"Okay, I'm sorry," she said as she picked her bag up and headed down the hall.

As she was walking away, she heard the coach say, "All right, whose girlfriend was she? I'll be checking your rooms tonight — so no stowaways."

"She's my *wahine* (woman)."

"Kuna, you expect me to believe *that* girl is your girlfriend?"

"What, coach? Just because I am not pretty like Iakona here, doesn't mean the ladies don't like this hot bod." The team laughed as Kuna rubbed his belly.

"Hey, Devan," Kuna yelled down the hall. *"Aloha wau iā ōe."*

She set her bag down and blew him a kiss. "I love you, too."

"Okay, fine. No bed buddies tonight," the coach said firmly.

"Yes, sir. I will *not* let her in my bed until after the game."

Kale stomped on Kuna's foot. Kuna laughed, looking a whole lot like Buddah as he did.

Kale laughed with him. "Thanks."

"Anything for my braddah. I figured if he thought she was mine, he wouldn't be checking on you."

"Good thinking, except we're sharing a room," Kale said and laughed, shaking his head.

"Aw shit! That's right. Sorry. But hey, I gotta tell ya, she's more beautiful than her picture, bro. I can see the attraction. I can also see her love for you runs deep — it's in her eyes. You must tell her *aloha wau iā óe* all the time, since she knows what it means."

Kale wasn't sure when she'd learned that phrase or what it meant, but he knew he'd never said it to her even though he wanted to.

A few hours later, there was a light knock on Devan's door. She opened it and there stood Kale. "I'm sorry about earlier. I couldn't help myself." He winked at her and sat on the bed. "You look different."

"Well, I should. You haven't seen me in two years." She giggled.

"Come here let me get a good look at you." She walked over to the bed. "I pictured you a lot whiter," he said and laughed.

"Yeah, well they have these things called tanning beds now."

"You don't need that, Monty,"

"So, you don't like what you see?" she asked, hands on her hips.

"Oh, *wahine*, I always like what I see when it comes to you. You look more grown up. I can't really explain it without sounding weird."

He reached out to her and drew her closer. "I've wanted to hold you for so long," he said, pulling her into his embrace.

I've missed this, she thought.

He kissed her lips gently. She pulled back and took her sweater off, revealing her tight low-cut camisole.

He looked at her arms. "Have you been working out?"

"A little," she said, while grabbing Kale's shirt and trying to take it off. When she got it off him, she threw it on the floor, then pushed him down on the bed and ran her hands down his chest. "You're asking me about working out? Is it just me or have you bulked up a lot more?"

"Just 10 pounds. Don't worry it'll go away after football season."

Mmm, but it shouldn't have to, she thought.

Kale snatched her hands from his chest and pulled her down on top of him. He looked intensely into her blue eyes, then kissed her passionately.

She reached down and started to unbutton his jeans. "No, wait. I want to enjoy this." He kissed her again, this time deeper. He pulled her tank up until it was around her neck. The warmth of his naked skin on hers sent shivers down her spine.

He slid his hands lower to cup her ass and push her harder against his erection that was threatening to burst right out of his pants.

"Devan, we have to stop."

"I don't wanna stop."

He chuckled. "I know, but I have the game tomorrow, and—"

"It's late, I know."

"Yeah, but I want to enjoy you for just a minute longer." He kissed her again.

She was too riled up to just let it go. So, she straddled his pelvic region and put her hands on his chest. Then, she slowly began grinding against him with her nails digging in. He didn't stop her right away, but then he licked his lips, grabbed her hips and lifted her off him. He flipped her over on her stomach, grabbed a handful of her hair, and got up behind her.

She could feel his hot breath on her neck. "I told you to stop." He put his mouth on her neck and brushed his lips against it before biting.

That sent her into a frenzy. "Please, don't stop," she begged. He continued to tease her neck with his tongue and teeth. "Oh, my God! Just give it to me already," she pleaded.

He knew at this point he really should leave, but the ache in his groin kept him there. He looked at the clock and saw it was already past midnight. *I need to get back to my room!* He released her and grabbed his shirt. "Sorry, Monty. I gotta go to bed."

She jumped up off of the bed and shot daggers at him with her icy blue eyes. "What the hell?"

"I'm sorry. I didn't realize the time." He grabbed her around the waist and said, "You know I wouldn't leave you like this if I had a choice. I promise I'll make it up to you tomorrow." He kissed her on the forehead and walked out the door.

The game was great. It was close, but the Warriors won. Afterwards, Devan went back to her hotel room and took a shower. The phone rang just as she was stepping out.

"Hey, how about I take you to dinner?"

She looked at the clothes she'd laid out on the bed. It wasn't much, only Kale's jersey and a pair of underwear. "No, we should order in."

"Okay. I'm gonna take a shower and be right over."

He showed up half an hour later and knocked on her door. She answered, wearing nothing but his jersey.

"Did you wear that to the game?" he asked walking in.

"No, I wore the sweatshirt."

"Oh, okay. So how hungry are you?" he asked, while looking at a menu.

She walked over to Kale, took the menu out of his hand and dropped it on the floor.

"I'm starving, but not for food," she said in a low voice and stepped out of her underwear without tearing her eyes away from his.

Her hands undid his belt buckle and the button of his jeans, and then pulled down his zipper. He didn't say a word. She pulled the belt all the way out, letting his pants fall to the floor in a heap. *Mmm, he's commando today.*

He broke the intensity of their stare by picking her up and kissing her thoroughly. She immediately wrapped her legs around his waist and her arms around his neck. He took a few steps and gently laid her on the bed.

He took his shirt off, exposing his bulging biceps, rock hard pecs, and tight abs. He grabbed her feet and pulled her down so her legs were hanging off the bed, then he stepped between them and put his hands on her knees.

His hands moved up to her thighs, then slid up top her navel. He lifted the jersey up, resting it just below her chin. His hands caressed her firm breasts then moved back to her thighs.

He knelt down and kissed her smooth stomach and worked his way up to her breasts, giving them both some much-needed attention. When his lips found their way to her neck, she gasped.

He moved away, looked her straight in the eyes and smiled. Within a second, he'd flipped her over onto her front. He took both of her hands in one of his and spread her legs farther apart, then thrust himself deep inside. The pleasure/pain of this was pure ecstasy.

An hour later they were exhausted. He kissed the top of her head and said, "I hate being so far away from you."

"This is too hard," she said to him.

"What's too hard?" he asked.

"I don't want a boyfriend I can't see or touch. Hell, we hardly even talk to each other."

He sighed. "I know. It sucks, and we've got two more years of this."

"I'm not saying I want to date other people," she continued.

"Good, because I'd kill them," he said, laughing a little nervously.

"Maybe we should just play the friendship card for a while. You know, less worries."

He thought about it. *She's absolutely right. This relationship isn't much of a distraction because we're so far away, but I do miss her and think about her all the time. We both really need to put all of our energy into school so we can graduate on time.* He hated the thought of breaking up. *What if something happens and she finds someone else?*

"Have you even thought about your future after college?" she asked.

"Yeah, I have, but all of my future plans involve you." He kissed her cheek. She smiled.

"What about you? Are you planning on staying here?"

"No, I want to go back home and get a job there. I was hoping you'd come back, too. If you're planning on staying in Hawaii, then my plans might have to change a bit."

He grabbed her hand and looked into her eyes. "I want to be wherever you are. If you wanted to go to Alaska, I'd buy a parka. If you wanted to go to Texas, well, I guess I'd get a cowboy hat."

She kissed his lips. "I like that plan."

Chapter 14

Summer of 2001, Four weeks before graduation

"Good morning, Kale, looking fine as usual," Jeane said to him as he came into to work.

God, I hate this woman. He had to force himself to even acknowledge her. "Hello, Jeane. How're doin'?"

She swung herself around his lifeguard chair, and her long dark auburn hair almost got caught in the leg.

"I heard that you've got a friend coming to work with us."

"Yeah, Devan. She'll be here in a few weeks." *I don't feel like making small talk. I'm trying to watch the kids in the pool. Go away.*

"Devan, huh? A girl? That's more of a boy's name, isn't it?" she asked with a smirk that Kale wanted to smack right off her face.

He sighed. "It's a unisex name based on its' spelling…Just like Jeane is."

"Hmph. Anyway, where will she be staying?"

It's none of your business. "With me. If you'll excuse me, I have to check the pool levels." He hopped down off the chair and walked away.

"I have to get back to work anyway."

"Thank God," he muttered under his breath.

Jeane was the afternoon bartender. She was 25, acted like she was 16, and usually dressed completely inappropriately for work. She favored dresses that left nothing to the imagination, hooker heels, and shirts that looked like they'd been made for a seven year old girl. She worked little and played hard.

She'd come into the picture when the new owner, Alistar Cadence, took over. She was his great niece, which meant she could get away with anything and everything, and she did.

She'd been pursuing Kale since she met him. He was nice to her at first, but after the constant sexual harassment, he stopped trying to be polite. He'd even been forced to talk to his boss about her on more than one occasion.

She had flings with a few of the other employees, which usually resulted in their dismissal when the fling was over. The only reason Kale still had his job was because he'd been there for a long time and had an in with the hotel manager, who'd stayed on after the hotel changed hands.

Jeane Cadence was nothing but trouble and Kale did his best to stay away from her.

Kale and Devan's college graduations were two weeks apart. The Iakonas went to Hawaii for Kale's ceremony and came back just in time for Devan's. Afterwards, the Montgomerys and Iakonas took Devan out to dinner.

As they were waiting for dessert to be served, Nāhoa, Kale's dad, handed Devan a card and said, "He really wanted to be here."

"I know. I'm so glad you two could make it," she said giving him a hug.

"We came back a few days early so we wouldn't miss it. We're so proud you both."

"Open the card," Cassandra said, so excited she couldn't sit still.

Devan opened it and it read: "Welcome to Hawaii." It was one of the cards they put in hotel rooms. "I'm confused."

"Look at the back," Nāhoa said.

She turned it over and her eyes grew big with excitement. "Oh my God! Is this for real?" She was holding a one-way ticket to Hawaii. A note was written on it that said: "See ya soon, Monty!"

She hugged Kale's parents as her mom walked over with another card.

"You board in two hours." she said handing her the card.

"What?"

"Look at the ticket, it has today's date on it," her dad said. "Mom has you all packed. Your luggage is in the car and there's a prepaid card in there with a few thousand on it so you can get whatever else you need."

"The four of us will be joining you there in a month. We'll celebrate Kale's graduation then," Chris continued.

"Will I be coming back home with you?" she asked.

"No. Your first week there will be your vacation. After that, Kale has a job lined up for you at the resort. We thought you could use a break after all that time you spent studying. You'll be working for the summer, but you'll be working in paradise."

"Am I dreaming?" she asked with wide eyes.

"Do you need me to pinch you?" her mom asked with a giggle.

On the long flight Devan wondered how awkward it was going to be to see Kale again after all this time. The last time they saw each other in person they'd decided to "just be friends."

We'll always have a close bond, but how am I going to keep my hands off him? How can I not kiss those full lips? She hadn't been with anyone since Kale.

I'll just play it cool, she thought, trying to enforce the idea that they were just friends. *It's going to be hard to remember he's not mine anymore.*

When the plane landed, she went to baggage claim and grabbed her luggage. She looked around but didn't spot Kale. Ten minutes later, she finally saw him.

Oh my God! There he is and he's wearing board shorts, sunglasses, flip-flops and no shirt! He was bigger, had longer hair, a darker tan and a scruffier look than last time she'd seen him. He'd also put on another 10 pounds of pure muscle. *He's a whole lot of hot!*

He dropped the sign that had her name on it, ran over and picked her up. He swung her around and said, "I've missed you, Monty!"

"Missed you, too, Lettuce Head." Being in his arms again brought all of those wonderful feelings of security back, but looking at him made her hot all over. *I don't know how long this "friend" thing will last, but I'll give it a shot.*

When they got to Kale's bungalow, he took Devan's bags inside. She watched every little movement he made — the way his muscles rippled when he lifted anything, the sweat that dripped off his brow, and the way he smiled when he looked at her.

"So, do you wanna chill out for a bit or do you wanna go do something?" he asked.

"I think we should stay here for a little bit," she said and bit her lip. *I want to rip your clothes off!* "Do you mind if I take a shower?"

"Oh, no problem. There's a towel in there for you and I got you a loofa, too."

"Thank you, it was sweet of you to think of me." She walked into the bathroom, shutting the door behind her — but only halfway.

He heard the water come on and went into the other bedroom. When he walked back by, he noticed a pile of clothes on the floor through the partially open door. He lingered a little longer than he should have, catching a glimpse of her long legs stepping into the tub.

Oh, how I'd love to have those legs wrapped around my waist. He shook his head to get rid of the naughty thoughts. *I can't think like this, we're just friends now.* He walked into his room and remembered he hadn't told her how to work the tub.

"Hey, you know that's a Jacuzzi tub. Hit the middle button to turn the jets on."

"What?"

He walked up to the bathroom door but didn't dare look in. "Hit the middle button to turn on the jets." He took a deep breath and walked away when he heard the jets start. *Picturing her sleek body stepping into the hot steaming tub is almost more than I can take. No, no, Kale Kai Iakona! You cannot have these thoughts.* He looked down at the bulge in his shorts and thought, *You need to go away.*

Devan soaked in the hot aromatic bath and couldn't stop thinking about Kale's biceps, chest, and flawless face. *I want those huge man hands all over my body.* She sighed, turned the jets off and stepped out of the tub.

He heard the jets turn off way too soon. He got up and stood outside the door. "Hey, everything okay?"

"Not exactly," she said pulling the door open to expose her towel wrapped body.

"Um, uh, wh- what's wrong?" He kind of forgot how to talk as he stared at the water dripping down her legs.

She grabbed his hand and put it on her forehead. "Do I feel hot to you?"

Yes! "No, not really."

She let go of his hand and grabbed the waist of his shorts, pulling him close to her. "That's weird, because I feel *really* ..." she put her other hand on his cheek, *"really hot."* She released her grip on his shorts and put that hand on his chest.

Oh my God! Is this really happening? He was hooked. He couldn't look away from her beautiful blue eyes. He lowered his head so he could reach her lips. *She tastes like strawberries and champagne.*

She pushed him into the hallway wall. Her hands were on his arms and chest. *I'm in charge!*

His mind was saying no, but his body was saying yes, yes, *yes!*

Somehow they ended up in the bedroom. Devan was on top, taking full control of the situation — and Kale liked it. His shorts had disappeared to God knows where. He was thoroughly enjoying what was going on. He let her ravish his body — all of it.

A few hours later, Devan woke up starving. She tapped Kale on his shoulder trying to wake him up. "Is there a pizza delivery place around here?"

He opened his eyes slowly. "What?"

"I need food. I used up all my fuel."

He laughed. "Get dressed. We're going to dinner."

They got dressed and jumped into Kale's Jeep. He drove a short distance, then pulled up to a roadside cafe called Happy Hookers. "So, should I expect a lap dance with my dinner?" she asked, as she warily walked toward the front door.

He put his arm around her and said, "No, but maybe you'll get one when we get home."

There were mounted fish, old fishing nets, hooks, and lures hanging on the walls, making Devan doubt Kale's choice of restaurant.

Kale noticed her reluctance and said, "Trust me, Monty, they have the best Mahi-Mahi anywhere, and the poi's to die for."

Much to Devan's surprise, the food was superb and satisfying. At the end of their meal, a small Japanese man came up to their table. "Oh, Mr. Kale! Who you bring here tonight? She very pretty lady."

Kale smiled. "This is Devan, my ... girlfriend. Devan this is Mr. Moshi. He owns the joint."

Devan shook his hand and said, "Nice to meet you, Mr. Moshi."

Moshi picked up her hand and kissed it. "Your boyfriend here save my grandson last year. He a very great man. You eat here for free."

Kale handed him the check with cash. "No, sir. You know my rules. I was only doing my job. I pay for my food, period."

"No you don't! You have good day. Bring Miss Devan back Wednesday ... all you can eat sushi. *You no pay!*" Moshi took the bill and left, after throwing Kale his cash.

Devan laughed. "He's a funny little man."

"Yeah, he's a cool guy. I always leave the money anyway."

"So, when did I become your girlfriend? I don't remember agreeing to that."

He wiped his mouth with a napkin. "Well, *you* threw the friendship thing out the window."

"*Me?*"

"Would you like a reminder of what happened between us earlier?"

"Yes, I would."

"Mmm, that can be arranged."

Chapter 15

Kale had been moved up to the head lifeguard position over the winter, so he would be in charge of training Devan. *How in the hell am I going to concentrate on training while she looks so hot?* he wondered.

She was sitting right next to him, and he was fighting with the demon in his swim trunks. *I just want to reach across and slide my hand right up her silky calf.*

A cool breeze swept through the resort, causing her nipples to become erect and eliciting a twitch in his shorts. He awkwardly tried crossing his legs to hide what was going on, but it wasn't easy.

This was the third day of this torture he'd had to endure. Soon, she would get her own pool right next to his.

"Hey, I bet I can dive better'n you," slurred a guy with bleach-blonde hair.

"Well, this pool is only five feet deep. If you want to dive, you'll need head over to the big pool past the lagoon," Kale said politely.

"Shut up, pansy boy! We're paying guests here!"

"You'd better listen, Mark. He's the lifeguard!" warned his friend, another blonde holding a beer.

"I'm sorry. You'll have to leave the pool area. There's no alcohol allowed past the gate," Devan said, while jumping down off her chair.

Kale got down as well.

"Ha-ha, the little girl yelled at you, Jameson," the guy said, while jumping in the water holding his beer.

Kale walked over to him and extended his hand to help him out of the water. "Come on, man. This isn't allowed. You guys need to leave."

Devan took the beer out of the other guy's hand. As that guy was apologizing, another drunk college guy with dark hair slammed into them, pushing both him and Devan into the pool.

"I can't swim! I can't swim!" he yelled, struggling. Kale jumped in and swam over to help Devan.

"I can swim, dude. I'll save you!" the other blonde said. He was closer and got there before Kale. However, instead of helping, he made things worse by grabbing onto his friend and dragging him under.

Devan pulled the guy she'd been dealing with out of the water. He was coughing and sputtering water. Kale helped the other blonde, who gallantly said, "I almost saved you, Jay."

Still coughing he yelled back, "Fuck you, man. You almost drowned me."

"This is why you don't drink and swim. Are you okay?" Kale asked.

"Thanks to this honey," he said smiling up at Devan, while he was still lying on his side. "Thank you. I'm sorry. This won't happen again."

"It better not," Kale threatened.

Later that evening Kale ran into Jay again. This time he was sober.

"Hey, aren't you the lifeguard?"

Kale turned around and saw him. "Yeah."

"Thanks for helping us today. Please tell that girl you were working with, too."

"No problem, man," Kale said and turned to walk away.

"Wait! Um what's the story with her, anyway? She's pretty hot."

"Sorry, man, she's taken."

"Are you sure?"

"Yeah, I'm sure."

"Awe, man, that's too bad. I was going to ask her out."

"Yep, sorry." Kale walked away before the guy could ask any more questions.

They'd said they loved each other before, but things were different now. It wasn't like either one of them had come right out and said the exact words yet, but Kale wanted to. He also wanted the moment to be right.

"How would you feel about going on a date?" he asked.

Devan pulled the sucker out of her mouth and asked, "With you?" then laughed.

"No, the other guy you're sleeping with," he said sarcastically. "Yes, with me."

"Well, it's been a long time since we had an actual date," she said and put the sucker back in her mouth.

"Come on."

"Okay, but only if we can have sex after."

He rolled his eyes. "Well, duh."

"Okay, pick me up from work at seven; I'll be ready." She walked out the door and went to work.

I don't have to work today, so I'm going to go all out. I want this to be perfect! He went to the florist down the road first and ordered a beautiful bouquet with peach rose buds, white orchids and ferns. Next, he made reservations at the "fancy-schmancy" restaurant, as Devan called it.

He looked though his closet and realized he really didn't have anything to wear other than shorts and t-shirts, so he went shopping. He finally settled on a nice pair of khaki pants, and a white dress shirt. When he was getting ready to pay he remembered he hadn't told Devan to dress up. "Miss, I need to get something else, and I think I might need your help." He explained what he had in mind, and she led him to a section in the store where he could find cocktail dresses.

"What do you think of this one?" the sales girl asked, holding out a red dress with low cleavage and sequins.

"No, I think she'd smack me if I got that one. It's not her style at all." He looked at a few dresses, then saw something he thought she would actually like. "What about this?" he asked the salesgirl.

It was a striking pale blue halter-top dress with an A-line skirt that stopped above the knees. The chiffon overlay shimmered. "I think that's perfect!" she said.

He dropped off his purchase at the front desk of the hotel. "Hey, Leilani, can you make sure that Devan Montgomery gets this in the next hour or two?" he asked the woman working the front desk.

"Sure thing, Kale."

The afternoon flew by, and it was almost six o'clock. He looked at himself in the mirror and thought he looked pretty sharp, but something seemed out of place. He pulled his hair back in an elastic band and rubbed his chin, then decided to trim his thick beard into a neat goatee. When he was done, he headed to the hotel.

He pulled up to the entrance and got out of the car at the same moment Devan walked outside.

"Wow!" they both exclaimed simultaneously.

"You sure clean up nice, Mr. Iakona."

She's stunning, Kale thought, momentarily dazed as the light hit the top of her dress, making it shimmer. He realized the blue of the dress enhanced the blue in her eyes.

"Oh, these are for you," he said handing her the bouquet. "Wait there's something I need to do." He pulled one of the orchids out of the bouquet and put it behind her ear. *She smells so good,* he thought as he got close to tuck the flower into her shiny black hair.

"Thank you. I love this dress," she said. "It was a wonderful surprise."

"Well, it looks perfect on you," he said opening the car door for her.

At dinner he ordered a glass of champagne for her, and she joked, "Trying to get lucky, sir?"

"I *am* lucky! You're with me." He winked at her.

"This is true," she said, and sipped from her glass.

She's so beautiful. I could stare into those magnificent eyes all day long. "Devan, I wanted to—"

"Your lobster, sir," the waiter, who couldn't have picked a worse time to interrupt, said.

They enjoyed the delicious food, and conversation was sparse. The steak was tender and juicy, and the lobster was perfectly cooked with just the right amount of butter and lemon. Devan devoured her entire meal.

After he paid the bill, they decided to take a walk on the beach. It was dark now, and not many people were out. Devan took off her shoes, fastened them together, and swung them over her shoulder as Kale tied his and did the same.

"Beautiful night," she said looking up at the stars in the clear sky.

He clasped her hands and said earnestly, "Not as beautiful as you."

She smiled. *This is so romantic — the water coming in over our feet, washing away our footprints, my hand in his. It's something straight out of a romance novel.*

They walked a little farther and then Devan came to a grinding halt. She let go of his Kale's hand and stood in front of him, face to face. "I need to tell you something," she said with a sigh.

"Well, let me say something first." She let him continue. "The past few weeks have been amazing and—"

"I love you," she said quickly.

"I love you, too."

She didn't think he was really listening. "No, Kale, *I love you*. I really *love* you."

He grasped both of her hands and said, "I'm madly in love with you Devan Marie. I've been trying to work up the nerve to tell you; I planned this whole evening just so I could do it right. Then you go and blurt it out and ruin my moment," he said, and chuckled.

"I'm sorry. I didn't mean to ruin your game."

He leaned down and kissed her passionately. "Now that we've got that squared away—" he picked her up threw her over his shoulder and ran into the surf. He didn't stop until the water was up to his waist.

She looked into his bright green eyes and said, "All these years, it's only ever been you. The others were just decoys. I've loved you since the moment you rescued me at the cliffs."

"Well, you sure had a funny way of showing it. Wait— There were others?"

"Well, no, I was just trying to make it sound dramatic."

Kale laughed, threatening to drop her.

"Shut up, you liked it," she said kissing him.

"I will always rescue you. *Always.*"

The next morning, the covers were nowhere to be found and their clothes were wherever they'd been thrown the night before. Devan's legs were cold but the rest of her was nice and warm. She had one leg slung over Kale's, with her hand on his chest and her head on his bulging biceps. She didn't want to move, but she saw a sheet within reaching distance, or so she thought. She slowly lifted her leg off his and tried scooting away. She almost had the sheet when she was forcefully pulled in the opposite direction.

"Where do you think you're going?" his deep voice asked quietly.

"I was cold, so I was trying to reach the sheet," she said and laughed.

"Oh, that's not a problem. I can warm you right up." He kissed her soft lips, pressing his body as close as he could to hers. He ran his hand slowly down her arm over her breasts and onto her hips. Then, he flipped her over on top of his rock-hard body.

"Kale, we have to get ready!" she protested, pulling away and looking at the clock.

"Oh, we have plenty of time before they get here," he said and flipped her over again, positioning himself on top of her. He started with her breast, planting soft kisses as he worked his way up to her neck. She couldn't handle that. Her hands went straight for his ass, pushing his pelvis into hers.

He lifted his head. "Is that an invitation?" he asked as he lightly bit her bottom lip. Her toes started to curl.

"Knock, knock! Anyone home?"

Kale hopped off her and put his shorts on so quickly he looked like a blur. "Their flight must've landed early! I'll get the door. You run to the other room and get in bed like you're sleeping," he directed.

Devan grabbed her clothes and ran to the other room just as she heard Kale say, "Mr. and Mrs. Montgomery, we weren't expecting you until later. Mom, dad, how nice to see you. Please, come in."

"Kale I wish you would start calling us by our first names," Devan's dad said as he slapped Kale on the back.

"I'm sorry, Chris, just showing respect."

"You're such a good kid," Elaine said and kissed his cheek.

"Where's Devan?" Cassandra asked.

"Oh, she had a really long shaf— I mean shift yesterday. I'm sure she'll be up soon. Let me show you around."

When they got to his room, he'd forgotten what a disaster it was.

"Oh look at this view!" Elaine said, going over to the window. Chris and Cassandra went over as well.

Kale's dad kicked his foot. Kale looked at him and Nāhoa nodded his head toward the lacy purple thong on the floor. Kale kicked it under the bed just before Chris walked over to him and put a hand on his shoulder.

"Where's Devan's room? I'm gonna wake her up."

Kale knocked on the door praying she was decent. "Monty, you have company."

She opened the door wearing a tank top and boxers. "Good morning," she said and hugged everyone.

Nāhoa noticed the matching bra in the corner of the room. He looked over at Kale and shook his head. *Busted!* Kale thought to himself.

"Dad, hey, um can you come over here after dinner. Just you?" Kale asked on the phone later that day. "Devan's going out with her parents tonight, and I just need to talk to you. … Okay. Great! Thank you. See ya tonight."

"Hot date tonight while I'm gone?" Devan asked as she walked into the room wearing a string bikini.

"Mmm not with this hotness here," he said, grabbing her around the waist from behind. He started slowly kissing the back of her neck, and then untied her top with his teeth, letting it fall against her stomach. He cupped her breast and kissed her neck again.

"No, no, no! Kale Kai, I have to get ready."

"That's not for another three hours."

"Yes, but if I don't start now, I'll never be ready on time," she said and tried to slip away.

He wasn't letting her get away that easily.

"Damn it, Kale," she protested as he rubbed himself against her suggestively. *It's a lost cause; I'm putty in his hands.*

"You know you want it," he whispered as he nibbled on her ear.

"I can't—" she turned around to face him, and he looked down at her with that evil sexy grin. As she wrapped her arms around his neck, she knew she wasn't going to be ready on time.

He kissed her softly then lifted her up and set her on the dining room table with her legs dangling. She quickly untied the bottom part of her suit and he shimmied out of his. She put her legs around his waist as he kissed her, then lifted her up onto himself. She held on tight to his amazing arms and thought, *He feels so good!*

He carried her into the bedroom like that and they fell onto the bed. "We (thrust) will (thrust) hurry," he said.

An hour later they found themselves in the shower.

"Can you hand me my shampoo?" she asked. He stepped in behind her with the shampoo. "Kale—"

"Didn't you know we're conserving water on the island?" he asked as he squirted some shampoo in his hand and started lathering her hair, massaging her scalp while rubbing himself against her.

"Kale!" she exclaimed.

"What?"

"We're *not* doing this again right now," she said sternly.

He took his hands out of her hair and glided them down her breasts, then on to her stomach, sliding farther and farther until he reached her sacred spot. *One of the benefits of being tall is having long arms and big hands,* he thought.

She couldn't resist him, so she parted her legs. He entered her from behind and she cried out in pleasure. He bent her over so her hands were on the tub so she could steady herself. *He's so gentle; he's always afraid he's going to hurt me.* "Harder," she said quietly. He increased his momentum, but not enough. "Harder!" she said louder.

"I'm *not* going to hurt you."

"Harder!" she demanded.

"No!"

"Harder!" she yelled. That got him really hot. He grabbed her hips tighter and pushed harder and faster. "Yes! Yes!" she cried.

"You like that, huh? How about this?" he said as he pushed himself in even deeper and rougher than before.

"Oh- (thrust) *my-* (thrust) *God!"*

Her velvety walls gripped him so tightly he couldn't hang on. "I'm—" he started to say.

"Ahh!"

They climaxed together.

Chapter 16

"Hey, Dad, come on in," Kale said as he held the door open. They sat down in the living room. "Um, I'm not sure where to start. You guys love Devan, right?"

"As if she were our own daughter."

"Okay, good," Kale got up and started pacing. "See, I love her, too, and, well, I've been thinking about this for a really long time. Maybe not a super long time, but um—" *God, just spit it out!* "Do you think it would be weird if, well I mean—"

Nāhoa was amused by Kale's anxious behavior. He knew exactly what his son was trying to say. "Son, you want to marry Devan."

Kale took a deep breath. "What do you think Mom will say?"

Nāhoa got up and hugged his son. "That would make her extremely happy. Since you kids were younger we've always seen Devan and the Montgomerys as family. This will just make it official. You'll need to ask her father for his permission, though."

Kale's eyes nearly popped out of his head. "What if he says no, Dad?"

"Well, Kale Kai, you have two options. You can ask her anyway or you can respect his wishes."

"I don't want anyone else, Dad."

"So then you'd just ask her anyway."

"Mr. Montgomery has been nothing but nice to me, but I love his daughter."

"Kale, he's not going to say no to you," his dad said and chuckled.

Kale sat down again with a sigh of relief.

"Have you bought a ring?"

"Well, no. I mean I have a little saved up, but I needed your approval."

"Well, put that money toward the honeymoon then," he said and pulled a small wooden box out of his pocket and handed it to Kale. "Your grandmother said that no one but Devan could have this."

Kale opened the box to see a perfect half-karat solitaire princess cut diamond.

"She didn't even really know Devan."

"No, but when they came here when you were about two years old, your grandmother watched the two of you a few times. She knew then you were meant to be together."

"So, you brought this all the way from Ohio? How did you know?"

Nāhoa smiled. "No, son, it's been at Aunt Noelani's this whole time. I grabbed it on a hunch before coming over here this afternoon."

"Well, your hunch was right." He closed the box and thanked his father. *Now I just have to ask Chris for his daughter's hand in marriage and plan the perfect proposal.*

The next day he called Chris and asked if they could meet for lunch.

He sat in the booth, nervous as could be and sweating bullets.

"Do you have a guest joining you, Mr. Kale?" Moshi asked as he started putting down the place settings.

"Um, yes. Devan's dad. I'm going to ask him if — well, if I can marry his daughter."

Moshi looked at Kale and smiled. "If he no say yes, he a fool. I tell him how wonderful you are. How about some Jasmine tea to help nerves?"

"Yes, thank you for the tea, but no to the telling him I'm wonderful part."

"I kidding, I know he say yes." Moshi smiled and walked back to the kitchen.

Kale saw Chris walk in, took a deep breath and stood up to shake his hand.

"Kale, is everything all right, son? You look a bit pale."

"Yes, I'm fine," he said, wiping the sweat off his brow.

"Oh, good. You had me a little worried, especially asking me to come to some place called Happy Hooker," he said and chuckled.

Moshi brought Kale's tea and some water for Chris. "Hello, I am Moshi. Mr. Kale save my grandson. He a great man! What you want?"

Kale looked down. *Oh, no.*

"Well, Moshi, I'm Chris and yes, Kale is a great man! He's like the son I never had."

"Ha! See?" Moshi slapped Kale's shoulder.

"The house special sounds good, can I get that, a salad with ranch dressing and a Coke?"

Moshi nodded. "Mr. Kale?"

Kale couldn't even think of food. "Clear soup and a salad with ginger dressing."

Moshi shook his head. "Fine, I get rest of your order later."

"He's a funny little man."

"That is exactly what Devan said when I brought her here," Kale said, while shakily lifting the cup to his lips, then set it down without taking a drink.

"Son, what is it? Your hand's shaking."

Kale set the cup down. "You know you're like my second dad, and um," he stopped and took a deep breath. "Okay. Um, can I just take a sip of this?" He took a big gulp. "Hot! hot!" he grabbed Chris's water and downed it.

"I'm sorry," Kale said, embarrassed.

"As you were saying—" Chris urged him with a knowing smile.

"I—" he wiped the sweat off his brow again and inhaled deeply. "I want to marry your daughter," he blurted out.

"See, son, it wasn't that hard. I knew that's why you wanted to talk to me." Chris grinned.

"May I have your permission to ask your daughter for her hand in marriage?"

Chris grabbed Kale's hand. "Kale Kai, I would be pleased to call you my son-in-law. You didn't have to ask me, although it was fun watching you sweat."

Kale took a deep breath and finally relaxed. "Oh, thank God! I didn't want to have to ask her without you saying yes."

"You still would've asked her even if I'd said no?"

"Yes, sir."

"Good boy!" he said and winked.

Kale was so excited that he drove straight to the resort. "Can you page Devan Montgomery for me?" he asked the girl at the front desk.

"Yes, sir. 'Devan Montgomery, Devan Montgomery, you have someone to see you at the front desk.'"

Kale was pacing. *Wait! How am I going to ask her? I can't just do it here. Can I? No, she deserves something so much better.*

"Hey, Kale, is everything okay?"

I really, really want to ask her now. He pulled her into the lobby near some chairs in front of the television. "Have a seat," he said while fidgeting with his pocket. *Damn it, I can't do this now,* he thought and left the ring in his pocket.

Devan was looking at him with concern.

"Um, I was thinking we could take the parents out to dinner tomorrow."

Devan stared at him. "You could have told me this later, Kale."

"I know, I know. I'm sorry I just was in the neighborhood and—"

"You realize I am off in an hour, right?" she asked and raised her eyebrows at him.

"No, actually I didn't. I'm sorry. I'll see you at home."

"Okay," Devan said and giggled.

Kale had decided he was going to pop the question the next night at dinner. He didn't come out and tell anyone but all of them except Devan had a pretty good idea why they were at dinner.

"I'd like to make a toast," Kale said, raising his glass. Chris, Elaine, Nāhoa, Cassandra, and Devan raised their glasses. "To my beautiful Devan for ... graduating college."

His dad gave him a strange look.

"A-n-n-d to Chris and Elaine for raising such a smart girl."

Chris winced at Kale.

"A-n-n-d my parents for being so supportive. Cheers!"

He sat down and clinked his glass with everyone. *I'm such an ass!*

Devan got up. "Well, I'd like to make a toast, too. Congratulations to Kale for graduating college as well."

They all took a sip as they waited for Kale to say something. *The atmosphere is perfect, and both families are here. What's my problem? Something is missing, but I have no idea what it is.*

"What happened?" his dad asked as they were leaving.

"I don't know, Dad. It didn't feel like the right time."

"When do you think the right time might be?"

"I don't know. It's like ... it was perfect but ... there was something missing."

"You know we're all leaving tomorrow?"

"Yes, I know. Maybe I need it to be more private. I don't know. How did you propose to Mom?"

"I took her to the place where I met her. Now, I know you can't do that, but if you have a special place, that's where I'd take her if I were you." Nāhoa patted Kale's back and left.

Something finally clicked. *I know exactly what I'm going to do!*

A few days later, he took a drive up to the cave. He stepped into the cold water carrying a bag, and said a small prayer of sorts, "Ole Blue, you're forever beautiful. Please let today go smoothly."

When he got inside the cave, he set his bag down on the ledge and lifted himself up. He opened the bag and let the white coral pieces fall on the ground. He set the ring box in a hidden hole after taking the ring out and tucking it safely away in his shorts. He arranged all of the coral bits to say,

"Will you marry me, Monty?" He stepped away and looked at his handy work. *It's perfect. It feels right, too. I'm ready.*

Kale couldn't wait for Devan to get back home. He was in the kitchen making dinner when someone came up to the door.

"Kale?" Jeane called as she knocked.

He set down the wooden spoon and looked out the door. "What're you doing here?"

"I need to talk to you. Remember that party I had in the spring?"

"Jeane, I'm kind of busy. I don't have time to reminisce."

She pushed her way in and sat down at the table. "Kale, I'm pregnant."

"Congrats, I think— Is that why you've been gone? Why are you telling me this?"

"Kale, it's yours—"

"How is that even possible?" He sat down as his perfect plan fell to pieces. Jeane explained everything and it made little sense to him.

Devan found him sitting in the same spot two hours later.

"Hey, dinner smells um ... done." It was burning on the stove. He didn't budge. She turned off the stove and sat down beside him. "Kale? What's wrong?"

He wouldn't look at her. He slid something over to her. It was an ultra-sound picture. "She says it's mine—"

That night Devan sobbed on his bare chest. Her whole world had fallen apart, and it wasn't going to get better. *Kale's life is going to change drastically and I'll just be a distraction. I had our entire future together mapped out. Never in a million years did I think something like this could happen. It doesn't make any sense. We had a fairytale romance.*

Kale could feel her warm tears on to his skin. He was scared of what the future would bring, and he was scared more than anything that he'd lose Devan.

The next morning he woke up next to a letter instead of her body. He opened it and read:

Dear Kale,

I never thought I'd have to say goodbye again. This is only goodbye for a little while I hope. Please don't come after me. I'm going home. I can't stay here and be in the way of you becoming a father.

I love you, and I know I always will. Sometimes, things don't work out the way we want.

He threw the letter down and didn't finish reading it. *Maybe I still have time to catch her before she gets on the plane.*

He got to the airport as fast as his Jeep would take him. When he got there, he could see that none of the planes had left yet. He ran to the front desk and yelled, "Devan Montgomery. Is she still here?"

"I'm sorry, sir, just one moment." The man started searching his computer. "Montgomery ... Montgomery ... Gate 7." It was a busy airport, and Kale had to dodge crowds of people who all stood in his way of getting there in time. He finally saw Gate 7 and headed to it.

"Devan! Devan!" he yelled.

"Excuse me, sir, you can't go beyond this line."

"But my, you see— Fuck it! Devan! Devan!" he yelled into the loading area. He jumped the chain blocking his way.

"Security! Security to Gate 7," he heard over the loudspeaker. Just as they were shutting the door he got a glimpse of her solemn face. Her eyes were swollen and red from crying.

As the door clicked shut, he pounded his fists on the wall and all feeling left his body. He didn't even hear the security guards running up to him. He just stared at the door. "Hey, man. Hey, Kale. It's okay, guys. He's not a threat. I know him," the heavyset guard said.

"Thank God, I was afraid it would take all four of us to knock him down," the small guard said.

"I got it, you guys go ahead. Kale? *Kale Iakona!*" he yelled in Kale's ear while tapping his shoulder.

Kale slowly turned around to see a familiar face.

"Dude, you don't look good. Are you okay?" Kuna asked.

"No."

"What happened?"

"I just lost the love of my life," he said and closed his eyes, sighing.

"Monty?" Kuna asked.

Kale nodded.

"Oh, no! I'm sorry. Listen, I'm off in 20. Go sit down over there and I'll meet you after my shift. We'll go out for a beer."

"Kuna, I don't drink — especially now."

"You do today, braddah," he said pushing Kale forcefully into a chair. Kale was taller than Kuna, but Kuna was a lot bigger. He looked like a Polynesian sumo wrestler.

Kale just sat there, and didn't move. He didn't see the people bustling by him, and he didn't hear the loud speaker or feel the kid kicking the back of his seat. In the state he was in, days could've gone by and he wouldn't have noticed or cared.

When his shift ended, Kuna took Kale to his house and handed him a bottle of beer. "One beer isn't going to hurt you. Drink it."

Kale took a sip of the beer and realized it wasn't half bad.

"Now, what happened, braddah?"

Kale told Kuna the entire story starting from the time when Kuna met Devan to the present. "I'm sorry, man, but she isn't gone."

Kale took another drink of his beer. "What do you mean, Kuna? She's probably halfway to the mainland by now."

"No, bro, I mean she isn't gone from you. Look, I saw the two of you together. Even when you were miles apart, you were still in each other's hearts."

"Kuna, that was a few years ago."

"I know you think I'm crazy for believing in the magic of the islands and stuff, but I tell you, you two will always have the Aloha."

"Well, yeah."

"No, braddah, *Hohonu Aloha.* The deep love. She's the one you're supposed to be with — your soul mate."

"What if you're wrong?"

Kuna laughed. "Kuna's never wrong."

Kale gave him a weak smile.

"She'll come back to you. I promise."

On the plane

"Hey, is it okay if I sit here? My neighbor is, well, taking up most of my seat, too."

She looked to where the guy was pointing as he continued, "I went to the bathroom and when I came back out, she was slumped over like that. Don't worry, I checked and she's still breathing."

"No one's sitting here," Devan said. "Make yourself at home."

"Thanks. My name's Justin Jameson of Jameson Enterprises," he said extending his hand. She shook it gently.

He sat down and started to talk to her. *I just wanted to sit and sulk. I wish you'd just shut up.*

"Where are you headed?" he asked.

"Ohio."

"Me, too. That's crazy."

She looked up at him finally. He was a nice-looking guy. He was no Kale of course, but no one would ever hold a candle to that gorgeousness. Justin had blue eyes and blonde hair that was to his ears.

He looked at her like something just registered. "Hey, you're the lifeguard!"

She remembered him now.

He pushed her hair out her face. "There are those beautiful eyes. I hoped we'd meet again."

"Um, yeah. I see you've recovered nicely. Bet you'll never drink and dive again."

"Only when you're there to save me." He winked at her.

"That's not gonna happen," Devan said shaking her head.

"Well, we have the rest of our lives to argue about that."

Chapter 17

*D*evan didn't have to explain herself when her parents picked her up from the airport. Kale had already called them and his parents and told them everything.

When they got home, Nāhoa was waiting for her. "Devan, may I speak with you?"

She sighed. She didn't want to be rude, but she just didn't want to deal with reality. She stepped aside and let her parents go into the house.

"Kale called and spoke to your mom before he called us. I'm sorry about what happened. We're here if you need anything."

She'd been expecting a big long speech about how she should go back to Hawaii. This caught her off guard, and her big blue eyes started to water.

"I can't apologize for my son's actions, but I can tell you he's hurting. He told me you're his everything, and now he feels like he's lost you and he's left with nothing."

She could no longer contain the tears and openly sobbed.

"I love you like you're my own daughter, and I don't want to see you hurt just as much as I don't want to see my son hurt. Take your time to figure things out, but please—" he sighed. "Don't give up on my son."

He bent down to hug her, and when he did she thought she saw tears in his eyes, too.

A week had gone by and she still hadn't unpacked her bags. She dreaded seeing what was inside them. Everything would remind her of the wonderful time she'd had with the love of her life. *The man who shattered my dreams. The man who broke my heart into a million pieces. The man I know I'll never stop loving no matter what.*

She sat on the edge of her bed and stared at the bags like they were the bane of her existence. "Fuck it!" She got up, turned on the radio and opened the first bag. Halfway through unpacking it, she heard the DJ say, *"It's 3 o'clock! You know what that means, folks. It's request time. Our lines are open. Our first request peaked at number 44 on the Billboard Hot 100 and got to number three on Billboard's Modern Rock chart in 1994. Congratulations Michael and Diana on your wedding day, from Stacey. Here's "Fade Into You" by Mazzy Star!"*

Devan threw down the shirt she was folding and screamed, "Are you fucking kidding me?" The tears started flowing as the song played. She remembered all the dances they shared to this song and could almost feel Kale's arms around her and even smelled his Nautica.

Why can I smell his cologne? It's getting stronger. She followed her nose to the scent. The shirt she'd thrown had knocked over and broken a bottle of the stuff. It was the bottle she'd bought years ago when the Iakonas had gone back to Hawaii. She bent down and started picking up the pieces, crying even harder as she remembered why she'd bought it.

Every time she'd gone over to water their plants, she'd also sprayed a little Nautica in Kale's room, then she'd sit there and think of him. When that bottle was empty, she'd bought a new one. When he came home she'd put it with the perfume bottles on her armoire and forgot about it, until now.

Of all the bottles to fall and break, why did it have to be that one? It was like a slap in the face. *I'm glad Mom and Dad aren't home to hear me sobbing like a fool.*

She finally stopped crying 45 minutes later, took a deep breath and sighed.

"Okay, folks, our last request was number-one on the Billboard Hot 100 in December of 1985 for two whole weeks. This message reads: 'Devan, if you're listening, please look in your carry-on bag. I slipped something in there while

you were sleeping' ... Oh, that sounds potentially creepy!" The DJ chuckled. *"It continues: 'Listen to the lyrics, and I mean really listen to them. Always, Justin'* Okay, that was weird. From the album* Welcome to the Real World, *here's* "Broken Wings" *by Mr. Mister."*

Did I hear that right? Am I the Devan he was talking about? If so, who's Justin?

She went over to her bags, grabbed the smallest one and unzipped it and dumped it out on the bed. She finally saw something she didn't put there. It was an airline napkin with writing on it and a broken pair of airline wings pinned to it.

> Devan,
>
> I know you're hurting. I'm truly sorry for your loss. Things will get better. I promise. Life gives us tidal waves sometimes. We can choose to ride them out or drown. You're much too pretty to drown in a sea of tears. So take these broken wings and learn to fly again.
>
> If you need a friend – and I think you do – please call me at 555-867-0783.
>
> Hope to see you soon!
> Justin

"Oh, my God!" she said and giggled. This was the first time she'd smiled since that dreadful day. She had friends, but she needed a new one who wasn't close to the situation. *I just have to figure out who he is. The name sounds familiar.* She thought hard, said the name out loud a few times, and then it hit her. She picked up the phone and dialed his number.

The next day, Devan walked into the restaurant and looked around from the hostess station.

"Hello, miss. Are you meeting someone?" the hostess asked.

"Uh, yes. I don't really remember what he looks like. His name is Justin," she said, slightly embarrassed.

"Yes, ma'am. Right this way."

There at a table in the corner near the fireplace was a nice looking man with short light brown hair wearing a maroon button-down shirt, a maroon, gold and hunter green tie, and tan khakis. He stood up and said, "I wasn't sure if you were going to show."

She recognized him now, but something was different. He pulled out her chair liked a well-mannered gentleman.

He could tell her mind was racing. "It's the hair," he said.

"Excuse me?"

"The hair. You're wondering what's different about me — at least it looks like that's what you're thinking." He grinned.

"Oh, yes. Yes, that's it." She smiled.

"My dad said it was probably bad for business. Said I looked like a washed up surfer wannabe."

Devan chuckled. "I wouldn't take it that far, but your hair does look nice like this."

"Thank you. To be honest, I was surprised to hear from you. I didn't think you'd remember me."

"Why would you think that?" she asked, even though she barely remembered him.

The waiter came over. "Mr. Jameson, are you and your guest ready to order?" Justin looked at Devan.

"I'll just have whatever you're having," she told him.

"Okay. Two Rieslings, the house steak medium with garlic sauce on the side. Baked potato with butter and sour cream; house salad with balsamic vinaigrette; and shrimp cocktail for the appetizer."

"Thank you, Mr. Jameson. I'll be right out with your drinks."

I don't know much about him, but he's got good taste. That's exactly what I would've ordered. "So why did you think I wouldn't remember you?" she asked him again.

He smiled. "On the plane home you weren't exactly coherent. You were pretty upset about a longtime relationship ending, so I ordered you some wine to help you relax. It worked and you ended up sleeping for the majority of the trip."

"What did I tell you?" she asked, worried that she had divulged too much information, as usual.

"Nothing much, that's the funny thing. You just kept saying how this guy had broken your heart and your life was over. No name, not what happened, nothing. I didn't want to upset you more, so I didn't ask. I tried to console you, and I thanked you for rescuing me a few times."

Oh, yeah — Jay from the pool! He doesn't seem like that jerk I dealt with that day. He seems like a decent guy. "Well, it's a new day — let's not talk about my past. Tell me all about you," she said and gave him a big smile.

After dinner, he suggested they take a walk in the nearby park. It was a beautiful evening, and they watched the sun set. As they walked, they played 20 Questions so they could find out about each other.

When their evening was over, Justin walked her to her car, took her hand and kissed it. "Thank you for a lovely evening. I'd like to do this again sometime soon."

Devan thanked him for dinner and they went their separate ways.

The next day, she was surprised by a knock on her door. She opened it and a deliveryman presented her with a large bouquet of flowers. There was a thank-you card included. It read:

My dearest Devan,

Thank you for having dinner with me yesterday. It was so nice to see you smile. I really enjoyed getting to know the beautiful person you truly are.

I'll be leaving town for a few weeks on business. I'd love to see you when I get back.

Please feel free to email me while I'm gone. It would mean the world to me to hear from you.

I've included my business card. It lists every way you can reach me.

Always, Justin

Her dad walked by, saw the flowers, and asked, "Those from Kale?"

"No," she said flatly, as she grabbed the card and went to her room.

She sat on her bed and read the card again. *What am I doing? I shouldn't email this guy. I never should've gone out with him. I feel like I'm cheating on Kale. What the hell — we're clearly not together anymore so why do I feel bad? Kale made his bed and now he has to lie in it. I need to stop thinking about him.*

For the first time since I fell in love with Kale I'm thinking of another man — a man who seems sweet and smart, and clearly interested in me. Forget Kale! He's out of my life. She knew he'd never be out of her life completely because their families were so close, but he was out of sight for now and that was enough for her to move on with her life.

Decision made, she opened her laptop and looked at her email. She had seven new emails — all from Kale. She opened the first one and started to read:

Monty,

Words cannot express the pain I feel without you here. I screwed up. I ruined my life with this one mistake. I don't know how it even happened. I don't even like this woman.

There was a party in the spring, and I had a few drinks. The last thing I remember is talking to her, trying to be nice. Next thing I knew, I woke up in the same room with her and half my clothes were missing.

I wouldn't do anything to hurt you or our relationship.

I know that we weren't together at that time but—"

She didn't finish reading. She just deleted it, and all the other ones after it. Maybe things would've been different if he'd told her about that night right after it happened… Not telling her when they resumed their relationship *did* hurt her and their relationship.

She decided to block Kale from her email and deleted him from her contacts list.

She opened a new email and began to type:

Dear Justin,

Thank you for the beautiful flowers. They were a lovely surprise. I'd love to keep in contact while you're gone.

Well, now you have my email, too.

I hope you have a safe trip, and I really look forward to hearing from you. When you get back, it'll be my turn to take you out.

Devan

I'm determined to learn to fly again!

Chapter 18

Fall 2001

Devan finally caved and started dating Justin that fall. He was a nice guy, and a good distraction from all the pain. He didn't smell as good as Kale, wasn't as sweet or romantic, and definitely wasn't as tall. He was smart though, and good-looking, just not as good-looking as Kale. She tried not to compare the two, but she just couldn't help it. The only guy she'd ever dated other than Kale was James, and James definitely didn't count. No one would ever compare to Kale, so she decided she'd just have to settle for second best.

Back in Hawaii

"Kale, man, you gotta get up and do something fun. You've been on your couch for two months," Kuna said to him gently.

"I go to work every day, Kuna, so I *am* doing something," he said defensively.

"You go to work and you come home and sleep. When's the last time you had a real dinner or worked out?"

"Dude, if you're going to come over here just to kick me in the balls, you can leave!"

Kuna looked down at him and shook his head in disgust. "Call me when you're ready to be alive again, because this," he said pointing a finger at Kale slumped on the couch, "is *not* living!"

When Kuna walked out the door, Kale reached under the couch for his notebook. It was still there.

Dear Devan,

This is my last letter to you. I understand you don't want to speak to me. My dad says it's because you need to heal, and because you think you're doing the right thing by staying away. You're trying to do what's best for me, but you are what's best for me.

I don't want Jeane. I don't even like her. This isn't my kid. I think she made the whole thing up. Maybe I was drugged and tricked into it like you were all those years ago. I hadn't been with anyone since Colorado until you came to Hawaii.

It's you, it's always been you. I don't want anyone else. I never have, and I never will. No one will take my heart like you have. NO ONE!

Dad says you have a new boyfriend, and that he seems nice. For his sake, I hope he is.

I won't beg or plead anymore. I won't call, but I won't give up either. When you're ready, I'll *be here waiting for you. I know, one day you'll come back to me. There's no one else for me, only you. Just like it's always been – you, me, and the moon and stars.*

I love you Devan Marie Montgomery!

Winter 2001/2002

Devan got the letter three months later, shortly after Jeane and Kale's baby was born. There was no return address on the envelope, so she opened it. She'd given all the other letters to her mother so she could destroy them. When she saw the letter was from Kale, she started to rip it up, but stopped mid-tear and decided to read it.

She knew she had made a mistake. She decided to go and see the baby as an excuse to see Kale. The Montgomerys and the Iakonas had gone up to see the baby a few days earlier, and Devan snatched the address off her mom's note pad. Half an hour later, she knocked on the door with a bouquet of flowers in her hand and a gift for the baby. She took a deep breath and trembled with anxiety.

A slender woman with medium length auburn hair opened the door. "May I help you?"

"Hi, I'm—"

"Devan Montgomery. Won't you please come in?"

"I'm sorry. Have we met?" Devan asked, startled that this stranger knew her name. She was pale with dark brown eyes, high cheekbones and perfectly shaped lips.

"No, but I met your parents. I know you're one of Kale's close friends. I'm Serena Cadence, Jeane's mother." *Mother? She's had some work done; she looks young enough to be Jeane's sister.*

"Come on, dear, they're in the living room." Her formal tone set Devan back. She followed Serena into the room. There, she saw a woman with similar features holding a baby and smiling.

"You must be Devan. I've heard a lot of good things about you. You look just like your mom."

"As do you," Devan said, handing the flowers to Jeane.

"We never officially met, but I know we've worked at the same place before." She seemed nice, which made Devan feel bad for what she was about to do.

"Thank you for the flowers. Please have a seat. Would you like to hold the baby?"

"I don't think I—"

"Here, meet Joey," she said handing him over. "Just make sure to hold his head like this." She showed Devan what to do.

Devan looked down at the sleeping child and couldn't help but smile. He was beautiful. His red hair was so bright and soft. He opened his blue eyes and looked right at her. It was as if he could see into her soul. There was something special about this baby. She didn't know why or how but she loved him.

"I heard someone at the door." Kale turned the corner and saw a sight he knew he'd always remember — Devan holding his son. It was so beautiful; it almost brought tears to his eyes. There she was, perfect as always. He held the emotions he felt at seeing her again in check with some major effort.

"Hi," she said with a smile.

"Hi," he said, awkwardly. He wanted nothing more than to grab her and hug her.

"Congratulations, Dad," she said as she looked back down at Joey's perfect little face. She thought she saw a smile. "Did he just—

"Yes, he just smiled at you," Kale said and sat down beside her.

Devan took in a deep whiff. She missed his scent. "Oh, it was probably gas," she heard Jeane say from the other room.

Kale and Devan looked at each other. Their gaze caught for just a second before Jeane came back in and walked over to take the baby. "He probably needs changed. Why don't you two visit for a bit? I'll change him and put him down for a nap."

The moment Joey was out of Devan's arms, he screamed. She instinctively held her hands out and Jeane gave him back. He immediately stopped crying. "Um, well, the change can wait. Maybe you can be his nanny. I think he likes you," Jeane said.

"I think he does," Kale said softly.

I came to confess my love for Kale, but I can't do it now that I've looked in that baby's eyes. I could never hurt him; he's innocent in this. When she saw Kale look at his son, she also knew she couldn't do it to him either. He loved this little boy, even if he might not be his biological father.

⁂

When Joey was about three months old, Devan got a disturbing early morning call. "Hello?" she asked, trying to wake up.

"It's Kale. I didn't know who else to call."

"What's wrong?"

"I called my mom and dad and Jeane's mom, but no one's answering."

"Okay. Calm down. No one's answering because it is 3 a.m. What happened?"

"It's Joey! Jeane's out of town. It started with a cold. We went to the doctor on Monday, and he said it was just a cold. Well, now it sounds like there's something in his chest. I can hear it rattling. He keeps coughing and he's not acting normal at all.

"Okay. Take his temperature."

Kale did as he was directed. "Oh, my God, it's 104!"

"Okay, hang up and go to the emergency room. I'll meet you there."

She got out of bed and grabbed her purse and coat.

"Hey, where are you going at this hour?" Justin asked.

"It's an emergency with the baby," she said putting her shoes on.

"I'll drive you."

Justin dropped her off at the emergency room door. She ran in looking for Kale, but didn't see him. "Is Joseph Iakona here?"

"Yes, ma'am. They just went back. Are you his mother? If not, you'll need to wait out here, please."

"Yes, yes I'm his mom."

"Okay, go back between those doors to the right. They're in the second room," the receptionist said.

"Is he okay?" Devan asked, as she ran into the room.

The doctor was there with them. "Mrs. Iakona, please have a seat. Your son has acute bronchitis. After a few treatments and a round of antibiotics he should be okay. We're going to monitor him overnight to play it safe. I don't mean to scare you, but with him being so young, we need to watch him closely. We want to be prepared if he gets worse."

"Okay, thank you doctor."

Kale hugged her. "Thank you for coming. Did you tell them you were my wife?"

"Yeah. They don't allow non-family in the ER."

"Thank you. I don't know what I'd have done without you."

"You would've come to the hospital, Kale. If you don't know for sure when it comes to babies *always* go to the hospital."

They had been transferred to a private room when Devan remembered Justin had dropped her off. "I'll be right back."

She ran down two flights of stairs to the main floor and saw Justin sitting in the waiting room, reading a magazine. "Oh my God, Justin. I'm so sorry!"

He put down the magazine and greeted her with a hug. "How is the little guy?"

"He's okay right now, but I'm going to stay. Okay?"

"Sure, let me walk you back to the room."

Devan knocked on the door. "Are you family?" a nurse asked. "Yes, I'm Joey's mom and this is his ... uncle."

Kale raised an eyebrow as they walked in. The nurse left after checking Joey's vitals.

Everyone was silent until Justin broke the ice. He got up and extended his hand. "I'm sorry, I don't think we've met. I'm Justin."

He looked familiar to Kale, but he just couldn't place him. "Yes, my wife's brother," he said and chuckled.

"I'm actually Devan's boyfriend," he said and laughed.

"I figured."

Kale got up and shook Justin's hand. He completely towered over him.

"Jesus, you didn't tell me he was so huge!" Justin exclaimed as he turned to Devan. "Remind me not to piss this guy off."

"Um ... What else didn't she tell you?"

Justin sat back down when Kale did. "I just know that your family and her family are pretty tight, and you guys are basically like best friends. Hey! Now I know who you are!"

Devan looked at Kale like she had no idea what Justin was talking about.

"You're the lifeguard from the hotel last year!" He nodded his head. "I can't believe I never put two and two together."

Devan froze. This could turn out to be a very bad thing. "Yeah, yeah! I was one of the drunken idiots that fell in the pool. Later on, I asked you if Dee was single."

Kale's eyes got huge, and he smiled awkwardly. "No shit! That's you?"

"Yeah," he got up and hugged Kale.

"Well, I got the girl," Justin said in Kale's ear.

"So you did."

Kale politely hugged him back, but looked over at Devan, who was looking down at her hands and refusing to look at him.

Justin stayed an hour longer and then excused himself. "I have an important meeting at 10. Call me later and let me know how Joey's doing."

As soon as he left the room, Kale started in on Devan. "Monty, he's too short for you. The dude from the pool? Really? You couldn't have mentioned this in the past few months?"

"I know. He's shorter than you." She let out a long sigh.

"Oh, let me stop you right there. He's almost shorter than *you!*"

"Now listen here, Lettuce Head, he is six foot-ish."

Kale laughed. "Carry on."

"He's smart, kind of, and nice, and good-looking."

Kale sat there stroking his beard. "And he doesn't know anything about us. Does he?"

"Well, no."

"That's okay. I never told Jeane much about us either. Not really something I like to talk about," he said smoothing back his hair.

An alarm went off. Joey sounded like he was choking and his oxygen level went down significantly according to the machine. Kale ran out of the room screaming for a doctor.

"It's okay baby. It's okay," Devan cooed as she rubbed his back. His lips started to turn more of a purple color. She kept rubbing his back and his oxygen level rose a little.

A team came rushing in and whisked him to another room. "Someone will come and get you," a nurse said before leaving. Devan started crying.

Kale was pacing and muttering, "Oh, my God. Oh, my God."

Devan grabbed Kale and said, "Let's pray." They bowed their heads and held onto each other's hands as they prayed silently until someone entered the room.-

"Mr. and Mrs. Iakona, Joey is stabilized. He is in PICU. Follow me."

When they got there, he was in what looked like a large incubator. He had a vent and two IVs. He looked pitiful. Kale and Devan held one another for a while.

They were sitting by his side when a doctor came over. "Joseph seems to be improving. We aren't exactly sure what happened, but we think he was misdiagnosed. He actually has pneumonia. He'll have to stay longer than overnight."

Devan stayed the full seven days at the hospital with Joey because no one could reach Jeane.

As Kale was signing the release papers, Jeane came storming in. "Where's my baby?" She took him away from Devan, and Joey started screaming. Jeane handed him back to Devan quickly. She sat down and said, "I'm so sorry. The phones weren't working, and—"

"It's okay, Jeane. Joey's all right. He's coming home," Kale said, trying to calm her.

"Devan, my mom said you were here with Kale the whole time." She hugged her. "Thank you so much, and Kale thank you for taking care of him. I am so sorry," she said hugging him. Kale returned the hug stiffly.

A few weeks later, Devan and Justin picked up dinner and took it over to Jeane and Kale's place.

Jeane opened the door and gave Devan a huge hug. "My best friend," she said.

Wait, what? Best friend? Devan started getting a headache just thinking about it. *Ugh!*

Kale took their coats, and they set the food down on the table. "Jeane, this is Justin."

Jeane hadn't even looked at him yet. She turned around and her mouth dropped to the floor. "Justin?"

"Yeah, are you okay?" She looked like she'd just seen a ghost.

"Yes. You just look like someone I know."

"Well, maybe you saw me at the resort. We were there for a little while," he said as he smiled and extended his hand.

She took it and squeezed really hard. "Yeah, maybe."

Devan noticed this weird behavior right away. *Something's off here!* Her worry quickly faded when Kale brought Joey in and handed him to her. She loved that little boy so much.

As they were eating dinner, Jeane spoke up, "So, we were talking, and we'd like nothing more than for you to be Joey's Godmother, Devan."

"That is if you agree," Kale said.

"Of course!" Devan said with a surprised smile.

"Well, I'd like to add to the happy occasion," Justin said and got up. He pulled a box out of his pocket and got down on one knee in front of Devan.

Kale dropped his fork onto to the plate. Due to his height, it had a very long way to fall so it made a loud clattering noise as it hit the plate.

"Devan Marie, will you marry me?"

Kale didn't give her a chance to answer. "Isn't this kind of fast? Did you even ask her dad?"

"Well, we've been dating for a while. And no, I didn't ask. That's old school."

"That is not old school. It is respectful!"

"Kale!" Jeane said and kicked him under the table.

"Her dad is cool with me. I apologize. I didn't even think about it. I know how close you guys are — kind of like brother and sister. Kale, do I have your permission to marry Devan?"

Devan looked at Kale and he looked back at her, his eyes going from hard to soft as he answered. "If she wants to, man." *What else can I say?*

"Devan, will you be my wife?" Justin asked again, awkwardly.

Devan looked at Kale again, and then Jeane and little Joey — sweet little Joey. She looked at Kale once more and smiled sadly. She knew he wasn't even an option. "Yes," she said to Justin.

Jeane clapped her hands and Justin hugged and kissed Devan.

Kale muttered, "Congratulations," and excused himself from the table. He couldn't eat another bite — he was feeling nauseous.

Justin yelled into the hallway, "Hey, you gotta be a groomsman, man."

Now I really feel sick! He sat on the bathroom floor trying to keep the contents in his stomach where they were.

Chapter 19

August / September 2002

The closer it got to Devan's wedding day, the more Jeane hounded Kale about the two of them getting married. He did his best to ignore her.

Two weeks before the wedding, as they were cleaning up the bridal shower, Cassandra pulled Devan aside and gave her a box. "Open it when you're alone and don't tell anyone I gave it to you. If you need a safe place to keep it, bring it back to me."

Devan thought this was a little on the strange side but put the box under the seat in her car. When she got back to her parents' house, she took it to her room and locked the door. She slowly took the lid off and looked inside. There was a note t sitting on top addressed to her.

> Devan,
>
> Please look at every item in this box and feel them with your heart. I love you no matter what you decide.
>
> Cassandra, aka your other mom

Devan took a deep breath and began. There were three packs of pictures, which she decided to look at last. There was the necklace she'd made for Kale back when she was 16. There was a framed homecoming picture, a framed prom picture, and a framed picture of Kale and her at his football game back in high school before the Iakonas moved back to Hawaii.

There was also a cassette tape that had "Devan '96" written on it, an old dried up boutonniere from homecoming, the hat Kale wore when he pretended to be the driver for prom, and an empty bottle of Nautica.

She grabbed the tape and looked in her closet for her old boom box. She plugged it in, praying it still worked, and popped in the tape. Kale's voice came through the speakers:

Hey, Monty, it's your Lettuce Head. It's November 29th, 1996. I put together a few songs I knew you liked and some that reminded me of you. I miss you, and I hope you enjoy.

The first song was "Fade into You," by Mazzy Star. She sat back and opened a pack of pictures as it played. Some of the photos were from '94 in Hawaii, some of Homecoming '94, and there were also some random silly pictures of the two of them. There were others of her, Kale, Pete, and Kristy —the Fantastic 4.

The next pack of pictures was from prom. She smiled as she thumbed through them. *That was the best night ever!* She stopped when she a saw a picture she didn't remember. Kale was curled up around her on the Iakona's couch.

She opened the last packet. It wasn't pictures. It was letters, postcards, and cards. She opened the first one and sobbed as she read.

Kale,

The days go by and I wonder each morning
how I'm going to make it another day without you.
I'm lying on your bed wearing your jacket, writing

this while I cry. I'll never send this to you, but I had to write down what I was feeling. So here it goes.

I know we haven't said it, but I love you, and it's hard being here without you. Nothing matters anymore. Sometimes, I feel like I'm dying. Kristy thinks she knows how I feel, but she doesn't. It's awful – like I had my heart ripped right out of my chest. Some days it hurts to breathe.

I miss your beautiful smile, your gorgeous green eyes, and your strong arms around me. I miss every-thing about you. My heart hurts, Kale. I don't want to eat or see my friends or go to school. I just want to come over here and cry. It's the only place I feel close to you. I hate that you're gone.

Sometimes I wish we'd never met at all. This just hurts too much. If that's what love is, then I don't want it. It's an evil, evil thing.

I pray for you to come back every night. I want you and only you!

I love you, Kale Kai

P.S. Now I must go burn this."

Only I didn't burn it, obviously. I don't want to read anymore of this. I don't even want this box in the house. She gathered the things and put them back. She was getting ready to take out the tape when "Almost Paradise" started playing.

She sat down on the bed and listened to the entire song. *I almost had paradise ... we almost had paradise.* She sat there, rocking herself and crying, until the next song came on. When "Take My Breath Away" by Berlin began playing, she cried even harder, then took the tape out and put it back in the box. She changed her mind, took it back out of the box and threw it on her bed.

She stormed over to the Iakona's, her face all red and blotchy. Cassandra answered the door and Devan said, "I don't want this. I can't keep it."

"Devan, I didn't mean to upset you."

"Yes, you did. You know I can't have him, so why torture me? Where did you get this letter?"

"I found that the spring we moved back. It had fallen under Kale's dresser."

"I love you, Cassie, I do, but this was cruel. No one will ever hold a candle to your son. No one will ever make me feel the way he did. I know I won't ever love anyone like I love him."

"You're still in love with him, aren't you?"

"Yes, I still love him. I just told you, I will *always* love him."

Devan turned to walk away, but Cassandra stopped her. "That's not what I asked. Are you still in love with Kale?"

"Why do you think this hurts so badly? Why do you think I'm marrying someone else? I never fell *out* of love with Kale, but I can't have him. So, I'm stuck with second best. Hopefully my feelings for your son will just go away eventually."

"Devan, they'll never go away. I don't think they'll even fade."

"That's what I'm most afraid of."

That night Devan listened to the tape over and over again, finally crying herself to sleep.

Justin had scheduled his and Kale's tux fittings at the same time. *How the hell I ended up being best man I'll never know,* Kale fumed.

"What do you think, man?" Justin asked as he came out wearing an all white tux.

Kale looked at him. It wasn't the style he would've picked. "It's okay."

"No, no, *okay* is not good enough. It has to be *perfect*. I'm marrying my dream girl."

"And mine," Kale said under his breath. The seamstress dropped the pin she was holding and looked up at him. "Long story," he whispered.

"And you're the best man?"

"I am. The dude has bad taste in friends, because I am *not* the best man for the job."

Justin came back out with a fedora and a cane. "Yea, or nay?"

Kale looked down at the woman letting out the hem so his pants would be long enough. She shook her head no. "Yea," he said.

"Hey, when you gonna propose to Jeane?" Justin asked from the dressing room.

"I don't know." *I'm sick of being asked that question.*

"She's hot, man. I say go for it."

The day of Devan and Justin's wedding was bittersweet. It wasn't even close to how she'd pictured her wedding. Then again, she never saw herself marrying anyone but Kale.

Her mom, Kristy, and Cassandra were helping her get ready. Devan asked them all to leave for a few minutes, and she locked the door behind them and sat at the vanity. She looked hopelessly into the mirror, and noticed how different her eyes looked, like they'd lost something. They seemed an empty and darker blue. *I have to be imagining that — they're the same eyes I've always had. My makeup looks perfect though, and my hair is absolutely amazing.*

Sadly, she saw someone else when she looked in the mirror. This wasn't the Devan that she knew.

Meanwhile, Justin was chilling out in the groom's area with his dad, Chris, and Kale. Chris asked Kale to step out of the room with him, and Justin didn't even notice. He was too busy talking business with his father.

"Let's get some water," Chris said. Kale followed him down a long, dark hallway and they stopped at the water fountain. "You know, I really thought you were the one she was going to marry. I never would've guessed you'd be the best man instead."

"If this were a movie, we'd run off into the sunset and never look back, but it's not. Real life is unscripted and unfair," Kale said as he looked down at the man with sadness and regret in his eyes. "Too bad it's not a movie, 'cause I suck as best man."

"You know, she's not married yet ... I think her room's right here. Why don't you check on her for me?" Chris said with a wink.

Kale looked at the door. Chris gave him a shove and walked away. Kale knocked lightly.

Devan got up from the vanity and walked over to the door. "Yes?"

Kale cleared his throat. "Um, your dad wanted me to check on you. Can I come in?"

Devan pulled him in, and shut and locked the door.

She's the most gorgeous thing I've ever seen. Her hair was half up and the other half hung in dark ringlets resting on her shoulders. The silver eye shadow brought out all of the greys and blues in her eyes, and her plump lips were a kiss-worthy wine color.

He grabbed her hands and said, "You look, perfect."

"Thank you." *His hands are so warm.*

"I can't believe I'm going to do this," he said under his breath. She looked up at him with curiosity. He looked into her eyes and said, "I love you, and I know you love me."

"What are you trying to say?" she asked, frowning.

"I don't know. I just— Do you really love this guy, Devan?"

"Yes, I do."

"Do you love him more than me?"

There was a knock on the door. "Five minutes," she heard her dad say.

"Kale, I love you, *and* I love him. You already made your decision so there's nothing to talk about."

"Damn it, Dev, I made a mistake. Then, you left and you didn't even ask me what should happen. *You* made this decision, not me."

Tears started to form in her eyes.

"We're meant to be together," he continued.

"You had a year. A fucking year to do something about it, and you tell me five minutes before I walk down the aisle?" She shook her head. "Okay, I made the best decision I could for *you,* and today I'm making the best decision I can for *me.*" She kissed his cheek. "I love you more than anything, but Joey needs you more than I do."

He nodded. She saw a tear escape his eye.

"I won't lie. I would run away with you right now. But if I did that, you and I both know she'd never let you see him again."

"You are," he cleared his throat, "the love of my life."

"Your child is the most important thing in your life. I'm just in the way. You have to do what's best for him."

"You're right, but Devan Marie, I will always love you, and I will always try to keep you safe," Kale promised.

"I know that, but if we were truly meant to be together, don't you think we would be?"

He sighed and tilted her chin. He lowered his lips to hers. She hadn't felt the warmth of his kiss in so long.

She closed her eyes. The passion was still there. She was mesmerized by his kiss and didn't hear the second knock. She did, however, hear her father's voice. "The best man is needed. If you've seen him, please send him my way."

"He's coming, Dad."

Kale let go of her hands. "If you really want to go through with this, I'll stand behind you."

She nodded with tears streaming down her face. "It's what's best for Joey."

He opened the door, looked back at her, and said, "My heart will always belong to you." He ran back in the room. "Come on, Monty, let's just leave. We'll figure out the Joey thing later," he pleaded.

"You're making me ruin my makeup! You have to go," she cried.

"Are you 100 percent sure?"

She nodded her head and he left the room.

Chris was waiting for him down the hall. "Everything okay?" he asked.

Kale shrugged and wiped his eyes. "I guess as okay as it's going to be today."

"She wouldn't do it, would she?"

Kale gave him a look of shock. "Do what?"

"She wouldn't give you a happy ending to your movie."

"You were listening?"

"No, but I know how the story is supposed to end."

"Not today, Chris. Not today."

Chris patted him on the back, and stuck a note in his pocket. "Save that for later. You're going to need it."

"What is it?"

"Your speech."

He'd completely forgotten he had to make a speech. It was one of the best man's duties.

Chris went back to see Devan. His wife, Kristy, and Cassandra were lined up outside her door. "She won't open it for anyone but you."

"Devan, sweetie, it's Dad."

"Tell everyone to go ahead and line up."

He repeated what she'd said. Then she unlocked the door and let him in.

"Sweetheart, you look beautiful!" he said, taking her hands.

"Are my eyes red?"

"No."

"Okay, let's do this," she said, and grabbed her bouquet.

After her mother was seated, the music began, and Kristy walked slowly down the aisle.

Her dad turned to her and said, "You don't have to do this."

"Yeah, Dad, I do."

"Why?"

She could see the disappointment in his eyes. She looked over at Joey waving to Kale. Her father squeezed her hand. "I see."

She blinked back the tears, plastered a smile on her face, and let her dad walk her down the aisle.

At the reception, Kale reluctantly took the microphone and stood up. He pulled the paper out of his pocket and read, "On behalf of the bride and groom, thank you for coming. I'd like to propose a toast to Justin and Devan. May today be the beginning of a wonderful new chapter in their lives." He crumpled the paper in his hand. "Okay, I'm not one for speeches, but I will come out and say ... I've known Devan, or Monty as I call her, for many years. She's a kind, sweet loving person, and she means a lot to me.

"I just met Justin this year, and he seems like a nice guy. He has a great head for business, and is a caring man. I like him. That being said, if he ever hurts her I will kill him. Drink up." He set his glass down and took the bottle and drank ... all of it.

Everyone — well almost everyone — laughed. Justin thought it was hilarious. Which made Devan wonder if she'd really made the right decision. She knew Kale *would* hurt Justin if he ever hurt her.

A little later, the dollar dance began. Kale was eighth in line, right behind his father. As soon as he took lead, "Fade into You" by Mazzy Star started playing. It kind of shocked them both. She knew for a fact she did *not* have this song on the DJ's play list. *I should've written: DO NOT play "Fade into You"!*

"You remember this song?" Kale asked, and looked down at the bride.

"I do."

"You don't think it is a coincidence that it's playing right this very second?"

She smiled. He got closer to her and whispered in her ear. "I wasn't kidding. I *will* kill him."

"I know, and you're the worst best man ever. You tried to steal the bride and you threatened the groom."

He chuckled. "I'm a man of many talents. I'm gonna get another drink." He kissed her forehead and walked away.

Kristy was behind him. "Hey, BFF." She put her arms around Devan and started dancing with her.

"Have you seen Kale drinking a lot tonight?"

Kristy thought for a moment. "Yes, actually, I have. Is that so strange though? I mean he had to be best man for his first love's wedding *and* he's still in love with her."

"Well, when you put it that way, no. But mention something to his dad or my dad or Jeane. Kale doesn't drink."

"Oh, *that's* not good. I'll take care of it." Kristy couldn't find either father, so she said something to Jeane, who nodded and said she'd planned on driving home anyway.

The Iakonas decided to take Joey for the night when they saw how drunk their son was.

When he and Jeane got home, Kale tried getting out of the car, but actually fell out. Jeane helped him up.

"Thank you. You know," he closed his eyes for a minute, "I have never been drunk. I am damn near 25 and it's my first time."

She giggled. "Well, there was that one time—"

He gave her a dirty look. "I don't think that counts, because I know I didn't drink much—"

She cut him off before it could turn into something bad. "Okay, let's get you in the house."

"I feel fine. Really I do."

"Well, that's good. Did you enjoy the wedding?"

Kale stopped. "Fuck no! It was the second worst day of my life."

Jeane unlocked the door and helped Kale to the couch. "What was the worst day?"

"I- I don't want to talk about it."

"Kale, I know I've been hard on you lately, but I really think we should get married for Joey's sake."

He rolled his eyes. "Christ woman, give it a rest."

Jeane pulled something out of her purse. "If this is about money, I already have my engagement ring. I bought it a few years ago in France."

He looked at her with disgust. "Who the hell buys their own engagement ring?"

"I wanted it to be perfect, and the only sure way of that was to get it myself, so I did." She continued, "You know, Uncle Alistar said if we didn't get married soon, he's going to make me come back home."

"So?"

"So, I'll be taking Joey with me."

He knew what she said was true. "Fine, just fuck it. We'll get fucking married." He knew if he didn't give in, it would become a never-ending battle. *A perfectly fucked up ending to a perfectly fucked up day.*

"Great, we'll announce it tomorrow and I'll start planning. I love you!" She gave him a kiss on the cheek and went to bed.

"You have no idea what love is," he mumbled then passed out.

Chapter 20

November 2002

Over the next two months Jeane and Kale planned their wedding. When Devan heard they were engaged, it made her sick to her stomach. So much so that very time Jeane brought it up, Devan had to excuse herself.

When Jeane asked Devan to be a bridesmaid, she almost threw up and ran to the restroom. Jeane was waiting for her outside when she opened the door. "How long have you been feeling this way?" she asked.

"What do you mean?"

"Devan, don't ignore it. I think you might be pregnant."

"What? *No!*" *There's no way!*

"Devan, when was the last time you—"

"Oh my God!" she exclaimed. *I hadn't even thought about it. I haven't my period since before the wedding!*

"Let's go to the store."

Sure enough two lines showed up on the stick. "Now do you believe me?" Jeane asked, looking at all ten positive pregnancy test sticks lined up on the counter.

"I can't be in your wedding. Who knows how big I'll be by then!"

"You'll be just fine. We'll just order the dress a few sizes bigger. Congrats! This is so exciting. I'm going to be an aunt!"

Devan got nauseated again at the thought of her baby calling Jeane "Aunt Jeane."

February/March 2003

Devan was seven months pregnant when it was time for Kale's wedding, but somehow she fit into her bridesmaid's dress. She hated being pregnant. She always felt bloated, hot, and just gross, but she loved feeling her little girl move around in her womb.

She hadn't seen much of Kale. She hadn't seen much of Justin either. Jeane's Uncle Alistar hired Jameson Enterprises, and they were both working on a big project for him, so Devan spent a lot of her time at her mom and dad's house.

Due to Jeane and Kale's schedule, the Iakonas babysat Joey most of the week. Since Devan hadn't taken on any new writing assignments, she was able to help take care of her favorite little man, who was now a little over a year old.

Two weeks before the wedding Nāhoa and Cassandra were called out of town, and Jeane and Justin were in Vancouver on business. Devan stayed at her parents' house and took care of Joey. Kale came and picked him up at seven o'clock every night. That Thursday, Kale was so tired he fell asleep in the Montgomery's chair while talking to Chris.

When he woke up, it was already 10 p.m. "Oh no! I am *so* sorry." He got up and started gathering Joey's bottles and diaper bag. Devan was already asleep with Joey's crib next to her bed.

"Kale, what time do you have to be at work tomorrow?" Chris asked.

"Wait! Tomorrow's Friday. I have a tux fitting and a meeting at the hall. I'm actually off work tomorrow," he said, smiling and suddenly in a good mood.

"Listen, son, you aren't going anywhere tonight. You're going to stay right here. You have bags the size of Texas under your eyes."

"Oh, I'll be fine, Chris."

"Kale, you aren't going anywhere. You passed out mid-sentence and slept for two hours."

Kale sat back down in the chair.

"Have you even had dinner?"

"Well, no."

"Stay there." Chris went into the kitchen for a few minutes and came back with a large sandwich, chips, and a drink.

"Eat. Bedsides I want to talk to you while Elaine and Devan are asleep."

"Thank you," Kale said taking a big bite.

"What's going on? You haven't been yourself since before Devan's wedding."

Kale was wide-awake now. He set his food down, took a long drink and looked Chris right in the eye. "Well, you are like my father and it's not like I can tell him. So, I guess I'll tell you."

He took a deep breath and let it all out. "I felt like a part of me died when your daughter got married. I got trashed that night and I don't drink. The next day I woke up and found out I was engaged. I'm still not sure how that happened.

"Since then, I've been working my ass off for Jeane's uncle while trying to take care of Joey the best I can. Thank you, by the way, for helping me with him. You guys and my parents have been amazing. Jeane is never home, so I am pretty much a single parent. Which, in all honesty, is fine with me."

"Why are you marrying her?"

"Simple answer, and there is only one — Joey."

"Kale, I have attorneys who could help with that sort of thing."

"What if they do a paternity test and find out what we've all been thinking is actually true? What if he isn't mine? Then what happens to my son? Jeane can't be trusted to take care of him. We might not share the same blood but he *is* my son."

"Good point. I think that fight would be difficult."

"If I marry her, then my chances are slightly better. At least that's how I look at it. Besides, it's not like I'll ever have what I really want anyway," he said as he wistfully looked at a picture of Devan and Justin hanging on the wall.

"I'm sorry son. We'll help you any way we can. Don't ever forget that."

Kale nodded and went back to eating his dinner.

The day before the wedding, Kale was too busy finishing up last minute things and didn't have time to pick Kuna up from the airport. Justin offered to do it for him, but got held up in a meeting. Devan ended up taking his place.

"I didn't expect to see you, *pua nani aó*," Kuna said and wrapped his large arms around Devan, squeezing her tight.

She hugged him back. *"Pua nani aó?* Should I be insulted?"

"No, I'm pleasantly surprised. *Pua nani aó* means beautiful flower." He put his hand on her belly. "She's hungry, let's get some chow."

"You're a funny man," she said, kissing his cheek.

"What? I can sense these things," he said with a chuckle.

They stopped to eat at a little mom and pop place. While they were waiting for their food Kuna said, "I don't want to upset you, but I need to talk to you about some things that have to stay between us. Okay?"

She nodded.

"You know Joseph is not an Iakona."

"I suspected."

"You know when you left, a part of Kale died, and another part of him died when you got married."

"Did he tell you this?"

"I'm Kuna, Kale told me nothing — I just know. When you left him, I tried to pick up the pieces. I don't like this Jeane. There's something wrong about her. Don't trust her ... *ever!*"

"Okay, I won't."

"You both feel like she killed true love, but true love still lives within you. It will prevail one day, but there will be agony first."

"What are you, a walking fortune teller?"

"No. I'm just Kuna."

Devan sat back and enjoyed her food and the company of this great man. She couldn't, however, help but wonder about what he'd said. *I know it's true. True love is still there between us, but will it really prevail one day? Will we ever get our happily ever after?*

When Pete showed up at the rehearsal, Kale was surprised. "Hey, I didn't think you'd be able to make it tonight."

"Yeah, it was rough, but I told them I was your best man and had to be here tonight and tomorrow."

Devan saw Pete and tried to get out of her chair. It took her a little longer than usual, but she finally managed it.

"What a sight! Baby in bloom! Congrats, Dee!" he said giving her a big hug.

They actually had a fun night. There were times that Jeane and Justin should've felt out of place, but they seemed to keep each other company.

The next morning it was a rush to get everything coordinated. Devan wasn't feeling that well, but she made it through the hair, makeup and getting dressed, then went out and sat in the pews next to Kristy to rest a bit an hour before people would start to arrive.

After about half an hour, Pete came looking for Devan. The second he saw Kristy, he couldn't keep his eyes off her.

"Dee, Jeane is asking for you. Here, let me help you up," he said still not looking at her.

Devan walked down the hall to where Jeane was waiting. As she approached, she saw someone leave the room in a hurry. When she got there, she asked Jeane, "Who was that?"

"Oh, that was Justin. He just came to wish me luck."

"Oh." *That's a bit strange, but I guess they're business associates and forced family friends, so maybe it's not all that weird.*

"Can you do me a big favor? I want to make sure Kale looks perfect. I don't want him to see me, but I trust your judgment. Can you make sure everything's how it should be?"

"Yeah, sure." Devan said, and went to find him.

When she got to the room where he was getting ready, she knocked and asked, "Are you decent?"

He opened the door, and wearing nothing but his pants and socks.

"Oh my Lord, Kale! Why aren't you ready?" She walked in and shut the door.

He was fidgeting terribly. "I can't find my shirt!"

"How in the hell did you lose your shirt?"

"I don't know. Wait, why are you here? I thought Pete was coming back."

"Jeane had Pete find me so I could check on you. When he found me, he found Kristy."

"Enough said," he sighed. "Well, I'm glad you're here. I needed to talk to you anyway." He took a long deep breath and continued, "Okay, look, there's something I really have to do before I get married. If I don't do it, I'll regret it forever. I'm really sorry but—" He grabbed her head and kissed her. Not a peck, but not really a sexual kiss, either. It was passionate and tinged with sadness.

I don't want to stop. I know once I stop, it's really over. This is my goodbye kiss.

Devan sensed the finality, too. It stirred up so many feelings and made her feel weak at the knees.

"I'm sorry. I had to—"

"Get it out of your system?" she asked with a smile.

"Yeah," he said and sighed.

"Well, did it work?"

"No, not really."

"Um, well, I should go. They'll be looking for you." She turned toward the door.

"Hey, wait!" he said and grabbed hold of her hand. "Please, help me find my shirt."

They looked around the room and both felt like idiots when they saw it hanging on the back of the door. Devan stayed to help Kale finish getting dressed. As she was tying his tie, he made her stop and pulled her around to face him.

"I still don't know if this is the right thing, but whether it is or not, Joey and I need you in our lives. Please don't go away."

"Why do you think I'd go away?" she asked sincerely.

"Because that's what I wanted to do when *you* got married. Plus once you have your baby, you won't have much time for us, which I completely understand."

"Kale, I'll *make* time. Our lives may be busy, but we'll always make time. You can't get rid of me that easily."

"Promise?"

"I promise, Lettuce Head."

He let go of her. "I'm only doing this for Joey. You know that, right?"

She nodded her head.

"I don't love Jeane. I still love you. You'll always have my heart."

The door opened and Kuna came in. "Your husband's looking for you."

"Kuna, how did you know where I was?"

"I'm Kuna."

"Right," she said, and left.

"How was it, braddah?"

"How was what, Kuna?"

"Your goodbye kiss?"

"How did— I know, I know, you're Kuna."

"That's right. Tell me though, how close are Jeane and Justin?"

"Close, I guess. They've been working together a lot."

"Hmm—" Kuna didn't like what he heard.

"Why?"

"Just wondered."

As Devan walked down the aisle right before Jeane, she started feeling woozy. She shook off the feeling and continued to her place. *I'll be okay. I'll rest when the wedding's over.* She looked over and smiled at Kale and then turned to look at Jeane as she walked down the aisle.

Even though Kale's eyes should've been on his bride, he could only look at Devan. She looked ill. She was sweating and swaying. He saw her start to drop and slid across the floor to catch her just in the nick of time.

"Someone call an ambulance!" he yelled.

Chapter 21

March 2003

Kale tried to ride in the ambulance with Devan, but Kuna and Pete stopped him. "Kale, I'll call your mom as soon as we find out anything," Elaine told him.

"Kale, let's get married now, and between the wedding and reception we can go check on her ourselves. Okay?" Jeane politely suggested.

He nodded halfheartedly.

They were married and as soon as the ceremony was over they headed to the hospital. On the way over, they got a call from his mom. Kale put it on speaker: "She's okay. They think she has something called preeclampsia. Apparently she has high blood pressure and a lot of swelling in her legs and feet. They're waiting for the results to come back from the lab to see if the protein is too high in her urine. Right now, she's okay and so is baby Calista."

"Oh, they named her!" Jeane said, delighted.

"Okay Ma, we're on our way over."

"No, you guys go on to the reception. We'll meet you there shortly. They're going to keep her overnight for monitoring. She's resting now."

"Kale, we'll go visit her after the reception," Jeane promised.

Kale nodded and said goodbye to his mother.

The reception went well, but Kale really wasn't enjoying it. He was too anxious to see Devan. As they were all cleaning up, Justin walked in. "What are you doing here?" Kale asked. "Is Devan okay?"

"She's fine Kale. I'm here to help clean up. I already talked to Jeane. Why don't you go ahead and go to the hospital to see Dee. I'll make sure Jeane gets home safely. I think Devan wants to thank you for rescuing her, anyway."

Justin gave him a weak smile. "Oh, here, take my car," he said as he threw Kale his keys.

Kale ran out to the car and stopped abruptly and stared at the vehicle. Justin's car was a Miata. *How am I supposed to fit in that little clown car? Oh, Christ, I hate these things!* He unlocked the car and tried to get in. He pushed the seat all the way back, but still barely fit.

When he got to the hospital and opened the car door, he practically spilled out onto the pavement. He went to the front desk and asked for Devan's room number.

When he got there, he heard Kristy and Devan laughing about old times — old times with the Fantastic 4.

"How are you feeling?" she asked Devan.

"Better, thank you. Laughter really is the best medicine."

"No, Dee, I mean about the wedding. I just feel like it was so stressful for you to see the man of your dreams marry some psycho. I think it made your BP soar."

"No, this was underlying and just decided to show its ugly face today."

"So, Kale getting married had no effect on you whatsoever," Kristy said sarcastically.

"Well, it's not on my top 100 list of fun things to do, and it definitely wasn't on my bucket list."

"I'm sorry. I'm sure it didn't help that he looked *so* hot," Kristy said fanning herself.

"Oh, God, I know. I haven't seen him almost clean shaven since our date back in Hawaii."

"Knock, knock ladies," Kale said and tapped on the door.

"Come in." They both answered.

"How are you?" he asked, pretending he hadn't overheard their conversation.

"Kale, shouldn't you be at the reception?" Devan asked, sounding surprised.

"It's over. Justin came and relieved me somewhat," he laughed.

"What do you mean?" she asked worried.

"He came back to help clean up and said he would— Wait, you knew he left. Right?"

"Yeah, I told him to go enjoy what was left of your day. I didn't expect him to send *you* here."

"Well, I'm here, and now I feel like I can breathe. I wasn't enjoying it anyway. I would've much rather been here with you," he said while stripping off his jacket and vest.

"Okay, not something you should admit in public, Kale — especially on the day you married someone else," Kristy said and snapped one of his suspender straps. "I'm going to go get some coffee. I'll be back in a little bit." She kissed Kale on the cheek. "I'd put money on it that she'd rather have you here than Justin," she whispered.

"I'm sorry for ruining your wedding," Devan said, almost in tears.

"No, I'm sorry for upsetting you and — everything." He tried crawling into the bed with her, but he was just too big, and fell on his ass. She laughed. He got up and bent over to pick up the keys that were in his pocket and ... rrrip.

He turned to look at her and she was laughing so hard she was crying. He sat down in the chair next her and joined in on the laughter.

Suddenly, nurses came rushing in to check the monitor on Devan's stomach. After a few minutes one of them said, "Okay, false alarm."

"What happened?" Kale asked.

"We lost the baby's heartbeat, and an alarm went off at the station. She must've moved and the monitor lost it. It's okay. We're going to do an ultrasound in a few minutes to double check."

Kristy came in frantic. "What happened?"

"It's okay. The baby moved and her heartbeat was lost." Kale said, repeating what the nurse had said.

A few minutes later, the ultrasound technician came in with the machine. "Can they stay?" Devan asked.

"Sure." The technician moved the wand around and a face came up on the screen. The baby was sucking her thumb.

"Awe, she already looks like you, Dee. I can tell by her nose," Kristy said holding Devan's hand.

The wand moved over the baby's heart. "Look at that! It's beating how it should. I'm going to turn it up so we can hear it." The sound was a perfect steady beat. "Looks good, mom!" the technician told Devan.

The medical staff left the room, and Kale and Kristy stayed around for a little longer. "Come on stud, you need to get home to Mrs. Iakona," Kristy said.

"My mom is the only Mrs. Iakona."

"What?" Kristy and Devan said simultaneously.

"Jeane kept her last name — I'm 100 percent fine with that. She doesn't deserve the Iakona name!"

Wow, that's a bit harsh! Devan thought.

Half an hour later, Jeane and Justin showed up. "How are you?" Jeane asked as she gave Devan a hug.

"Oh, I'm okay. Listen I am so sorry for—"

"Shhh ... don't you say another word. As long as you and the baby are okay, everything is fine."

"No, really Jeane, I'm sorry."

"Devan, it's not like you sabotaged my wedding," she said and laughed.

A doctor knocked on the door. "Hi Devan. I'm Dr. Arlynne. Your urine came back positive for protein. I'm sorry, but we'll need to keep you here for a few days. We're also going to start you on blood pressure medication.

"Now, your husband can stay, but everyone else has to leave," she said. Kale stood up and the doctor stopped him. "You can stay, Mr. Jameson."

Justin stood up and said, *"I'm* her husband!"

It was obvious the doctor was confused, and she didn't hide it well. "Oh, I'm sorry, I just— okay. Well, we'll be back in about an hour to draw some blood."

Justin walked over to Devan and said, "Dee, I have some bad news. Well, actually we both do," he said looking at Jeane.

Jeane looked at Kale and said, "We have to leave in the morning to catch an early flight to Montreal. My uncle can't make the meeting, so he is sending us. I'm sorry."

"Okay, we'll postpone the honeymoon, but Justin can't go. He needs to stay here with Devan. I'll go with you instead," Kale told Jeane.

"No, honey, Justin needs to be there. I'm sorry. We both thought maybe you could stay with Devan until her mom can come."

Kristy looked at Jeane and Justin, convinced that something was up.

"Oh, don't worry about it. I'll be fine. I don't need anyone to stay with me. I'm being monitored, so it's all good."

"No, I'll stay." Kale said and put his hand on hers.

"That okay with you, Dee?" Justin asked.

"I guess, but you really don't have to stay, Kale."

Kale looked at her swollen feet and the bags under her eyes and just smiled. He really didn't want to be anywhere else.

Justin kissed Devan and hugged her, then gave Kale a hug. "Thanks, man. I know nothing bad will happen to her if you're around. You' re kind of like her guardian angel, aren't you?"

"Oh, if you only knew," Kristy said under her breath.

Everyone but Kale left, and Devan said, "Kale, go home and be with Jeane before she leaves. It is your wedding night after all."

"Right, so I can consummate a marriage I was pretty much forced into. I'm good, Monty. *That* is the last thing on my mind."

"Thank you for staying and thank you for saving me *again*."

"I wouldn't have it any other way," he said and kissed her forehead. *I'll always be your protector,* he silently vowed.

Chapter 22

Calista's arrival

Devan was able to leave the hospital after a few days, but was ordered to have complete bed rest. A few days later, Kale went over to visit with her while her parents went away for a three-day weekend.

He knocked on the door, but there was no answer. He found the hidden key and unlocked the door. He called for her, but there was still no answer. He looked in every room in the house and he still couldn't find her.

Finally, he went to the basement. "What are you doing Monty?" he asked with relief and bit of frustration.

"What does it look like — laundry," she replied sarcastically.

"You're *not* supposed to be out of bed. I'll finish this. Come on; let's go back upstairs. I'll help you."

"Where's Joey?" she asked looking around.

"Still in his carrier in the living room."

"Can we just go there, instead? I promise I'll just lie on the couch."

They went upstairs and Kale got her some pillows and a blanket from her old room. When he came back into the room, she was sitting up playing peek-a-boo with his son. "Damn it, Monty! Lay down," he said angrily.

She grunted a few unpleasant words but did as he said.

Satisfied, he went back downstairs to finish the laundry. Half an hour later, he came upstairs and noticed she was still lying down but her face was red. He felt her head, and it was hot. "Are you feeling okay?"

"I have an awful headache," she groaned.

"Where's your blood pressure machine?"

"It's on the stand next to the bed."

He quickly retrieved it, and took her blood pressure. *185/102? That can't be right!* He moved it to her other arm and checked again — 189/103. He remembered what the doctor said and went out to his truck and started it. After it warmed up, he put Joey in and went back inside. He noticed that Devan seemed disoriented. He picked her up, put her in the truck and drove straight to the hospital.

"Are you Mr. Jameson?" the nurse asked, looking at the insurance card.

"Yes. Can you please take her back now? I can handle this."

"Calm down, Mr. Jameson. Someone is coming with a gurney."

When they came and got Devan, he finished the paperwork and was then led back to a triage room.

Devan opened her eyes and asked, "What's going on?"

"Your blood pressure was really high. I brought you to the hospital."

"Oh, Kale, I don't want to be here."

"I know, but you have no choice."

A doctor and nurse came in the room. "Hello, I'm Dr. Stafford and this is Nurse Turner. We're going to draw some blood and check your blood pressure again."

"Okay," Kale said, "I'm going to step out and call my parents so they can come and get Joey."

When he got outside, he pulled the cell phone out of his pocket and called his mom. "Ma, I need you to leave work right now. Come to the hospital and pick up Joey."

"Why? What is going on?"

"Devan's blood pressure spiked, and I had to bring her in."

"Okay, I'm on my way."

When he came back into the room, the doctor said, "Mr. Jameson, her blood pressure is pretty high. The baby seems to be okay right now, but I'm waiting on some test results to know for sure. Right now, we need to get her to the ultrasound room so we can see what's going on. Why don't you wait here with your child and we'll take her to radiology."

The doctor came back just after Cassandra had picked up Joey and said, "Okay, Mr. Jameson, the baby's not in distress right now, however her placenta is pretty much dead. The baby is only four and a half pounds, and at 34 weeks she really should be bigger. She is not getting many nutrients at all. We're going to need to induce labor."

Kale rubbed his head. "When are you planning on doing that?"

"Well, we're moving her up to Labor and Delivery so we can get her setup in a room. Once we do that, we'll be starting her on Pitocin and giving her Cervidil as well."

Before going up to her room, Kale sent out a mass text to Devan's parents, his parents, Justin, and Jeane:

KALE: Devan being induced, placenta not working anymore.
       Need to get baby out.

Eight hours after they started the drugs, Devan started having contractions.

"You know that time we jumped off those cliffs?" she asked.

"Yeah?"

"I'd rather be doing that!" she said, huffing and puffing. "All right, all right I can breathe," she said after a few minutes. "Tell me something fun."

He thought for a moment and looked at her with an ornery smile. "Do you remember the waterfall at the lake?"

"Uh, yeah."

"That was fun."

"Come on, Kale!"

"Okay, okay. How about prom? I bet you didn't know I was nervous as hell."

"Why were you nervous?"

"Monty, I hadn't seen you for a really long time. I wanted everything to be perfect, and I wanted my being there to be a really good surprise."

"Kale, that was the best surprise in my whole life."

He smiled and looked at her puffy, yet beautiful face. "I'm so sorry," he said, looking so sad.

"About what?"

"I'm sorry Justin isn't here."

"Ugh, don't be sorry. He drives me crazy sometimes. He's all business. You're much better company."

The pain hit her again, harder and faster, and the doctors came in to see if she was dilated. "Only one centimeter," was the bad news.

The contractions calmed down for a little bit, and Devan fell asleep. Around 4 a.m., she was awakened by them again.

"*Ahhh!*"

Kale jumped up.

A nurse came running in. "Let's see where you are." She looked. "Still at one. I'm going to call the doctor."

While she was gone, Devan felt a strange sensation, almost like a little pop in her lower abdomen. "Awe, hell!" She looked down to see that she'd wet the bed.

"What?" Kale asked.

"I just pissed myself."

Kale started laughing, which really set Devan off. "This isn't funny! I'm in pain *and* I pissed myself. How can you laugh at a time like this?"

"Monty, I don't think you wet the bed. I think your water broke."

She thought for a moment. "That must've been the popping sensation. Okay, that makes sense."

The nurse came rushing back in. "Okay, we're going to prep you for an emergency C-section."

"Why?" she asked concerned.

"Well, your heart rate is really high and so is the baby's. It will be safer for both of you if we do a C-section."

Suddenly Devan was terrified. Kale could feel her fear, and he was afraid for both her and the baby.

"Sir, I need you to scrub up really well and put these on," the nurse said as she handed him a complete sanitation outfit. He did as he was told, then sent out another mass text:

KALE: Doing emergency C-section NOW!

He realized they'd given Devan something when he came back into the room, because she was in good spirits. She laughed at him when she saw him. The booties covered only part of his feet and the gown was so short most of his forearms were showing. She could see his man bun was covered with the cap, and he looked absolutely ridiculous.

"Okay we're going to start. Can you feel this?" the doctor asked tapping her shin.

"Feel what?"

"Okay, that's good. How about this?" He tapped her on the opposite foot.

"Nope."

"Okay, you're ready."

Devan took a deep breath and grabbed Kale's hand.

"Devan, you're going to feel some tugging and pulling," the doctor said.

"Okay."

Kale's height allowed him to easily see everything that was going on. He didn't turn away fast enough when they started slicing her. "Ohh—" he whimpered, then turned around and squeezed her hand tighter. "I sure as hell hope you didn't feel that," he said cringing.

"Nope."

About 20 minutes later, the doctor said, "She's out. Okay, pulse is strong and weight is 6 pounds. Great! She's bigger than we thought. Come on baby, let's hear you cry."

There was silence that seemed like it lasted forever, then "Waah!"

Devan could feel warm tears cascading down her face. "Oh, thank God!"

"Color is good, length 18 inches. Let's clean her up."

A few minutes later, they handed the baby to Kale. Devan felt more tears stream down her face. *She's beautiful. Just beautiful.*

"She looks like you," Kale said, "perfect. This is the most amazing thing I've ever witnessed!" A few tears rolled down his face, too.

"Devan, do you still feel okay?" the doctor asked.

"Oh, yes, now that I know she's okay."

"Good, we're going to finish up now. You'll feel some tugging again. We're just putting things back where they belong and sewing you up."

Halfway into it, she tensed up. "Something's wrong, it hurts!" she cried out in agony.

"Can you feel this?" the doctor asked while tapping on her leg.

"Yes. I think I feel your hands on my intestines— *Ahhh!*" she screamed.

A nurse rushed in and took the baby from Kale. "Sir, I'm sorry but you need to leave."

"No! I can't leave her!" he yelled as he was escorted out.

"Sir, please come with me."

"I love you, Kale. Take care of my baby!" Devan cried out.

Kale was taken out to a waiting room, where he saw his parents and Joey. His mother immediately knew something was wrong by the look on his face.

"Oh, no," Cassandra put her head to her hands.

"Kale, what is it?" his dad asked.

"They made me leave. She started screaming. I don't know."

"Son, have a seat. They'll tell us soon." Nāhoa took Kale by the arm and led him to a chair.

Twenty long minutes later, the doctor reappeared. "Mr. Jameson?" Kale stood up. "Your wife is in recovery. She's okay. We had to put her out completely. The epidural stopped working — nothing to be worried about. You should be able to go and see her in about two hours. You can, however, go see your daughter in the nursery now."

"Thank you," he said and gave the man a huge hug.

"Is there something we need to know, son?" his mother asked.

"No. I had to say I was her husband or they wouldn't let me go back with her."

When Devan woke up, Kale went back to see her. "Hi. How are you feeling?" he asked with a weak smile.

"Is Calista okay?"

"Yes, I was able to go back and see her. Mom and Dad are here, but I haven't heard from Justin or Jeane. Oh, and your parents are on their way."

"Please call them and tell them to just stay. I probably won't be allowed to leave for a few days anyway."

"Well, Mom and Dad need to leave soon. Joey's getting restless."

"Oh, please bring them and Joey back."

A moment later Joey came teetering in. "Mem-Mem."

"Mem-Mem?" Cassandra asked.

"I think he's trying to say Monty," Kale said.

"No, I think he is calling her 'mom,'" his dad said.

Devan was only allowed to visit with them for a few minutes before the orderly came to take her up to her room. "Wait, Kale. Please, don't go!" she said as they were wheeling her out.

"I'm not going anywhere," he said, grabbing her hand.

He said goodbye to his family and then followed her upstairs. Once she got there, she was reunited with her daughter and finally got to hold her.

"She's the first brand new baby I've ever held in my life," Kale told her.

"Other than Joey."

"No, I didn't even get to see him until he was a day old. Jeane wouldn't let me," he confessed.

"I didn't know that. I'm so sorry."

"Eh, it's done and over with."

"You know, I forgot something today with all the excitement," she said and reached for his hand.

"What's that?" he asked.

"It's your birthday! Happy birthday, Uncle Kale."

He'd completely forgotten. "Well, this the best birthday gift anyone could ask for," he said as he bent down to kiss Calista on the head. "Happy birthday, little girl."

Chapter 23

After Calista's birth, the families grew even closer. Justin and Jeane were constantly away for work, and pretty soon it seemed like Kale and Devan were playing house and raising their kids together. As much alone time as they had, neither of them made a move on the other — it was all about the kids.

Joey continued to call Devan "Mem" but called Jeane "Ne-Ne."

A little more than a year after Calista was born, Jeane announced she was pregnant again. Sage was born in October of 2004, and she looked just like Kale's dad. No paternity questions there!

Jumping ahead to 2007/2008

The morning of Calista's fourth birthday, Justin and Devan found out they were pregnant again.

"Hey, guess we're trying to catch up with you, man." Justin said and nudged Kale.

"Oh?"

"Yeah, we got a bun in the oven. The past few months of not traveling for work have been *productive*." Justin winked.

"No kidding, man, we do too." Kale said shaking his hand.

"That's crazy. Congrats! I'm going to go congratulate Jeane."

He walked over to Jeane and hugged her. The look on his face wasn't a happy one.

Devan sat down next to Kale, and saw Jeane and Justin in the distance. "What's that about?" she asked Kale.

"Oh, we're pregnant, too. I just told Justin," Kale responded.

"That's wonderful!" she said and hugged Kale.

Devan looked over at Jeane and Justin again and saw they were deep in conversation. Jeane caught her staring at them and immediately put on a smile as she walked over and hugged Devan.

"Congrats!"

"You, too!" She hugged her back and thought, *Something's fishy here. I can smell it.*

Justin was in a foul mood over the next few weeks. He stayed late at work and they had to cancel their plans with Kale and his family on three different occasions.

Months went by and things didn't get better. Justin's attitude toward Devan had shifted in a negative way. Several times when he came home she could smell alcohol on his breath. For some reason, their relationship had changed drastically and it never did get back on course.

Jeane had to be hospitalized, and had the baby four weeks early. The moment Kai was born, Justin's attitude lifted. He was nicer to Devan again and drank a lot less, or so she thought.

"Oh, my god, he looks just like Kale," he said when Devan and he went to visit Jeane and Kai at the hospital.

Three weeks later, Cyrus was born.

Over the next year, family-related matters took center stage, and the couples didn't have a lot of time to spend together. Once a month, though, they made sure they had Sunday Family Day.

"We have an announcement to make," Jeane said on one such occasion. "We're moving to Seattle to help my uncle with his new hotel. I'm going to be project manager and Kale is head architect."

"Why am I just being told this?" Justin asked, acting less than pleased.

"Alistar called us this morning with the opportunity and after he told us all the benefits, it's just an offer we can't refuse," Kale explained.

"Don't worry, Justin, my uncle has some great opportunities coming your way, too," Jeane said.

"This isn't permanent, it's just for a few years," Kale reassured him.

"Well, congratulations. We'll miss you guys," Devan forced herself to say cheerily.

"Hey, what if we do something really fun together before we leave?" Jeane suggested.

"That's a good idea. What did you have in mind?" Devan asked.

"How about a vacation," Jeane asked with enthusiasm.

"Yeah, I like that." Justin winked at her.

"How about that lake you guys went to when you were younger?" Jeane asked Kale.

"I don't—"

She cut him off. "Come on, it's family friendly."

"I'm sure they're booked up." Devan said.

"Come on, let's call," Jeane said, handing her phone to Devan.

"I don't know the number," Devan lied.

"Okay, fair enough. What's the name of the place? I'll look it up."

Jeane looked it up and called them. "Okay, so you don't have anything for all of June and July?"

"Jeane, let's just find someplace else, please," Kale urged.

"Hold on," she said and shushed him.

"Oh? Um it'll be a tight squeeze, but yeah. Please book it ... four adults and five kids. Okay, yes ... Great you can put it under Jeane Cadence." She finished giving her information over the phone and flipped it shut.

"Okay, first week of August," she said, all smiles.

"Jeane, that's right before we have to leave." Kale said, unhappily.

"No biggie, we'll just finish packing early."

"Can't we just book a stay at one of your uncles' hotels?" he practically begged.

"No, honey, I'm doing this for you. I know how much that lake means to you, and I'm sure Devan loves it, too. Plus, the kids will have a great time."

Kale put his head to his hands and peeked at Devan. *She has to be just as freaked out about this as I am.*

The next day when Devan found herself alone, she called Kristy to vent.

"I mean, yes, I totally want to go but—"

"But that place has significant meaning to you and Kale. This sucks — you guys have been doing great being just friends."

"Well, there is that, yeah, but that lake will bring back so many memories and—"

Kristy interrupted her again. "Wait, the lake... first kiss, oh… *the water-fall.* You're afraid you won't be able to keep your hands off each other."

"No," Devan said and sighed.

"No?"

"Well, over the years he and I have had more than our share of—"

"Heartache, hiding your feelings for each other, crying every night because you can't be with the one you truly love? Oh, hello officer!"

"What? Who are you talking to?" Devan asked suspiciously.

"No, no. Sorry, um ... Where was I?"

"Go to the lake, Dee," Devan heard someone say in the background.

Her mouth dropped open. "Is that *Pete?*"

"Well, maybe he just got home from deployment and maybe he stayed the night."

Devan laughed. "That's *great,* Kristy, really great. But you tell that Marine to not say a word to Kale."

"He won't. Maybe he had this exact conversation with a certain muscle-bound someone just a few minutes ago."

"No, no *NO!* There's no way we're going to the damn lake now."

"Devan, come on. When was the last time the two of you didn't have at least three kids climbing all over you every second of the day? Now you have two more babies to add to that. You two won't ever be alone, so don't even worry about it."

The Lake, 2008

They'd only been at the cabin on the lake for about an hour when Devan decided to take a shower. Afterward, she got dressed, walked out into the open living area and looked around. "Uh, where is everyone?"

Kale sighed. "J and J took the three older kids out to play, and the two little ones are sleeping."

"I was only in the shower for like 10 minutes."

"I know, I was outside checking the water temp and Joey ran down to tell me that they were all going to the park. He ran back up before I could say anything."

"Do you have any idea when they'll be back?"

"Nope."

Kale turned on the TV and just sat there. Devan wished they had better cell service so she could call or text Kristy to tell her how wrong she was about thinking they'd have no alone time.

She sat down in a chair as far away from Kale as she could, and prayed that one of the babies would wake up soon. She got her wish, and they both jumped up at the same time. Kale got there faster because he was closer, and picked up Cyrus and cradled him.

Devan just stood there watching. *Kale's such a good father. Even though Cyrus isn't his child, he treats him just like he is.*

"What?" he asked when he caught her staring.

"You're so good with children."

"Well, I *am* a dad."

"Yeah, but so's Justin, and he doesn't have the touch."

"The touch?"

Oh shit! Well, he definitely doesn't have that *touch either. Oh, my God —* stop it! "What I mean is, Justin just isn't a hands-on, caring father like you." *Like he doesn't already know this.*

He nodded, "Yeah, we have the same problem in our house."

Kai started screaming. "I got that one," Devan said going over to pick up the baby."

They changed diapers and made bottles, and the babies were quiet again. "Hey, you wanna go ahead and rent the boat?" Kale asked, while slipping on his sandals.

"Yeah, let's get the babies' life jackets and get them in the strollers."

They walked down to the marina and looked around for a while.

"Hey, it's Stretch! I almost didn't recognize you with that beard. How many years has it been?"

Kale couldn't believe it was the same boat rental guy from years earlier. "Hey, man, still here after all this time?" he asked as he shook the guy's hand vigorously.

"Living the life, my man. Lake living is heaven. Awe, who's this little guy?" he asked, bending down to get a better look at Cyrus.

He stood up quickly and smiled when he saw Devan looking at some sunglasses. "Now that's awesome. You guys stayed together — see that waterfall *is* magic. He looks just like her."

He walked over to Devan and leaned over to look at baby Kai. "Now, this one though looks exactly like you. Wait fraternal twins?"

"No, he has mine and I have his."

"How is that possible?"

Devan realized what he was asking and said, "Oh, we're together, but not together-together."

"So, you ended up with different people? That's an awful shame." He looked disappointed, but smiled anyway. "It's cool you're here and I'm guessing still really good friends."

"The best," Kale said.

As he passed, the guy whispered in Kale's ear, "You need to go back to the waterfall and fix this." He patted Kale on the back and walked away.

Chapter 24

Kale couldn't sleep that night. He kept hearing the marina guy in his head. "You need to fix this!" *I want to fix it. Hell I've wanted to fix it since she left me in Hawaii. I didn't want to come on this damn trip to begin with. I knew it would stir up all these old feelings.* Truthfully he wasn't having them again; they'd always been there. Tired of tossing and turning, he got up and went to the kitchen for a glass of water.

"Couldn't sleep?"

He jumped and nearly hit his head on the light fixture. Devan was sitting on the couch with Cyrus in one arm and a book in another.

"Good Lord, you scared me."

She giggled.

"What are you reading?" he asked as he sat down next to her.

"*Dancing with Danger*, it's a romance novel. You wouldn't like it."

"Gimme that." He snatched the book out of her hands, opened it, and began reading. "Now that she saw him face to face, she remembered those seductive eyes. So daring, yet sincere. She needed him, and she needed him now. She started tearing his clothes off piece by piece—"

"Shut up, Lettuce Head. It doesn't say that."

"Hmmf, well it should."

"You're not allowed to make fun of this book. They're turning it into a movie. Remember that actress who grew up not too far from us?"

"Sam ... Sam something?"

"Samantha Lane. She's got the lead role."

"Really?"

"Yep," she said, yawning.

"I can't sleep, so why don't you give me Cyrus so you can go to bed?"

"If I go back in there, I'll wake up Justin and I really don't feel like dealing with that asshole right now."

"Um, is there something going on?"

"No. I'm sorry, it's just — I don't know. He's been acting really strange. He's snippy, never home, and drinking a lot again. I don't know what's going on with him."

"Do you want me to talk to him?"

"Oh God, *no!* I'll kill you if you do, Kale Kai. Just pretend I didn't say anything," she said, glaring at him to make it clear the threat was real.

He took Cyrus out of her arms and started walking around with him. "Is he hurting you or the kids?"

"No! Nothing like that. I wouldn't put up with that shit. Just forget I said anything."

"Okay, well if you can't go to your room why don't you go ahead and lay down out here? If Cyrus starts fussing I'll take him to my room."

Why does he have to be so damn perfect? Instead of keeping the thought to herself she just came out and asked him, "Why do you have to be so damn perfect?"

"Excuse me?"

"I don't get it. You can't be real!"

"I assure you, Dee, I am." He chuckled. "Do you want to pinch me?" He turned around and stuck out his rear end, offering it to her. She giggled.

"Okay, you're beautiful, and—"

"Oh God, *stop*, Monty!"

"No, you're insanely in shape, you're nice, funny, a great father, romantic," she said that one quieter for fear it would awaken more of her demons.

"You make me sound perfect, and I'm not. You forgot — push over, murderer of love, loser—"

"Shut up. You aren't any of those things."

"I'm not going to sit here and argue with you."

"Good, because I'm right. There's nothing to argue about."

He rolled his eyes then gave her that mesmerizing smile. "I *so* hate you right now," he said with a smirk.

"Good, that'll make this trip easier." *Oh shit, I said that out loud!*

Kale cleared his throat and pretended he didn't hear the last comment. "So, what are the plans for tomorrow?"

She shrugged. "I don't know exactly, but I bet sleeping will be involved." She yawned and stretched.

Cyrus had fallen asleep, so Kale went in the other room to put him in his crib. When he came back, Devan was asleep. He stayed awake for a half hour or so, just staring at her and dreaming of what should've been.

"Kale, wake up. They did it again," Devan said, furious.

"Did what?" he asked when he opened his eyes.

"They left without us."

"What the hell?"

"Oh, and here's the note: Going into town, needed to fax something. Taking Justin and all the kids with me. Going to chill out there for a bit. Be back around dinnertime. Will bring food. Have a good day. — Jeane."

Devan slammed the note down on the table. "I thought this was supposed to be a *family* vacation!"

"Well, I'm not going to sit around all day and wait for their asses to get back. Go put on your swimsuit and grab your ski jacket."

They walked down to the marina and rented a WaveRunner. When they hopped on, Devan realized she'd have to hold on to Kale as they rode through the water. *Oh God, it feels so good to have my arms around him again. I've missed that.*

After they got out on the open water, Kale stopped at an island. "Feel like exploring?" he asked with a wink.

"Sure."

He tied up the WaveRunner and they walked up to drier land. They both wandered around for a little bit, enjoying the natural beauty of the island, until Kale called out, "Hey, come look at what I found."

Devan ran over and saw he was staring at a hole in the ground. "What did you find?"

"You can't see it?"

"I see a hole."

"Look closer," he said and pointed.

She bent down and saw what looked like an old locket. She reached in, pulled it out of the dirt and opened it. The locket was definitely weathered but wasn't as old as she'd hoped. There was a picture that was pretty much ruined on one side. She could tell it was a guy. Then on the other side was a pretty girl with an '80s hairstyle.

"Let's hold on to this and see what else we can find," Kale said as he put the locket in the pocket of his trunks. They looked around the island some more, but didn't find anything else interesting. They were having a great time just being together.

"Okay, what's next, Monty?" he asked as he headed down the hill.

"I'm kind of hungry. Can we go back to the marina and eat, then go back out on the water?"

"Sounds good."

At the marina they parked, took their ski jackets off and sat down at one of the outdoor tables.

"What can I get for you two?" asked the boat rental guy.

"Hey, you work here, too?"

"Jack of all trades, that's me. Now, what can I get ya?"

"Ill have a chicken salad on rye," Devan told him, after looking at the menu.

"I'll have the same," Kale said.

They were so intense in their conversation about nothing they didn't even notice when their food arrived.

As the guy walked away, Kale said, "Oh, I forgot, I was going to show him the locket." He got up and went after the guy.

"Hey, we found this today when we went out exploring," he said as he put the locket in the man's hand.

He looked at Kale like he was spooked by something and then opened it. "Where'd you find this?" he asked with a quiver in his voice.

175

"Over on that island when you first leave the cove, the one to the right."

The man rubbed his thumb over the photo of the woman. "Can I keep this?" he asked Kale quietly.

"Sure, man. Wait — you know her, don't you?"

"Yeah, you know her, too. Only yours is still within reach," the man said nodding towards Devan.

"Excuse me?"

"True love."

Kale was quiet during the rest of lunch, lost in thought. *Whoever that girl was to that guy she must've been* his *Devan.*

After lunch they went back out on the water. Kale really wanted to take Devan to the waterfall, but thought it wouldn't be the best idea. Instead, because they had a few more hours left with their rental, they just cruised around and jumped some waves.

When they turned in the rental, they ran into Justin, Jeane, and the kids.

"Hey, we were just picking up pizza for dinner. Did you guys have a good day?" Jeane asked.

"Yeah, we had fun. Did you get your work done?" Devan asked.

"Yes, but we have to go back tomorrow for a conference call on the laptop. I hate that this place doesn't have decent cell and Wi-Fi service."

Devan silently agreed with her. "Okay, we'll take the kids out on the boat tomorrow and you guys can do what you have to."

Jeane walked near Justin. As she was talking to him, Devan noticed a few things that bothered her. *He's acting happy, something I rarely see anymore. Jeane leans in a little closer than a "friend" would. It also seems like Justin is a little too affectionate with her.*

She wasn't the only one who noticed. Kale was looking at some shirts when the marina guy came up to him.

"That your wife?" he asked nodding in Jeane's direction.

"Yeah," Kale said looking up.

"Who's the guy she's flirting with?"

"Oh, that's Devan's husband," he said, ignoring the flirting comment.

"Hmm ... looks like something's going on there, if you ask me."

"I didn't ask you," Kale said coldly.

"Look, I'm not trying to piss you off, but they have almost as much chemistry as you and her," he said looking in Devan's direction.

I never really thought about that before — maybe because I really don't care or because I really don't love Jeane. Probably because I'm always too consumed by thoughts of Devan when she's around.

The guy started walking away, and he quickly said, "Wait. What happened to the girl in the locket?"

The man sighed. "I haven't talked about that in a long time and I can't get into it right now. Meet me down here at six a.m. tomorrow. No one will be around and I can talk."

Kale told him he'd be there at six.

The next morning, Kale got up bright and early. Everyone was still asleep when he snuck out of the cabin.

"Hi," he said as he walked into the store.

"Hey, how do you like your coffee?" the man asked.

"Black."

"Okay, black it is." He poured Kale a cup and they went out to a table outside and sat down.

The marina guy started talking almost as soon as they were seated. "I haven't even mentioned her name in 20 years, and I wouldn't today if I didn't feel like you need to hear this story."

He took a sip of his coffee and set his cup down. "I met Alison in 1982. My aunt and uncle had bought this place a few years earlier, and Alison was the daughter of one of the families who came every summer. She was the same age as me, 15.

My parents made me stay with my aunt and uncle because I was a troubled kid. I was always getting into shit I shouldn't and I needed something to make me turn my life around. So, I started pumping gas down here.

I remember the day I saw her like it was yesterday. Her parents pulled up in their boat and needed gas. She was pretty, with dark curly hair and piercing blue eyes. I was a scrawny kid — not much different than I am now. I was staring at her for so long that the gas ran over. It was so embarrassing. As I was cleaning the gas off the boat, she came up to me and asked my name."

177

"Dude, what *is* your name?" Kale asked with a chuckle.

"It's Will. Guess I should've introduced myself a long time ago," he said and laughed.

"Well, nice to meet you, Will. I'm Kale."

"Like the vegetable?"

Kale sighed. "It's Hawaiian. It means man."

"Well it's good to officially meet you, Kale."

Will continued with his story. "She told me her name was Alison and she'd be here for a few weeks. I told her I was here all summer and to let me know if she needed anything.

"I didn't see her the rest of that week. But the following week, she came down to the marina and started talking to me. I was shy, but I tried to keep up my end of the conversation. She was a talkative little thing, and her smile, man, it just sent butterflies flappin' in my stomach.

"So, we became friends and we talked every time we saw each other. I kept trying to ask her out, but I'd always blow it because I got too shy every time I tried. Finally, I worked up the nerve to do it — two days before she had to go back home.

"I waited and watched for her, but she never came back to the marina. I found out later they'd had a family emergency and had to leave the last day I talked to her."

"Well, that sucks," Kale said, feeling sorry for the man.

"The following summer I hoped and prayed they'd be back, but May turned into June and June turned into July and her family never showed. My last week working before I had to go back home and start at school, I saw her. You better believe I had some serious palpitations going on, too.

"She came right up to me and gave me hug. I thought for sure she wouldn't remember me, but she did. That day, I asked her out. A few days later, I took her on a picnic right over there by the beach."

"It was comical! I made bologna sandwiches that were awful — the bread was soggy— Ugh, it was gross. We laughed about it and enjoyed ourselves though. I walked her back to her cabin, but we stopped right at that old willow tree. You know, that the one by the woods?"

Kale nodded. He knew that willow tree well.

"And I kissed her. It was my first kiss. I was scared I was going to mess it up. She put her arms around me and it was magic. I saw her a few times after that, but then I had to go back to school. She gave me her address and asked me to write to her, and I did.

"We wrote back and forth a few times. In her last letter that year, she said she had a boyfriend and we could only be friends. It hurt; I can't lie about that. I also knew how high school romances worked, so I wasn't too worried.

"That summer, she came back and she was single again. She told me she thought about me the whole time she dated her former boyfriend. She said she broke up with him right before the summer. Needless to say, I was a happy camper.

"We hung out the whole time she was here. There were a lot of kisses by that old willow tree, let me tell you."

"Yeah that willow tree has seen a lot of action," Kale declared.

Will nodded and continued, "We kept in touch that following year. I dated a few girls, but none of them made me feel the way she did. The next year, I graduated and decided to move down here. I really love this place and I thought if I went to go college I could go here.

"I called her a week before she was supposed to come down, from that payphone right over there. Let me tell you, it took a ton of change, too. I asked her to make sure she packed a dress because I was going to take her on a real date in town.

"The second night she was here, I took her out. At this point, I felt like I was a cool son of a bitch. I had myself a mustang. Now that car, oh she was beautiful — a 1967 convertible with fire engine red exterior and black leather interior. I kept her shiny as hell, too. To this day she was the smoothest ride I've ever owned — V8 engine with 4 BBL chrome dress up kit and dual exhaust.

"Anyway, we went into town. We were both 18, so we could get into a club. That was one of the best nights of my life." He smiled, looking out at the lake. "The next day, one of the locals told me about this special place on the lake. Said I had to take her there."

"The waterfall?" Kale asked.

Will nodded. "Yes, sir. Something just took over when we got there. It was beautiful, with the mist coming off the lake and the canopy of trees. It was amazing. We made love right there in the water. It was the first time for both of us. I've never experienced anything so magical.

"We spent the rest of her time here together. We'd sneak off to the willow tree or take a walk in the woods every chance we got. We cherished every moment we had. I truly fell in love with that girl." He took a deep breath and Kale watched as his shoulders slumped down.

"Then, she went back home. I wrote to her and after a few letters she finally responded — almost a year later. It was almost time for her family to come back. Hell, I was gonna try to get her to move here with me. Her letter said she'd met someone and was marrying him, so her family wouldn't be down that summer."

"Oh, man, that's harsh." Kale frowned.

"I was torn up. I saw myself marrying that girl. You might say I wasn't ever the same after that. That was 20 years ago and there isn't a day goes by that I don't think about her."

"I am so sorry. What happened to her?" Kale asked. He knew the story couldn't end there.

"I wrote and called, and finally her dad said I couldn't call anymore. That was it."

Kale was dumbfounded. "What do you mean that was it?"

"That's the last I heard of her."

That's not good enough! "What about social media? You could look her up on Facebook," he suggested.

"Man, I'm not into all that techno bullshit. Clearly she doesn't want anything to do with me, so why bother. I told you this because I saw the way you looked at that girl back then and I see the way you still look at her now. How in the hell did you two end up with other people?"

"Can I have another cup of coffee?"

"Sure, man." Will got the coffee pot and filled his cup. Kale looked at the clock on the wall and said, "Well, looks like we have a little bit more time. I'll condense my story the best I can." Then, he told Will his and Devan's convoluted story.

"Ouch, so coming here was a major kick in the balls, huh?" Will asked wrinkling his nose.

"You could say that. This was our special place, too."

"Hey, what are you doing?" They turned around to see Devan standing there.

"Just having coffee with an old friend, sweetheart," Will said and got up and gave her a hug. "I'm Will, by the way."

"I'm Devan. It's nice to put a name with your face."

"I know. Listen, I gotta get to work. Do you want some coffee, Devan?"

"Sure, that would be great. Everyone's still sleeping at the cabin and I came down to see if I could buy a cup."

"It's on the house, darlin." He got her a cup and poured some coffee.

He looked at Kale. "The waterfall is looking pretty drab these days. Too many people discovered that little treasure. It's still there, just not as magnificent as it was. I'd go visit it before ya'll go home. It might not be there the next time you come," he said as he walked back into the store.

Chapter 25

That day, while Justin and Jeane went into town, Kale and Devan took the kids out in the boat. They had fun playing in the water, and Kale even surprised Devan by picking her up and throwing her in the lake. The kids giggled because they never got to see their parents acting like that.

After the long day, Kale pulled the boat into the slip. Before anyone got out he asked, "Who wants ice cream?"

Sage, Joey, and Callie started screaming, "I do! I do!"

As they walked to the marina, Kale had Sage sitting on his shoulders, Cyrus in his baby backpack, and was holding Callie's hand. Devan had Joey's hand and Kai in his baby backpack. Will laughed at them as they walked in.

"Quite the man, aren't you?" he chuckled. "You sure they aren't all yours?" he asked Kale with a raised eyebrow.

"I wish—" Devan said walking past him.

Will was shocked. "Did you hear that?"

Kale smiled.

"The waterfall." Will whispered.

It was dark and Justin and Jeane hadn't come back to the cabin yet. The kids were already in bed, so Kale asked, "Hey you wanna play UNO?" as he slid the pack of cards across the table to her.

"The last time we played Uno was— Oh."

"Yeah, so I think it's been too long. Sit your pretty little ass over here and amuse me." She sat down at the table as he dealt the cards.

"What time is it?" he asked.

She looked at the microwave clock. "It's 9:47."

"What do you think is keeping them this time?" he asked, picking up his cards.

"Does it matter?"

"Nope." He laughed then slammed down a draw four.

"Seriously?"

"All four." He slapped the table.

"Damn you, Iakona." She pulled them into her hand one by one.

Jeane and Justin walked in at 11:45. Kale and Devan were still up. "Oh, you guys missed a great time!"

Kale lifted his head to see his wife and Justin in disheveled clothing. "Looks like you had enough fun for the rest of us," he said, dryly.

"Oh, Kale, don't be so *snarkly*," Jeane said.

Justin almost fell over laughing. "It's snarky."

"Whatever. You guys are just jealous." Jeane pursed her lips.

"Are you drunk?" Devan asked.

"Is there a better way to be?" Justin answered.

"Stay in here," Kale told Devan. "I'm gonna check on the car."

He opened the door and stepped outside. "Where the hell is the car?" Kale yelled coming back in and slamming door.

Devan shushed him. "You'll wake up the kids and they don't need to see their parent's like this."

"Well, it's not like we could call your phones, so we left it at the bar," Justin said, like it was the obvious thing to do.

"Ha, we aren't dumb enough to drunk and drove," Jeane laughed.

"You mean drink and drive. Okay, I think you guys should go to bed now. Don't wake up the kids."

"Yes, boss," Justin said to Devan.

Kale walked outside, ready to explode. Devan followed him.

"What the fuck was that?" he asked, throwing his hands up in the air trying to be more expressive than loud. "Wow, things are just the same here as they are at home. I thought this trip would help, even though I totally did *not* want to come here," he said kicking a ski jacket near his foot.

"Kale, please sit down," Devan said, as she took a seat.

"I'm so sick of this shit— I gotta walk or something," he said and started down the steps.

"Please, stay here. Don't leave me alone with a house full of kids and two drunks."

"I'm sorry." He came back up the steps and sat down next her on a towel on the deck floor.

"I hate her sometimes. She's never home. She doesn't help me with the kids or the house or anything else, and *then* she does shit like this."

Devan scooted behind him instead of staying by his side. She put her hands on his tight shoulders and began massaging them. "I know how you feel. Justin is the exact same way."

"What the hell? Our kids deserve better!"

"Good thing they have us then, huh?"

"Us — yeah until we move all the way to the other side of the damn country."

I forgot all about that. I don't want him to leave. I don't want his kids to leave. I wish he could stay and Justin and Jeane would just move away. Those assholes deserve each other. They sure as hell didn't deserve anyone else. She wrapped her arms around Kale and put her chin on his back as he put his hands over hers

"Is it really worth it?"

"What? The move? Yeah, money-wise it is," he said as he dropped his hands from hers. She decided to run her hands through his hair to try to sooth him. She messed with the tousled curls, and he didn't say anything for a few minutes.

He felt himself starting to calm down from her touch, yet get excited at the same time, and he reached behind his head and grabbed her hands. "Please, don't do that," he asked nicely.

"Oh, I'm sorry. Am I pulling it?"

He sighed. "No, it's just I'll have to do something if you keep it up."

"What?"

He turned his head so fast it almost gave him whiplash and twisted his body around so he was facing her. His hair got in his face, and she moved to push it out of his eyes.

He grabbed her hand before she could do it. "Don't. Anyone else can touch my hair and I don't mind, but *you* absolutely can't," he said and let go of her hand.

"Okay."

He looked at her and all he could think was, *God she's beautiful.*

She broke the silence. "So, why can't I touch your hair?"

"Because when you do, it makes me want to do this." He kissed her on the lips not one, but two lingering kisses.

She didn't kiss him back. "Kale."

"I know. I'm sorry."

"Don't apologize. You realize, though, that I'm going to touch your hair if I want." She grabbed a handful of his hair and pulled him toward her, then kissed him for a good two minutes.

"Um, I'm gonna go check on the babies and the drunks," he said, as Devan sat there, shocked by what she'd just done.

A few minutes later, Kale came back out. He reached down and helped Devan to her feet, then led her to the willow tree by the dock and pulled her into his embrace.

"Now, where were we?"

They looked into each other's eyes for a long time before Kale moved his lips over hers. *I'm in heaven,* she thought. His arms were wrapped around her, and the softness of his beard tickled against her chin. It was so nice, but it wasn't smart.

She pushed him away. "As much as I hate Justin right now, and as much you hate Jeane, this is wrong."

He picked her up and set her in the tree. "Come on, Monty. You can't tell me you aren't enjoying this. All of these memories from when we were kids—"

"Kale, we aren't kids anymore."

"No, but we can pretend." He tilted her chin down so he could kiss her lips.

She didn't fight back. He put his hands around her lower back and she draped her arms around his neck and wrapped her legs around his waist. He picked her up and gently set her on the clay pebbles beneath the tree.

"I miss this," he said brushing her hair out of her face.

"So do I, but it can't happen anymore, Kale."

"Okay, but how about one last kiss—"

"No."

"Just one little peck—" He kept getting closer to her face.

"No." She smiled.

He did it anyway. "Okay, I'm done," he said as put his hands in the air.

They walked back up to the cabin, said goodnight and walked into their rooms, then walked right back out.

"Um, where's Jeane?" he asked, worried she'd wandered off into the woods. *I really don't feel like playing find the drunk bitch tonight.*

"In bed with Justin," Devan said with a straight face.

"What?"

"Come look." She opened the door and Kale peeked inside. There was Jeane, spooning Justin.

"Wow," Kale said. "Get your baby and we'll put him in with mine, just in case someone gets sick or something."

"Just … wow!" He kept shaking his head.

"You don't want to wake them?"

"Let sleeping dogs lie, Devan. You know, she *never* spoons *me.*"

I'm sorry," Devan said, laying Cyrus down with Kai.

"Oh, I'm not complaining. Hell, I'd rather not share a bed with her at all. I'm just— wow! Here, you take my bed. I'll take the couch," he said grabbing a pillow.

"No, it's fine. I'll take the couch," she said, just as they heard crying and the sound of little feet coming their way.

"I had a bad dream," Sage wailed.

"Come here, little girl," Kale said and held his arms open for his daughter.

"Can I sleep in here with you guys?" she asked with tears running down her face.

"Honey, I'm gonna go sleep on the couch. You stay in here with your dad," Devan told her, while wiping her tears away.

"No, I don't want you to go. That's what my bad dream was. You went away, and I never got to see you again."

Devan hugged her tight.

"Just let me cuddle with you guys, just for a little bit. Please?" she begged.

Devan gave in and lay down on the bed next to her. "You need to hold hands," Sage said grabbing Devan and Kale's hands and putting them together.

"Why do we need to hold hands?" Devan asked.

"That's what Mommy and Uncle Justin do when they're together. So you guys should do it, too."

Devan and Kale shared a look of bewilderment.

The next morning, they woke up to the loud sound of banging pans and the scent of hickory-smoked bacon. They opened their eyes, saw one another and then looked down and saw Sage cuddled between them. They both smiled as Kale got out of bed to see what the racket was about.

Jeane and Justin were making breakfast, very loudly. "Ah, the booze hounds are up," Kale announced, when he saw them.

"Where's my wife?" Justin asked.

"She's cuddling with Sage," Kale replied nonchalantly.

"Oh," was all Justin said.

At breakfast no one brought up what had happened the night before.

"So, what are the plans for today?" Jeane asked.

"Well, Justin and I are going to go get the car, while you and Devan get stuff ready for our all-day boat trip," Kale said.

"Okay. Hey, while we're out, can we stop and get some aspirin?" Justin asked.

"Sure thing."

The trip to get the car took about half an hour. Neither man spoke until they got to the bar, then Kale asked, "Are you and Devan having problems?"

"What do you mean?" Justin asked, and grimaced.

"I just sense some tension."

"Oh, if this is about last night — dude, I didn't touch your wife."

"No, Justin, that's not what I am talking about. Is something wrong at home?"

"Ha, you're asking the wrong person. She's been a complete needy bitch the past year. I don't have time to deal with her bullshit and deal with everything at work, too."

"Maybe you should open up the lines of communication," Kale suggested.

"Open up the lines of communication? I ask her all the time why she's quiet and what's wrong. She always says the same shit — 'You're never home,' 'You don't help with the kids,' 'You don't do this, you don't do that.'" I gave up trying to make her happy. Nothing works. Hell, she won't even let me have a beer after work."

Kale knew when Devan was quiet it wasn't a good sign. "Maybe plan a date night, or give her flowers for no reason."

"Dude, you have it made. Your wife is perfect. Devan ... is a pain in the ass," Justin said, opening his door.

"Devan is the most amazing person I know. If you don't start treating her better, I *will* hurt you!" he said grabbing Justin's arm.

"I get it, man. I know she's like a sister to you. That's why you'll never see her the way I do," he said, and slammed the door.

Kale glared at him, with his eyes turning a dark shade of green. Through clenched teeth he growled at Justin as he got into the other vehicle. "Think what you will, but know this — my toast on your wedding day was a promise. I *will* kill you if you ever hurt her!"

The rest of the day was slightly awkward but went smoothly. Everyone seemed to be having a good time skiing, swimming, tubing, and just riding around in the boat.

Sage wouldn't leave Devan's side, and wanted nothing to do with her mother. None of the kids ever wanted to hang around Justin or Jeane if Devan and Kale were around.

After dinner that night, they decided to let the kids stay up a little longer than normal and make s'mores. Sage dropped hers on the ground and cried.

"It's not a big deal, Sage. Just get another one," Jeane said, rolling her eyes.

"But I don't want to wait any longer!" Sage whined.

"Too bad," Jeane said, shoving her own treat into her mouth.

"Here, Sage, why don't you take mine? I'll just make another one," Devan said, handing her the treat.

"Thank you so much, Aunt Dee. I love you," she said giving her a big hug.

Seeing that hug warmed Kale's heart. *Why can't Jeane be nice like that? Justin thinking Jeane is better than Devan, clearly proves he's an idiot. Jeane's a cold woman.*

Devan soon excused herself and put the kids to bed, then went to bed herself. She hadn't been sleeping well lately, and she wanted to be rested for their last full day at the lake.

She woke up at 1:25 a.m. Everyone else was asleep, so she made herself some tea and sat down to drink it. It didn't help make her sleepy, so she decided to take her MP3 player down to the dock and do some meditating by the water.

She sat down on the edge of the dock and dangled her feet in the quiet water. She put her earbuds in and searched for some calming music. She meditated for a few minutes, then a song came on she didn't remember putting on the list — "Fade Into You," by Mazzy Star. It was their song, hers and Kale's. *That shouldn't be on there — there are too many memories attached to that damn song!*

She remembered dancing with Kale as this song played just like it was yesterday. The ambiance, the smell of his Nautica, Miss Jenkins giving them a hard time. She smiled at the memory.

When the song was over, she hit the back button. For some reason, right now she liked how it made her feel. All those years ago the only true stress in her life had been remembering to bring homework home and worrying about who liked who. *How big those stresses seemed at the time. I never expected life would turn out to be this hard. No one warned me about the heartbreaks, the pain, and the true reality of life. I want to go back, just for a day, just for an hour, even for just that 5-minute dance.*

I don't want to think about what an asshole my husband is. I don't want to think about Kale moving across the country, either. I just got him back! She rested her head on her hand and just stared at the moon's reflection on the water. The man in the moon seemed to be laughing at her.

Devan looked up into the sky and yelled, "Why do you keep throwing him in my face? It can't happen. It *never* will. I'm tired of hurting! Life isn't fair; I know that. I just don't want to hurt about this anymore. It's been too many years and too much pain. You keeping taking him away then bringing him back! What the hell did I do to deserve all this suffering? What, moon? Tell me!"

She saw a shooting star race across the sky and asked, "What the *hell* does that mean?"

She couldn't fight back the tears any longer, so she just let them go. She rocked herself back and forth and sobbed. She hadn't cried this hard in a long time. She didn't understand the whole point of her life anymore. She knew Kale would always be in her life in some way, but it wasn't enough. *I need him — all of him — heart, body, mind, and soul. Is this how the rest of my life is really going to be — living in a fantasy of another time and not letting go of the past?* She felt foolish, and cried even harder because she was mad at herself for crying over something that would never be resolved.

Kale was awake, too, and made his way outside. He looked toward the dock and couldn't tell for sure, but it looked like someone crying. He walked slowly and quietly down the hill and heard, "Why? *Why?*"

It's Devan! He walked up behind her, sat down and wrapped his arms around her.

She thought she was just imagining it at first, and continued to cry. *When will these arms belong to me?*

He pulled the ear bud out of her left ear and whispered, "Why are you so sad?" then rested his chin on her shoulder.

I wasn't imagining it. "I hate you! I fucking hate you!" She turned around to face him. "I hate how you're always coming into my life just to leave again.

I hate your stupid captivating smile, your stupid sexy voice. I hate you!" She was sobbing again. "Most of all I hate how you make me feel."

He hugged her tight, pulling her to his chest.

"No!" she shouted as she pushed him back. "I hate how happy and sad I am every time I see you! I hate how perfectly you kiss me and how it sends shivers down my spine. I hate myself for wanting to be nowhere else when I'm in your arms. I hate the fact that you're a better father to my kids than their own dad. I hate that I can't let go of you and what we had. And I really hate that I can't get over you!

"I thought marrying someone else would take care of that, but it didn't. I hate that we're here and I have to relive every emotion I've had for you here at this place—" she stopped took a deep breath and finished. "Coming back here just made those emotions slap me in the face a million times over."

He took her chin into his hands.

"I hate that I love you. I fucking hate that more than anything," she finally finished.

He brought her lips to his and brushed them very gently. "I hate all those things, too. We've been dealt a shitty hand. You aren't the only one who's suffering. There isn't a minute that goes by that I don't think of you and how wonderful it feels to have your body next to mine. How amazing it is to taste your sweet lips, to just be around you and wake up beside you."

He pulled her in and held her tight, not letting her go. "But I truly believe that one day — it could be 10 months from now or 10 years — but I know we'll be together again. That's why we haven't lost touch with how we feel. I feel just as strongly about you now as I did the last time we were here."

She was soaking his shirt with her tears. "Then, if that is true, why all the pain and sorrow?"

"That, I can't answer. Come on, let's go up and get some sleep so we can enjoy tomorrow. It's our last day here, so let's make it count." *I know what I have to do now!*

He helped her up and she wrapped her arms around him and looked up at him looking down at her. "One last kiss," she said.

His mouth cradled hers. It was probably one of the most passionate kisses either of them had ever experienced.

Chapter 26

Devan had the best sleep of her life after purging her emotions. She and Kale both slept in, and woke to find that Jeane and Justin had taken the kids and left them alone again.

"Get up!" she said, and smacked Kale's foot trying to wake him.

"What?" he groaned.

"They left us again!"

"I know."

"What do you mean, you know?"

"I told them to let you sleep, and we would meet them later."

"Kale, it's our last day. How could you do that?"

"I made plans. Chill out and sit down," he demanded. "I rented a boat again today, just for us. I have a surprise for you later."

"And Jeane and Justin okayed it?" she asked in a smart tone.

"Yeah, I said 'I want to surprise your wife because you are a fucking loser and can't ever do anything for her.' No, smart-ass, I didn't tell them anything." He rolled his eyes.

They headed down to get the boat and Kale took them out onto the lake as Devan sat back and enjoyed the cool air in her face and warm sun on her skin. Some of the trees were already starting to turn; fall wasn't far away. She hadn't noticed the last time they were out. The reflection of the yellows, greens, oranges and reds rippled as they sped through the smooth water was beautiful.

"Where are we going?" she asked.

"You'll see."

Half an hour later, they were on the other side of the lake, and clouds started covering the clear blue sky. Devan saw something on the shore. "Hey, slow down. Go over there. Do you see that?"

"The house?"

"Yeah. Let's go check it out."

He beached the boat on the shore and tied it to a tree. They walked up the short hill to an abandoned stone house that was slowly turning to rubble. "Be careful where you step," Kale said. "The structure seems steady, and it's all made of stone, but the floors could be rotted."

She tiptoed over to the fireplace. There was wood in it. She looked around and saw more firewood stacked nearby, and a cigarette lighter rested on the mantle. Someone had been there recently.

The house, possibly built in the early 1900s, had crumbling delicately flowered wallpaper and moss was growing on the plaster walls. A chandelier hung from the ceiling, there were a pair of decaying leather boots sitting on the floor beside the door, and there was a rug, which at one time was burgundy and green, lay on the floor, shredded by time.

Devan turned her head to see what Kale was doing. He was looking at a portrait hanging on the wall of a beautiful young girl sitting between a man and woman. Devan guessed they were probably her parents.

There was something odd about the girl, though, so she got up to get a closer look. The girl's eyes didn't seem quite right. "There's something creepy about this picture, I just can't put my finger on it." Devan finally figured out what it was. "She's dead!"

"No shit, Sherlock. They all are. This has to be from like — look there it is —1889," said, pointing to the year printed on the bottom of the portrait.

"No, look at her eyes. Do you see how they look like they're looking somewhere else? Look at how dark the circles are under them," she said, pointing.

"And?"

"Look at how awkwardly she's leaning on her mom. Her hands are just kind of weird."

"Yeah? Who would take a picture with a dead family member?" Kale asked with a turned up nose.

"Lots of people. Post mortem photography was popular in the Victorian era. Photography was so expensive back then, most people would have this done to have at least one lasting memory of their child. The infant mortality rate was so high, a lot of the pictures from those are of babies and small children who died," she explained.

"That is *super* creepy. How do you know so much about this?"

"Do you remember Nate Cavendar?"

"Yeah?"

"His dad owned the funeral home in town and I got stuck doing a report on it in eighth grade. Nate was a huge help."

"Nate the great! I remember him. He was a cool kid. It was a shame people gave him such a hard time about being a funeral director's son. Whatever happened to him?"

"I think he took over the mortuary."

A gust of wind blew open the shutters, startling them both.

"We should probably get going," he said as he turned toward the door.

"Wait a minute," she said as she looked out the hole that was once a window. "Come on," she grabbed his arm and headed for the door.

They walked around to the other side of the house. The grass was high there but she'd seen something dark in the yellow blades — a headstone that read, "Edith Lenter, 1878–1889, Beloved daughter."

"A grave?" Kale asked.

"Yep, and I'm willing to bet it belongs to the girl in the picture."

"Okay, Monty, you've had your fun and you've creeped me out. It's time to go."

"I'd like to look around a little more."

"I know, but we really are on a schedule. Come on."

As Kale was untying the boat, Devan thought she saw someone walk into the house out of the corner of her eye, and a chill ran down her spine.

After they got back out on the lake, Kale pulled into a completely secluded cove. As he beached the boat, she could hear the waterfall and smiled.

"Why'd you bring me here?" she asked in somber tone that erased the smile on her face.

"Well, I thought it would bring something back for both of us."

She looked long and hard at him wondering, *What the hell is he thinking? Hasn't this whole trip brought enough painful memories back for both of us?*

She watched the muscles in his arm ripple as he tied the boat as tightly as he could to a tree. *Damn's he hot!*

He pulled a bag out from under the driver's seat and said, "Time to get out, Monty." He helped her out and didn't let go of her hand as he practically dragged her through the wooded area to the falls.

What a disappointment! Devan thought. *There's only a trickle of water flowing over the rocks now.* It was still beautiful in its own way, but the erosion they saw was too severe to be natural. The hand of man had destroyed the natural beauty.

Kale let go of her hand. "Strip down to your suit and get into the water," he said as he started stripping, too. When they were both undressed, they got in the water.

Kale stood there, staring at her beauty, as her long black hair swirled around her while she treaded water. She smiled at him and asked, "Are you getting in?"

"In a minute, I want you to close your eyes. Don't open them until I say."

She did as she was told and Kale pulled the bag out and opened it. He grabbed a handful of what was inside and threw it into the water around her. Then as he dumped the bag right on top of her, he said, "Open your eyes and look straight ahead, then close them when I tell you to." She opened her eyes and saw red, pink, white, yellow, peach, and purple rose petals raining down on her. It was beautiful. As the last few rose petals fell, Kale told her to close her eyes again.

He slipped into the water behind her and put his arms around her waist, then whispered in her ear, "Please don't say anything. Just listen to my voice."

That's easy; I could do that all day long.

"I want you to remember when you ran into me that first time in Hawaii."

195

She remembered how she'd stumbled into him and how the smell of lime, coconut, and sunscreen had smacked her in the face. She smiled as she thought about "Kai and Dee."

He whispered in her other ear, "Now think about the first time we kissed."

She did, and she could feel the raindrops like they were falling on her now.

He laughed. "That couldn't be more perfectly timed," he said about the light rain that had started to fall.

"Homecoming 1994—"

She could almost hear Mazzy Star singing in her ear.

"Think about the hospital when you woke up in the spring of '95, when we kissed."

She did. It started to rain slightly harder, but there was enough of a canopy above them that it was pleasant.

"Prom ... dancing with you ... looking into your eyes, I could see forever—"

Her eyes started to sting. *Why is he doing this? It was nice at first but it's starting to hurt.*

"The first time our lips locked at the willow tree..."

She felt him move and then felt his lips on hers — his soft, perfect lips. She'd been kissed by a few guys in her lifetime, but not one of them could make her feel the way Kale did.

"Think about the first time we came here..."

She remembered every detail. It seemed like yesterday. Oh, to be 18 again.

She opened her eyes and he was staring right back at her. "Why are you doing this?"

He could see her eyes welling up with tears. "Because our lives don't have to be this complicated—"

"Kale, wake up. Complication is our life."

"You asked me the day of your wedding if we were really meant to be together. Well, Devan, we *are* together, *always*. Can you honestly tell me that a piece of me isn't in your heart?"

A fat tear rolled down her cheek. "You own the majority of my heart. You always have."

"Then let's leave here with a plan. Jeane hates me — I know it. Hell, I think the kids know it. Do you really think she'd even miss me if I left? And the kids? Who do you think takes care of them 99 percent of the time?"

She knew what he was saying was true, but it didn't matter. "Kale you're insane. It's not going to happen."

"Why, because your life is so fucking perfect?" he snapped at her.

"I didn't say that—"

"Damn it, Devan, open your eyes and see what you have right in front of you." He grabbed her face.

"Kale, what's gotten into you?"

He dropped his hands. "The very worst day of my life was supposed to be the best." He turned his back to her.

"What are you talking about?"

He turned around and faced her. "The day I found out Jeane was pregnant, I was going to ask you to marry me."

"What?"

"I'd asked my dad, and took your dad out to lunch and asked him. I almost proposed to you like three times. I wanted to do it the moment I got the ring, then at dinner with our parents, and—"

No one ever told me this!

"Something was missing each time, and I thought it had to be perfect. So, I went to the cave that morning—"

"What cave?"

"'Ole Blue. You know, forever beautiful. That's where I really saw you for the first time. I saw your beautiful eyes looking back at me, and I wanted to kiss you so badly, but I was afraid. A kid's nerves, maybe, I'm not sure — but I didn't kiss you then, and I've regretted it all these years. You see, it wasn't just that I wanted to kiss you, I actually fell in love with you that day."

She couldn't believe her ears. "The summer of '94?"

"I remember it like it was yesterday. You in your black floral two-piece with the broken string. I remember how your blonde hair tangled around it, and your sun-kissed cheeks and sparkling blue eyes. I remember fighting the urge to just grab you and hold you."

"So why didn't you?"

"I don't know. I was a stupid kid. Anyway, I had it set up, and it felt perfect. I got white coral and spelled out, "Will you marry me?" with it on the ledge. I was going to take you back there right after we had dinner. It was going to be perfect."

It started raining harder.

"And then Jeane happened." She sighed.

"I need you Devan. I need *all* of you." He grabbed her tight and kissed her hard.

She didn't hold back. Their kiss turned into something much more. Her hands were in his hair. His hands were untying her bathing suit top.

"Kale, we can't."

"Yes, we can."

His mouth was on her neck, and she moaned. Before she knew it, they were both naked in the water. His hands were all over her body. She wrapped her legs around his waist as he kissed her deeply.

"Kale, stop!" she pushed herself away from him before any more damage could be done.

"You want this just as badly as I do," he said grabbing her and pulling her close again.

"Want it, yes, but just because I want it doesn't mean it's right. You and I both *know* this isn't right." She tried escaping his grip.

"I need this. You need this!" He kissed her and she didn't push him away. She let it happen like it was the natural thing to do. When the kiss was over, he looked down at her. "I want and need you more than anything else in the whole world."

She felt frozen in time. She wanted and needed him too, but she was also a realist. *Would my life be enriched if it were suddenly okay for this to happen between us? Justin's hardly ever around, and he doesn't treat me very well. He's not evil, but he isn't kind either. Maybe he and Jeane have something going on and maybe they don't.*

Kale ... well, Kale's perfect, at least he is for me. He has a fantastic personality. He's smart, tall, gorgeous, a good friend, and a great father. Would Justin even miss me if I decided to leave him? Probably not. I'd get full custody with no problem, since he wouldn't have a problem with me having the kids. He definitely wouldn't want to deal with them. Would I be okay? Yes.

Kale on the other hand, even if he is the one who takes care of his kids, has a vindictive wife to deal with. Jeane will do everything she can to keep him away from them, I know it. That would destroy Kale. His kids are everything to him.

"We're just caught up in the moment right now, Kale. This," she said, pointing to each of them, "can't ever happen."

"But it did, Devan. It did."

"Damn it, Kale. You'll lose your kids!"

"No, I won't. Jeane doesn't want them. Don't you see? It could work."

She could see the hope in his eyes, but had to continue, "Clearly you don't see. Jeane is a conniving bitch. She'll take those kids from you so she can make your life *and* theirs miserable. She'll do it just to hurt you."

"I don't think—"

"You aren't thinking. Jeane will destroy you. Maybe you can't see it, Kale, but I can. I know how that woman thinks. Kuna told me to *never* trust her!"

"You're going to bring Kuna into this? What does he know? Shit, anyone can see Jeane is only out for herself and can't be trusted. Yeah, she threatened to take Joe before we got married. Hell, that was the only reason I married the miserable bitch. The kids won't go with her."

"Kale, you don't get to make that decision. Courts usually favor the mother."

"You're unbelievable, Devan. Are you really going to just tell true love to go fuck itself?" He glowered at her.

"If it means saving you and your kids, then yes."

He shook his head. "Unbelievable! So, if the kids weren't part of this, would you follow your heart?"

Why is he so stubborn? "The kids *are* a part of this, Kale. Look at us — we aren't teenagers anymore. Our little fairytale just wasn't meant to last. Nothing is the same now. Hell, even the damn waterfall is dying."

"I think this hurts worse than the day you left me in Hawaii." His eyes turned cold.

"I don't want to cause you pain, but if your kids get taken away from you, that will hurt a thousand times worse than this."

She got out of the water and put her swimming suit and clothes back on and headed for the boat.

"Tell me you don't love me," he demanded, while untying the boat.

"Will that make you stop this foolishness?" she asked.

He gave her a blank stare.

"Fine, I don't love you, Kale." Her warm tears mixed with the cold rain. "Are you happy now?"

"No, because I know it's not true." He wrapped his arms around her and kissed her. Lightning flashed across the sky and thunder boomed all around them. The wind picked up, blowing the boat around, and the sky had turned an ominous dark grey. It wasn't safe to be out on the water.

"We need to get back and quick," he said, letting her go.

She fought the tears as they practically flew through the downpour. *I have to put an end to this.*

After they docked, she grabbed his hand and led him down a path into the woods, instead of going straight to the cabin. Nothing was said as the rain kept pouring down.

The trail led to an opening near the willow tree. She pushed him against the tree just like she'd done years ago. He leaned down, his hair dripping water on her as she met his lips. She kissed him like it was the last time she'd ever see him.

He wrapped his arms around her and held her close, but she broke the embrace. "I let you go—" A bolt of lightening lit up the sky and the thunder roared.

"What?"

"Kale Kai Iakona, I release you from my heart and from my soul," she said as tears streamed down her face.

"You aren't making sense—"

"I can no longer love you, I can no longer care about you. You're free to live your life without me."

"Devan, don't—" He dropped his arms and stepped back.

"This is my goodbye. I can't keep doing this to myself. The same goes for you. Things went way too far today. I won't be able to look Justin in eyes for a long time." She was trembling, and the rain wasn't letting up.

"Devan, nothing really happened—"

"It did though. Once again, we stepped out of bounds. This whole trip has been nothing but us going out of bounds. You might be okay with it, but I'm not."

"Then what was that kiss?"

"That was goodbye, Kale. After today, I think it's best if we don't talk for a while." She looked away from him.

"Devan Marie—"

"You're moving and I think maybe that's the best thing for us."

"Well, I'm glad this is *so* easy for you, because it fucking *sucks* for me!" He took another step back.

"It's what's best for you, for me and for our children." She was right and she knew deep down Kale knew it, too.

He got in her face. "You know, you've constantly complained about me rescuing you over the years, well I'm sick of *you* making decisions for *me!* You don't want to see me? *Fine!*"

He started walking away, and a cold gust of wind chilled her to the bone.

"Kale!" she yelled. He slowly turned around. "We can't keep our hands off each other. I'm not saying it will be forever."

"Poof ... I'm gone," he said and turned around.

Streaks of pure white danced across the sky and thunder echoed all around them. Devan stood in the rain for a long time, sobbing. When she'd wrung out all of her tears, she walked back to the cabin and saw that everyone but Kale was sitting at the table eating.

"Hi. How was your day?" Joey asked. Devan forced a smile.

"Wet. Where's your dad?" she asked, grabbing a towel.

"He went to the marina to return the boat."

Kale walked up to the counter at the marina.

"Hey, Kale, how did it go today?" Will asked.

Kale slammed the keys down on the counter and said angrily, "Worst day of my life." He turned to walk away, then turned around. "Make that third worst day of my life."

"What happened?"

"Thank you for all your help, and I'm glad I got to know you better. Good luck." He shoved the keys closer to Will and started walking to the door.

"Stretch, wait—"

"How long did it take you to get over that chick?" Kale snapped.

"I never did."

"Okay. How long did it take for you to let go of her?"

"I never did."

"Fuck, man. How have you survived?" He looked Will up and down.

"Oh, that? It takes time. One day you'll wake up and realize all hope is lost and you'll go numb. You don't have to worry about that. I see the way she looks at you."

"Well, if you see her again, maybe you can remind her about that." He left, slamming the door behind him.

The next morning, Devan went down to the marina to pay the tab and turn in the cabin keys. Will asked if they'd had a good vacation, even though he already knew the answer. She gave him a half smile and nodded her head.

"Do you have a minute?" he asked, taking her hand.

"Well actually—"

"I need to show you something." He led her to a room that must've been his office, and turned on the light. "Please sit." He opened a drawer in his desk and pulled out the locket she and Kale found and opened it. Then, he told her the same story he'd told Kale, looking at the picture the whole time.

When he stopped he looked up at her with tears in his eyes. "I've only told this story one other time."

"Why are you telling me?"

Will let out a long sigh and reached across the desk, clasping both of her hands in his.

"*You* don't find true love, *true love* finds you! It's rare gift that few get to experience. You're one of the few. I'm begging you from the depths of my soul, don't let him slip away." He let go of her hands and got up. Before walking outside, he looked back at her sitting in the chair not moving a muscle.

"They say true love has a habit of coming back. I'd say in your case that's happened time and time again. How many times are you going to let it go? If it was me and I had one more chance with Alison, I'd grab ahold of her and never let her go!"

Chapter 27

Fall 2010

The next few years came and went. Jeane sent Christmas cards, so did Devan, and she'd hear from Joey once in a while via email — but Kale and Devan didn't speak to each other at all.

Devan found that dealing with her feelings was manageable with Kale so far away. No one but Pete and Kristy knew about their falling out.

One day, Devan's phone rang.

"Dee, it's Pete. I need your help with something. Can I come over?"

"Sure, it's just Cy and me."

"Good, because I'm at your door."

She set the phone down and went to let him in.

Pete gave her a huge hug and said, "It's time." He sat down on the love seat in the living room and dropped the bomb. "I'm gonna propose."

Devan squealed. "That's the best news I've heard in a long time!"

"I want it to be perfect, so I need your help."

"Do you have the ring?"

He pulled a folded pamphlet out of his pocket and handed it to her. "I think she'd like the one I circled."

Devan opened it and saw he'd circled a beautiful half-carat marquise cut set in white gold and surrounded by diamond chips.

"That's perfect Pete."

"Okay, good. Now, how do I make this romantic?"

"How soon do you want to do it?"

"In the next few weeks," he said as he shakily smoothed his hair back.

She could tell he was nervous and excited all at the same time. "Okay, what's going on with football?"

"Well, I didn't tell Kristy this yet, but Davis is retiring at the Homecoming game on the 24th, and they're announcing me as head coach. Do *not* tell her!"

"Oh, I won't. That's great Pete!"

"Thanks."

"Wow, Homecoming is a lot earlier than it used to be. Okay, when can you get the ring?" she asked as she handed the paper back to him.

"Tomorrow, if they have it."

"Great! Is Maggie Frasier still coaching the cheerleaders?"

"Yeah..." He said slowly.

"Perfect! Here's my plan." She explained everything to Pete, and he liked her idea.

"Okay, go get that ring, but don't give it to her yet — even though I know it'll be burning a hole in your pocket."

"Yeah, that happened to Ka— my cousin Kate's husband," he stuttered. *Shit, I almost mentioned he who must not be named!*

"Well, if you want you can bring it here so you don't have to worry about it. I'll message Maggie right away."

I've got two weeks to set up Pete's surprise, and I'm determined to make everything perfect!

The October sun's golden light was fading as Devan admired the beautiful colors of the leaves. They'd all turned magnificent shades of red, orange, and yellow practically overnight. The only green she saw was on the dimly lit football field and the opposing team's jerseys. She thought back to the last time she'd been here and could almost see Kale running onto the field.

"She doesn't have any idea?" Maggie asked, interrupting Devan's trip down memory lane.

"Nope, she doesn't even know he's going to be named head coach." Devan looked back to see one of the players escorting Kristy down to the field on the opposite side, and pulled her hood up so Kristy wouldn't recognize her.

Coach Davis came on the field and everyone clapped. He took the microphone from a ref and said, "Welcome to our 2010 Homecoming Game!" The crowd roared. "We normally have the Homecoming Court come out here now — and I promise we'll do that in a minute — but first I need to make a few announcements.

"Tonight's game is my last as head coach. I'm retiring, and finally making my wife happy." People in the stands clapped and laughed. "I'd like to introduce you all to my replacement. He was a great player for me years ago, and has been a great assistant coach since he came back from the military — Coach Peter Monahan."

The crowd cheered as Pete came out on to the field.

"Here we go," Maggie said. "Okay, girls, as soon as he starts talking run out and get in formation."

"Thank you, Coach Davis. Filling your shoes will be rough, but I'm gonna to do the best job I can."

The girls ran out carrying boards and surrounded Pete as he spoke. They sat down like they were posing for a team picture. "I know I'll need lots of help and support from our fans, the team, my family and friends, and most of all my beautiful partner in crime." He waved at Kristy, and she waved back.

"Hey, team!" the head cheerleader yelled.

"Yeah?" they replied.

"Can you read?"

"Hell, yeah." All the girls replied.

"Shout out what these boards say!" The head cheerleader flipped over her board.

"Kristina McDaniels!"

"Will"

"You"

"Be"

"My"

The last board was flipped around.

"Wife?"

"What's it say?" She yelled as loud as she could.

"Kristina McDaniels, will you be my wife?" the girls yelled, and holding their boards, ran behind Pete in order.

Pete got down on one knee and said into the microphone, "Will you marry me, Kristy?"

She ran out onto the field screaming, "Yes!"

Maggie and Devan hugged. Both had tears in their eyes. They were so happy for their friends. It really was a long time coming.

Everyone clapped and whistled. Kristy put the ring on, flashed her hand to everyone, and then took the mike. "Yes, I will marry you, Pete Monahan!" Her answer echoed throughout the stands.

Maggie and Devan congratulated them with open arms.

"Oh, my God. I didn't even you see you!"

"That was the point," Devan said taking down her hood.

"You have to be my matron of honor, Dee! Oh, please say yes!" she begged and squeezed Devan tight.

"Of course I will. I'd be honored."

∽◎ ◎∾

A few weeks later, Kristy invited Devan over to help her plan the wedding.

"So, we finally set a date — June 25th, 2011."

"That's not that far away, Kristy. We need to get started. You need to see if there are halls available and—"

"It's already booked."

"Oh, great. Where?"

"Hawaii," she said, and looked down, refusing to look Devan in the eye.

"Okay. Where in Hawaii?"

"The hotel you and Kale worked at. Please don't be mad at me. They had a really good wedding and honeymoon package and—"

"Kristy, why would I be mad?"

"Well, there's more—" Kristy looked at Devan and continued. "Pete asked Kale to be his best man, and he accepted."

Devan shrugged. "I kind of figured it would work out that way."

"Please say you'll still do it? I can't picture anyone else standing by my side."

"Yes, Kristy, I'll still be your matron of honor. Calm down."

"Oh, thank you! Thank you!" she said hugging Devan tight.

The next day was parent teacher conferences, so naturally Justin was out of town. Devan had to ask her parents to watch her kids so she could go.

"Shut the door, please." she heard a woman say when she got to her last conference. Devan shut the door and sat down, waiting for the teacher to turn around.

"I'm Miss VonStross, Calista's art teacher. I'm filling in for Mrs. Smith tonight." She turned around and Devan almost fell off her chair. "Roni?"

Her childhood friend came over and gave her a hug. "I should've put two and two together. She does look like a mini Dee."

"Vernonica VonStross? Didn't you get married?"

"Yeah, and we can discuss that divorce over some wine later. While we're doing that, maybe *you* can tell me why your child's last name isn't Iakona," Veronica said and stepped back behind the desk to retrieve her folder.

"Fair enough."

"Well, she has here that Calista is a well behaved child who likes to talk a little too much, but she doesn't let that get in the way of her school work. She's getting all A's and B's, Devan.

"Oh there is one concern," she said, and began reading. "When asked about her family, she only talks about her mother and brother. Knowing that she had a father, I asked her about him and she replied: 'I want lettuce.'

It says here she won't draw pictures of her dad, either." She looked up from the paper, concerned.

"Aside from that, though, she's doing okay?" Devan asked.

Veronica nodded.

"So what's up with her dad?"

"When are you done here?" Devan knew this wasn't going to be a five-minute conversation.

"At nine. I have one more parent to see."

"How about we get that drink then?" Devan asked and stood up.

"Okay. Urban Myth at 9:30-ish?" Veronica asked walking Devan to the door.

"Nah, I need a quieter atmosphere. I live just down the road. I'll give you my address and you can meet me there." She pulled out a pen and paper and wrote everything down.

Devan picked up the kids at her parents' house, took them home, gave them baths and put them to bed in record time. She'd just pulled out a few bottles of wine when there was a light tapping at the door. "Come on in."

"Wow, nice place, Dee," Veronica said, looking around.

"Thanks. Red or white?"

"White."

"Zinfindel or Moscato?" Devan asked holing up the bottles.

"Moscato."

"My favorite." Devan set the bottle and glasses on the table.

"You go first. Divorce?" Devan poured the first glass handing it to her friend.

"Eh, good-looking guy, who was arrogant and mean. Cheated on me with someone we both know." Veronica swished the wine around in the glass.

"Who?"

"That slut Desireé."

"Seriously?" *That really doesn't surprise me much.*

Veronica nodded her head. "Your turn. Why doesn't Calista want to acknowledge her dad?"

Devan took a sip. "I'm guessing it's because he's never around, he's always *working.*"

"Hmmm. The way you said working doesn't sound very convincing ... do you think he's having an affair or something?"

"I don't really know and I don't care." Devan took a big gulp.

"Okay, that's kind of strange. So what happened with Hawaii? Last time I saw you it was college break and you were head over heels for him. He was coming to visit you."

Devan smiled and leaned back in her chair. "Ah, yes. Hawaii vs. Colorado. That was a fun few nights."

"I want to know all about it. Don't leave anything out. I had a huge crush on that guy." Veronica swallowed the remaining wine in her glass.

Devan laughed. "Oh, that's right. You have a thing for tall guys, too. What happened to the guy you dated in school — what was his name?" She tried to remember while pouring another glass for her guest.

"Ugh! Jasper." Veronica said, and cringed.

"Yeah, him."

"Nothing. He moved away and that was that. Okay, enough about me. What's the deal with Kale?"

Devan looked at the clock and asked, "How much time do you have?"

"All the time in the world — no school tomorrow." Veronica sat back.

"Let me see if I can find another bottle of Moscato. This one is two thirds gone already."

When Devan came back with another bottle, she told Veronica everything she could. She admitted things she shouldn't have, and by then both bottles were empty and they'd laughed and even cried a bit.

"Dee, that's the saddest story I've ever heard," she said wiping a tear away.

"You can't tell anyone. Promise?"

"I never told anyone about the time you let all the frogs go in biology."

Devan laughed. "I forgot all about that. You know, I didn't do it alone."

"Who helped you?"

"Nate Cavendar. He said, and I quote, 'Such beautiful creatures should be free, not die an agonizing death so they can be someone's learning tool.'"

"Nate said that?"

"Oh, yeah. He was different, but not in the way people thought. I think he'd seen too much death, so rescuing the frogs was important to him."

"Okay, since you told me all that stuff, I'll tell *you* a secret. I had another crush in high school. Well, actually, he was my main crush. I'd hook up with him in a heartbeat."

"Who?"

"Nate. Ugh he was *so* dreamy. Dark hair, dark eyes, tan skin ... mmm."

"Really? I guess I could see that. He was nice looking, and—"

"Tall!" They said in unison.

"Wasn't he like the tallest guy in school or something?" Veronica asked.

"I think so. I know Kale was tallest in football, but I'm pretty sure he was an inch or two shorter than Nate."

"Well, you remember that Goth phase I had?"

"How could I ever forget? Looks like you didn't grow out of it that much," she said looking at her friend's odd clothing.

"Yeah, I'm *artsy*. Anyway, he always seemed to be mysterious, and for a while I thought he was Goth. He kind of reminded me of a young sexy Poe."

"Poe? I was thinking Brandon Lee when he was in *The Crow*."

"His name alone was sexy — Nathaniel Cavendar," Veronica said in a slow, sultry voice.

Devan giggled at her friend.

"Yeah. So, now that we got all of that out of the way, why does your daughter want lettuce? Did you turn vegan on me? Not that it's a bad thing."

Devan put her head to her hands. "I think she means Kale. When Kale and I first met, we hated each other. We were kids so we called each other names. He called me Monty, and I called him Lettuce Head."

"And he was more of a father to her than Justin — that is what you said. Right?"

"Yeah, he was even there when she was born. He was the first one to hold her."

"Why wasn't Justin there?"

"Justin was out of town, working, like always."

"And she hasn't seen Kale since she was five?"

"Nope. We'll be seeing him next June at Pete and Kristy's wedding though," Devan said as she spun her empty glass around.

"That's right. I heard he proposed at the game. So, let me guess — you're the matron of honor and Kale's the best man?"

"You know it — and to add insult to injury, they're getting married where Kale and I worked in Hawaii."

"Oh, that has awkward written all over it."

"You have no idea."

Chapter 28

Present day, just before Kristy and Pete's wedding

Devan walked into the same hotel where she'd stayed during her first visit to Hawaii, and worked one summer after college. Being here again was exciting and sad all at the same time.

"Room for Iakona," she heard a man's voice say. She didn't have to look up to know whose voice it was. She'd immediately recognized its sexy, gravelly tone. It had been three years since she'd seen him, and she was so nervous that she didn't want to turn around and look at him. *I'll have to see him at some point,* she thought, *"but not yet, Lord. Please, not yet!"* She turned in the opposite direction, hoping he hadn't seen her. She'd planned to make a quick get away, but instead, she walked right into the brick wall that was Kale Iakona's chest.

"Monty?" he asked as he steadied her after their collision.

"Oh, hi Kale. Fancy running into you here," she joked lamely. "No one's called me that in years." She fondly remembered when he'd given her the nickname a million years ago when she was 12.

She finally looked him in the eye and saw that he was still as handsome as he'd always been. It had only been three years since she'd seen him, but it felt a lot longer. She blushed a little as he looked into her eyes. *It always feels like he can read my thoughts when he looks at me like that.*

He, on the other hand, felt like the world stopped spinning and she was the only person in the room when he looked at her. His pulse sped up like it always did when he was around her. It was like the last few years had never happened.

"Daddy!" Kale's daughter, Sage, yelled, as she ran toward him. "I have to pee!" she whispered loudly, breaking the spell Devan had put on him.

"Where's your mom?" he asked.

"I dunno," Sage replied with a shrug. "She went with some guy. Come on, Daddy, I really gotta goooooo bad! I don't wanna go in the boys' bathroom neither," she added, and crinkled up her little freckled nose. "It's gross!"

Devan bent down to her level, smiled and asked, "Do you remember me, Sage?"

"Yes. You're Aunt Devan," the little girl said and hugged Devan's neck.

Devan smiled into her adorable little face, "How about *I* take you to the bathroom?"

"Would you? It'll be better than going with Daddy, 'cause you're a girl, too. I *hate* going to the boys' bathroom. It always smells *bad*."

Kale watched the woman he should've married walk away, holding hands with his daughter.

"Doesn't Aunt Devan look fabulous, Dad?" Joey asked interrupting his father's thoughts.

Kale shook the image from his mind and asked, "Fabulous?"

"Yeah, fabulous."

Kale raised an eyebrow. *The kid's only 10, where did he come up with that description?* "Um yeah, sure."

Devan and Sage returned from the restroom a few minutes later and joined Kale and Joey in the lobby. Joey greeted Devan with open arms, "I missed you Aunt Dee!"

Devan wrapped her arms around the young man tightly, "I missed you, too, kiddo! You didn't mention how much you've grown when you emailed."

"Emailed?" Justin, asked as he walked up behind her. He turned his attention to Kale. "Mr. Kale Iakona in the flesh! How the hell are you?" Justin asked while shaking Kale's hand firmly.

Kale tried not to laugh. Justin always tried to act so manly. He used to think it was because Justin knew about his relationship with Devan, but he'd learned that Justin thought they were just "good friends" and chalked up the behavior to Justin feeling intimidated by his size.

"Darling Devan!"

Devan tried hard not to wince at the mere sound of Jeane's voice.

"Look at you! You do not look a day over 40!" Jeane said, as she embraced Devan.

Devan rolled her eyes while hugging the abrasive woman. "Thanks, Jeane. I'm not sure that's so good considering I'm only 33."

Jeane chuckled. "Oh, I tease you, my dear. You look wonderful as always," she said and air kissed Devan on both cheeks.

Since when is she European? Devan wondered. She could never quite figure out why she despised Jeane. *Sure, she's a smart-mouthed, snarky, stuck up bitch, but that's not it. Maybe it's jealousy?* Devan had always felt Jeane stole Kale right out from under her nose, and she definitely didn't trust her. Somehow, they were pseudo-friends. Anytime she heard Jeane's name, though, the phrase "Keep your friends close and your enemies closer," came to mind.

The concierge returned from the bar with Jeane's French Cosmo. She took a sip and gave him a nod of approval before saying, "Well, we're going to go get settled in. See you on the beach at six?"

"Why don't we meet down here at 5:30 and share a rental van?" Kale suggested.

"Great idea Kale." Justin winked at Jeane, and he and Devan walked away.

"Well that was awkward," Joey said to his dad.

Just a little, Kale thought.

The two families met at 5:30 as planned and all piled into the rental vehicle to drive to the wedding rehearsal. As they rounded the bend in the road, Callie, Devan's eight-year-old, screamed, "Oh, my God! What are they doing?"

Devan looked out the window and smiled when she saw kids running and jumping off a cliff so they could plunge into the water below.

"It's okay, honey. They're cliff diving. It's actually pretty fun." Devan chuckled. "If you're a local, that is." She wasn't about to tell her impressionable daughter she'd almost died while cliff jumping 17 years ago.

Jeane stopped the car and said, "This is actually where your dad used to cliff dive." The kids watched in awe as more people ran toward the edge, jumped and then plummeted to the warm water below.

I was scared I lost her that day. From that day on I vowed to always rescue her. Kale thought when he glanced over at Devan who just so happened to be looking at him.

"Really? Dad?" Sage asked incredulously.

"Well… it was a *long* time ago," Devan said and laughed.

Kale knew it wasn't going to be easy seeing Devan again. He'd been trying to keep her out of his thoughts for the past few years, but it never seemed to work. No matter what he was doing, she was always walking through his mind.

Now here I am riding in the same car with her and my wife, and all I can do is relive the past in my mind. I've got to stop this. I came here for Pete and Kristy's wedding, and nothing else.

Chapter 29

Everyone was already waiting on the beach when they got there. Devan ran down the steps to the sand. Skipping a step, she nearly fell and ended up grabbing onto Kale to regain her balance.

"Is it just me or is this déjà vu?" Kale asked. "You just keep running into me."

Any time Kale's near me, I seem to end up in his arms one way or another. She smiled helplessly, trying to keep her composure, "Thank you for not letting me face plant."

He studied her for a moment. "I couldn't let a pretty face like yours get hurt, now could I?"

Damn him with his sexy voice, sexy body, sexy smell, and — well, sexy everything! "Well thanks again," Devan said, while trying to get him to release her.

"Hey, can we talk later?" he asked, still not letting her go.

"Yeah, sure. At some point," she said and sighed. He still hadn't let go of her and she was starting to blush.

His eyes met hers and were pleading with her heart, "Devan, we need to talk. Alone. Please?" he asked softly.

Devan looked up at him and sighed again. "Okay, alone," she agreed reluctantly.

He finally let go of her and watched her walk toward the beach where everyone was gathered.

The rehearsal went smoothly, but by the time it was finished everyone was ready for the beautiful buffet at the bar. The buffet included fresh fruit and vegetables, five different types of bread, several types of cheese, salad, ham, roast beef and baked chicken. A pianist was playing softly off to the side, adding lovely ambiance to the happy occasion.

When they'd finished eating, Kale excused himself and joined the groom at the bar.

"Dude, I know I've already thanked you but I gotta thank you again!" Pete said, giving Kale a big bear hug. "I'm sure it's weird being back in Hawaii and even weirder having Devan here."

The bartender handed Pete his glass. "Thanks man," he said and took a sip of his drink.

Kale noticed the bar hadn't changed a bit; it looked the same as it did 10 years ago. There were old photos of surfers from the 1950s and '60s and ukuleles signed by famous musicians decorating the walls.

"It's cool, Pete," Kale said. "You're my best friend and you know I'd do anything for you."

The bartender handed Kale his drink. "Got anything special in there?" Pete asked looking into the glass.

"Nope, just good ol' coconut water," Kale said and laughed.

Pete patted him on the back. "Don't you at least want a beer?"

"No, thanks," Kale replied. His smile turned somewhat solemn, "I learned my lesson a long time ago. It's best that I stay away from alcohol all together."

"Well, I can respect that my friend. Now, go and be merry, for tomorrow I wed!" Pete joked, and then swallowed the remainder of his drink.

Kale left Pete at the bar and headed back to his seat at the table. When he got there, he noticed it was taken.

"Hi, honey! Justin was just telling me about a new opportunity Uncle Alistair presented to his dad. It looks like we'll be working together again."

Kale patted Justin on the back, "That's great Jay." Without making eye contact with anyone in particular, Kale asked, "Have you guys seen the kids?"

"Yeah, Dev has them just over there," Justin said pointing in the direction of the beach. Kale thanked him and went back up to the bar where he ordered a Moscato.

When he got the drink, he walked out of the dining area to the beach. When he saw Devan, he stopped and just watched her. *I've missed seeing her with my kids. I wish Jeane had that same natural maternal instinct, but it's a trait she never acquired.*

Devan didn't have to see Kale to know he was there. Somehow, she could always sense when he was near. She looked up, saw him approaching and instantly had butterflies in her stomach.

"Here," he said handing her the wine. "I know it's been a while, but I'm assuming you still like the sweet, bubbly stuff."

She smiled her award-winning smile; the same smile that always made his heart skip a beat. He wanted nothing more than to grab her and kiss her, but he knew that was way out of line. *I'm already on thin ice when comes to her. Better cool it, big guy.*

They both knew they needed to talk, but neither of them was up for the challenge just yet. Instead, they simply sat together and enjoyed watching the kids playing in the sand.

They've all grown up so quickly, Devan thought. *The last time I saw Kai he wasn't even a year old and now he's almost four.*

Kai and Cyrus were only a month apart. They played well together and were laughing at the seagulls trying to steal a man's fish while he was removing it from the hook.

Kale's daughter, Sage, was six and a half, about a year and a half younger than Devan's daughter, Callie. Kale's oldest son, Joey, who was almost ten, shared a special bond with Devan. She was his godmother and had helped raise him. It was love at first sight with him, from the moment she held him when he was a baby. Joey had always liked Devan more than his own mother, and she watched with pride as he built a sand castle.

Kale's voice interrupted her thoughts, "That kid misses you. Well, we all do. But I think it's hardest on him."

Devan's eyes grew misty as she looked at Joey's curly auburn hair. She smiled and said, "I miss him, too. We miss all of you."

Kale put his hand on top of hers, "I'm sorry," he began, "We shouldn't have—"

Devan stopped him abruptly, "Kale, not now. Please?" She slipped her hand out from under his and stood up. "I'm going to get another one of these," she said, brandishing her empty glass. "Can I get you something?" she asked sweetly.

"No, thank you. I'll stay here and watch the kids."

Kristy came over and sat down next to him after Devan left and asked, "Whatcha thinkin' about, stud?"

"Memories. Real ones and ones that should've been," he said sadly.

"Are you guys at least talking now?"

Kale looked down at the sand, grabbed a hand full and let the cool sand run through his fingers, "Yeah, I guess you could say we're talking. If you're asking if we've had a real conversation — the answer is no."

Kristy put her hand on his knee. "Don't worry. She'll come around. She's probably feeling as mixed up as you are."

Kale had no doubt that was true. They both needed to deal with their feelings and act like adults.

Devan headed back over to where she'd left Kale, carrying her full glass of wine. She was ready to have that serious talk with him, but Kristy was sitting there with him. *Well, dodged another bullet,* she thought and smiled to herself.

She sat down in the sand next to her friend and listened to her chatter about the wedding. For the first time in her life, Devan was glad she had a best friend who had the gift of gab.

The sun had long gone to bed and it was getting late. Everyone was making moves toward turning in for the night — that is everyone but Jeane and Justin. They appeared to be having too much fun drinking and talking about work.

Devan took her kids back to their room and readied them for bed. After they were both asleep, she sat down, opened her laptop and began typing.

The thing I feared the most is happening. I can't help but feel trapped by the sweet sound of his deep voice and the intoxicating smell of his—

She heard her phone buzz. It was a text.

KRISTY: What are you doing?

DEVAN: Trying to write. Why aren't you sleeping?

Devan set the phone down. It buzzed again. She looked at it expecting Kristy but it was a number she didn't recognize.

UNKNOWN: We need to talk.

DEVAN: Who is this?

Her phone buzzed again.

KRISTY: I'll go to sleep after I tell you something. I gave Kale your number. I hope you aren't mad.

Devan rolled her eyes.

DEVAN: WHY????

UNKNOWN: It's Kale. You know why.

Oops, thought I was replying to Kristy. Devan looked at the next text.

KRISTY: Please talk to him. I don't want tomorrow to be super awkward."

DEVAN: Fine! He's texting me now. Don't worry about it, everything will be A-OK!

She replied back to Kale's text.

DEVAN: Sorry. I was texting Kristy and I didn't recognize your number.

KALE: That's OK. Meet me outside your door in 5.

Oh, great, she thought as she set her phone down. She quickly looked in the mirror and tried to fix her disheveled appearance. "Damn it, Kristy!"
 A few minutes later, she heard a light knock on the door. She opened it and let him in.

Kale hugged her tightly. "I'm sorry, I just really needed to do that," he said sitting down at the desk. "What's that?" he asked, looking at her computer screen.

"Nothing," she said as quickly walked over and shut it. "It's just something I'm working on. Well, you wanted to talk, so let's talk," she said as she walked over and sat down on the bed.

"I don't want to get all into the 'elephant in the room' per se, but Kristy thought it was a good idea for us to—"

"Yeah, I know 'talk,'" she said as she made air quotes. "She's afraid it's going to be awkward tomorrow since we haven't talked in three years."

Kale wanted to laugh but decided not to. *Things are too tense and she might take it the wrong way.* "So, I'll go first. I'm sorry for leaving things the way I did at the lake—"

"Oh, please," Devan interrupted him. "Can we *not* go there? I'm too tired for that conversation right now," she said, rolling her eyes.

Irritated, Kale continued, "Look, we need to talk about that—"

"Okay, how's this?" she asked, interrupting him again. She sat a little straighter and uncrossed her arms, "I was wrong. You were wrong. It shouldn't have happened. Luckily, I stopped it before it got out of hand. I forgive you. Please forgive me. Let's get on with our lives."

Damn, she's feisty tonight. He stood up, walked over to the bed and sat down next to her. He turned to look her dead in the eyes and said, "Good, now that we have that out of the way…" and he attacked her with his lips.

Devan was surprised, but she never could fight him off — mainly because she never wanted to. His lips were so lusciously plump and soft. His kiss was forceful yet gentle and ended way too quickly.

When it was over, she smacked his face. He stood up and walked to the door, rubbing his cheek, "You and I have issues with our lips at weddings. I just wanted to get that out of the way now," he said and winked.

She couldn't help but laugh, "You, sir, are an ass!"

"I missed that laugh. Are we good now?" he asked raising an eyebrow.

"Yes, we're good. Now get the hell out of here before I change my mind," she said as she shooed him away with her hands.

She shut the door quietly behind him. *He's so hot...and that kiss...oh, Lord!* Devan thought and screamed her frustration into her pillow. She turned off the lamp on the nightstand and fell asleep with a smile on her face. Everything was going to be okay...

Chapter 30

Devan woke up to the scent of freshly baked bagels and Kona coffee. "Good morning, Peaches!" she heard Kristy's chipper voice say.

Devan stretched and yawned loudly. "How did you get in here?"

Kristy giggled, "Justin let me in. He got up early and took the kids downstairs to the breakfast nook so we could start getting ready. My mom and Jeane are supposed to meet us in my room in an hour and a half, but I wanted to spend some alone time with my BFF."

Devan smiled and poured a cup of coffee. She put her lips to the ceramic cup and paused. Looking up she asked, "Did you say Jeane?"

"Yeah," Kristy answered slowly. "Justin offered to take their kids too. He said he knows how long we women take to get ready and he knew Kale would want to be with Pete."

Shit! I don't want to be around Jeane right now, especially when my emotions are so mixed up.

"So, what happened last night?" Kristy asked suddenly remembering the texts.

Devan sighed and smiled.

Kristy raised her eyebrow, "Oh, do tell, my love!"

Devan took a long sip of coffee and said, "Okay, so he came over to talk, which we did for about two minutes. Then he kissed me and left."

"*What?*" Kristy shrieked, wide-eyed.

"He came over to talk, so we talked and then he left."

"No, no, no!" Kristy scolded. "Devan Marie, you're withholding precious information. You said he *kissed* you."

"Oh that? Yeah, that happened," Devan said, pouring herself some more coffee.

"But why?"

Devan took a bite of the warm bagel, "Well," she paused to swallow. "We talked about what happened at the lake and then all of a sudden his lips were on mine," she finished in a matter of tone.

"Annnd?" Kristy asked, leaning in.

"And, he left."

"Not that. How was it?"

"Mmmm you know when you've had the worst day and then something wonderful happens and makes all the bad the things go away? It was like that." Devan said, and smiled devilishly.

"Well good. So you guys are on speaking terms then? Today won't be as awkward as I thought?"

Devan didn't say anything. *It's going to be a strange and awkward day, but I'm pretty sure things will come together and we'll be okay with each other.*

"I was interrupted by my uncle, but I come bearing gifts," Jeane said, while setting down a tray holding a pitcher of mimosas and champagne goblets.

Devan walked past Jeane and noticed a familiar scent.

"You smell like aftershave," Kristy said and laughed while giving Jeane a hug.

"Yeah, my uncle's always giving hugs and I swear he takes a bath in that crap."

Devan had been around Jeane's uncle plenty of times, and knew he wore Old Spice. Every time he was near her the scent made her think of her grandpa. What she smelled on Jeane certainly wasn't Old Spice...

I should feel guilty being around Kale's wife after that kiss, but I don't. I feel giddy like a schoolgirl.

After they'd had their mimosas, the girls started getting ready. There was a lot of makeup and hair that had to be dealt with before they could head down the aisle.

Chapter 31

The time had finally come; they were almost ready to start walking down the aisle. In the distance, Devan could see Kale standing under the hand carved Banyan tree pergola. It was brilliantly decorated with lush palm leaves and magenta and white Plumeria.

Devan took a deep breath and looked down at her bare feet in the black sand. Her off white chiffon dress and long black hair blew around her face in the warm salty air.

"Wait, you need this," Kristy said as she tucked an orchid into Devan's hair and secured it with a bobby pin. She stepped back to admire her work and said, "Perfect, just perfect! Are you ready?"

Devan nodded and kissed her friend's beaming cheek as her pulse quickened with anticipation. *After all these years it's finally happening,* she thought as the ukuleles began to play.

After the first eight-count, Devan gave her son, Cyrus, and Kale's son, Kai, a gentle nudge, and they began their walk down the aisle toward the pergola. Cyrus had the same platinum blonde hair and bright blue eyes she'd had when she was his age, and looked like he came straight from the California coast. Kai was the spitting image of his father, with dark brown hair, green eyes and burnished skin.

"Remember, walk slowly," she whispered. She watched as the boys reached the pergola without incident. Cyrus went to stand next to Pete, and Kai stood next to Kale. *Now it's my turn...*

Pete nudged Kale as Devan started down the aisle. *She's breathtaking!*

Her hair was so dark it looked like it had violet highlights. Her tanned skin accentuated her pale blue-gray eyes, making them look sliver. The thin chiffon dress she wore was strapless and cut to flatter her figure perfectly. The top was snug and left nothing to the imagination, and the skirt flowed easily in the breeze.

She's always been the most beautiful woman I've ever seen, Kale thought dreamily, *but she's even more beautiful today.*

"Dude, I think you're starting to drool," Pete said under his breath and snickered.

The matron of honor and best man made eye contact, and smiled at each other.

I've waited for this moment since I was a teenager, she thought. *He's perfect. Too bad he's not mine.* His white muslin shirt was unbuttoned halfway, revealing his bronze, rock-hard chest, and a lei of white and magenta Plumeria rested on his shoulders.

When Devan took her place under the pergola, the music changed and the guests stood and turned to watch the bride come down the aisle.

"The time's finally here, man!" Kale said and patted Pete's shoulder. "She's all yours."

Devan smiled warmly at Pete as he watched Kristy's father walk her down the aisle. His smile got even wider as her father placed Kristy's hand in his. Devan took a surreptitious look at Kale and blinked back the tears. *This should've been us,* she thought sadly.

The wedding was beautiful, with its backdrop of the tranquil waters of the Pacific rolling onto the sandy beach. The temperature was in the mid 80s with a light breeze. Everything was picture perfect. Even the kids were well behaved during the ceremony — a miracle in itself!

Devan caught Kale staring at her more than once as they stood in the receiving line. They'd caught each other's eyes a couple of times during the ceremony, too. It must've been pretty obvious, because Pete had stepped on Kale's foot to remind him that Jeane and Justin were seated only a few feet away.

Kale couldn't help himself. Devan had been his, and he regretted letting her slip away. He would always regret what happened, but last night's kiss had put a smile on his face that wouldn't go away.

The bride and groom were on the dance floor, swaying to "Lucky" by Jason Mraz and Colbie Caillat when the music stopped abruptly.

"What's wrong? Why'd the music stop?" Kristy asked and dropped her hands from around her groom's neck.

Devan set her camera down and said, "I'll find out." She walked over to the DJ and saw he was frantically pushing buttons and unplugging cables, only to plug them back in with no luck. "Oh, man, I think it shorted out! I don't know what to do," he told her. Devan tried helping him find the problem but they couldn't get the music going again.

Kale walked over to the bartender and said, "Hey man, last night I saw you had a ukulele back there. Can I borrow it for a bit?"

Devan was determined to get the music going again. She hit another button, just as she heard the light strumming of a ukulele. She looked up and saw it was Kale. He began singing the very same song the DJ was trying to play. It was a duet and when he walked closer to her, she knew he expected her to sing the female part.

He kept playing the ukulele while she sang. The DJ put two working microphones in front of them, and it reminded her of the times they'd sung karaoke back when they worked together.

Kristy and Pete began dancing again. Kale only looked away from Devan once or twice to make sure he hit the right note, the rest of the time he was looking right at her.

Suddenly, someone started playing the piano in the corner. It was Kale's old manager from the hotel. He nodded to Kale and smiled. Once again, Kale had saved the day.

When the song ended, the guests all began to clap. Kristy hugged Devan and thanked her for saving their first dance as a married couple.

Devan laughed, "You shouldn't be thanking me. You should be thanking Kale."

Kristy turned to thank him, but he'd moved outside the pavilion and was talking to someone. He returned with a guitar and started playing "I Run to

You," by Lady Antebellum. Devan shook her head no but he continued to come closer. When he began singing into the microphone, she gave in and sang with him.

Kale loved hearing Devan's voice. He hadn't heard her sing in years, and it brought back so many memories. By the time the song ended, the DJ had fixed the sound system and "Fade Into You," by Mazzy Star began to play.

Devan tried walking off the dance floor, but Kale took her by the hand and pulled her close. He was so tall that she couldn't see over his shoulder — her face was level with his chest.

He swung her around and she saw her husband dancing with Jeane. Just then, Jeane leaned in and snuggled close to Justin. Devan found that a little odd but didn't really care. She was in the arms of her first love, her true love, and the DJ was playing "their" song.

She put her head on Kale's chest and breathed in his signature scent — Nautica. She closed her eyes and enjoyed the feeling of security she always felt in his arms. *I've missed this, but then again I miss everything about him — from the way he makes me feel to the size of his hands. He is and always will be the perfect man.*

Kale breathed in the fresh coconut fragrance of Devan's hair. He wrapped his arms around her a little tighter and kissed the top of her head, hoping no one saw but not really caring if they did. He searched the dance floor for his wife, and saw that she was clearly not paying attention to what he was doing. *She's probably too preoccupied by Justin's hands on her ass. I wish this time with Devan could last forever.*

Devan looked up at Kale's alluring green eyes as the song changed to "Right Here Waiting," by Richard Marx. When they looked at each other it felt like they were the only people in the room.

Kale whispered the lyrics just loud enough for her to hear as they danced, and watched as she began to cry.

This is so wrong! Not here, not now. "I can't," she said as she let go of him and walked away.

He didn't think anyone saw her leave, so he decided to follow her. He found her down the hill from the reception pavilion. She was leaning against a stone wall, gazing out to the west where the sun was melting into the ocean.

Devan saw him out of the corner of her eye, "Why did you follow me? Isn't it obvious I can't be around you right now?"

Kale wiped her tears away and said, "I think about you every day," he said as he held her face in his huge hands. "I miss those eyes and how they look back into mine. I miss the softness of your lips," he said brushing his thumb over them.

This isn't helping! she thought, and cried even harder, "This is why I didn't want to come! I didn't want to be in this predicament with you again. It never ends—"

"Monty," he pleaded.

Devan shook her head no, "I need you to go."

"Dev, I'm not leaving you here."

"Fine," she sniffled, "then I'll leave." With that, she walked away, worried he would follow and afraid he wouldn't.

Kale let her go and stood looking out to the horizon. *There really isn't anything I can say or do to make her feel better. I was afraid something like this would happen. Maybe I shouldn't have danced with her. Then maybe the feelings wouldn't have come flooding back.*

He turned around and saw her footprints leading back to the party. *I didn't tell her we're moving back to Seattle. How will she feel when I'm back? Whatever either one of us feels, what just happened can't happen again. I can't stand seeing her hurt like that — especially knowing I caused it.* Kale sighed and ran after her.

"Dev, wait up."

"Kale, just stop." she said as she snapped her head around.

He turned her around to face him. "No. Just let me say this. I have to say it. Okay? I have good news and bad news. The good news is we're moving back to Ohio. The bad news is Jeane found a house in your subdivision and we're moving just down the street from you."

"Isn't that a good thing?" she asked.

He looked into her grey-blue eyes, "Not if it's going to hurt you to see me. We'll definitely be seeing more of each other, you know. Certainly more than we have these last three years ... that's my fault, I know, and I'm sorry."

231

Devan shrugged her shoulders and said, "Well, welcome back to the neighborhood, I guess. Listen, I'm sorry about just now. There was no call for that kind of childish behavior. I'm sorry and it won't happen again. I'll put my feelings aside. Lord knows I'm pretty damn good at wanting things I can't have! And you...you *will not* pull a stunt like you did last night ever again."

Kale almost growled the words, "It seems like that is all we ever do — put our feelings aside. Monty, we didn't talk for three years! Isn't that punishment enough?"

She put her hand up to stop him. "With our past — and now our current situation — the only thing we *can* do is put our feelings aside and deny their very existence."

With that she walked back onto the dance floor.

Chapter 32

It had been a long day — both tiring and beautiful. Pete and Kristy were finally married, Kale and his family were moving back to Ohio, and the emotional struggles were starting all over again.

Devan decided to deal with stress the best way she knew how — write. Some of her friends did yoga, some ran marathons on their living room treadmills and others drank an extra glass or three of wine at dinner when they were stressed. Devan chose to use writing as her outlet. She opened her laptop and began typing, allowing her memories to fuel her work.

After a couple of hours, Devan stretched and yawned. It was going to be a long night. She'd never tried writing non-fiction, but she'd decided to write out her love story with Kale and it felt good.

She got up and brewed some coffee because there was a lot of writing still to be done. As she typed, she relived every moment she and Kale had spent together. She started at the beginning and tried to write all the pain and disappointment out of her system.

The more she remembered, the faster her fingers flew across the keys. It felt good to release all the feelings, even if it was just pouring them into a file on her laptop.

Soon, she didn't even realize she was typing. The memories had taken over and she'd been transported back to those happier times. She wrote more and more, trying to purge the longing from her soul.

"Mommy? Are you dead?" Cyrus asked and smacked Devan on the forehead. She tried opening her eyes, but it was too bright. She'd fallen asleep with her head on her laptop. She got up, stumbled over a pair of shoes and some clothes on the floor and somehow managed to shut the curtains without falling flat.

"Were you up all night?" Justin asked.

"What? Oh, yeah. I was working on a … project."

"What project?"

"Oh, a new policy book for the school. What time is it?" She yawned and stretched.

"It's two. Are you hungry?"

"Oh, shit, it's the afternoon already? Yeah, I'm hungry."

"Mommy that's a bad word. You need to say *poop* instead," Cyrus corrected her.

"Yes, Cyrus, it is a bad word. I'm sorry."

"I'll order you something from room service. We're going to meet Jeane and the kids at the beach. Dinner with everyone is at six." Justin opened up a menu and placed the call.

It was nice of him to order food for me. I'm surprised he didn't yell-at me for not coming to bed and then sleeping in so late.

Devan searched for her phone and finally found it as everyone was leaving. She thumbed through her contacts and dialed. "Roni?"

"Yeah?"

"Do you have a few minutes to talk?"

"Sure."

Devan spilled about everything that had happened since she arrived in Hawaii.

"Okay, well at least you found an outlet for all of those emotions. Wow, you realize you basically wrote a whole book last night?"

Devan looked at the last sentence and saved the file. "Yeah, but now what?"

"You're asking me?"

"Yes. What do I do? I'm going to have to see him later."

Veronica thought for a moment then said, "Be cordial and try not to cry? I don't know, Dee."

"What would you do?"

"I'd be all over that man. I wouldn't be on the phone with me, that's for damn sure. I'd be making that man scream my name."

"Roni, that's not helping."

There was a knock at the door. "Hold on, it's room service. Boy, that was fast." She opened the door to a soaking wet Kale wearing a wet suit. She picked up the phone from the bed and said, "Not room service."

"Well who is it?"

"Lettuce— Let us talk later."

"Lettuce Head! It's Kale! It's Kale!" Veronica shrieked.

"Bye, Veronica," she said as she hung up on her.

"Hey, are you feeling better?" Kale asked as he walked in.

"I wasn't sick."

"You missed breakfast and lunch, and Callie said you were in bed."

"Oh, I stayed up all night — writing."

"Oh yeah? Must've been good. What was it?" He stepped closer to her.

"Nothing. Why aren't you on the beach?" she asked as she backed away from him.

"I met Kuna for some waves, and I wanted to check on you. You didn't respond to my texts last night."

She looked at her phone and went to messages. *Holy cow! There are 21 new messages — all from Kale.*

"Sorry," he began. "I was upset and worried about the way we left things yesterday."

She took a deep breath. "It looks like we're going to have to have that long talk I've been avoiding."

"Before you start, let me get comfortable," Kale said and unzipped his wet suit, pulling it down to his waist.

He still has the same killer physique! That tight chest, those abs, and those arms! She shook her head to get rid of the fog. "Okay, first rule. You can't tease me like that."

"Huh?"

"Just keep your clothes on around me. Okay?" she barked.

"Um, okay. I brought my bag."

"Go in the bathroom and change, Kale."

He came out a few minutes later wearing a dark grey tank top and matching plaid shorts. *I wish he had a shirt on that covered more. He's just too hot, especially after all that writing last night and remembering all the details — and the sex. Oh, the sex! How in the hell am I supposed to have a serious talk with him when he's so damn sexy?*

"Can I talk now?" he asked in a snarky tone.

"Go!"

"I'm sorry about yesterday. I didn't mean for things to become so ... nostalgic. I definitely didn't mean to make you cry," he said sincerely. "The last three years have been pure hell for me. Jeane hasn't changed at all, and from the looks of it Justin hasn't either. The kids hated it in Seattle. Alistair has been a complete dick. I'm miserable. Most of all, I'm miserable because I can't be near you." He put his hand up to stop her from speaking. Before you yell, let me finish."

Devan crossed her arms and let him continue.

"I know we have to make our feelings disappear. I know I can't just kiss you like I did Friday night. I know there can never be an us like there was before."

"So what do you propose, Iakona?"

"I've been thinking about it, and for a few years there we were a pretty good team. We didn't let the *feelings* take over and ruin everything. What if we became that team again?"

She thought for a minute. "No pining after one another?"

"I'm always going to pine after you, but I won't tell you about it."

"Hmmm. So back to the basics — just friends."

"Exactly. We can help each other with the kids — God knows, I need it. I'll do the shit that needs done at your house like fix things Justin never gets around to—"

She interrupted him. "A team like when Callie and Joey were little?"

"Yes, nothing more. I'm not promising it'll be the answer, but I know it worked before —and I'll give 110 percent."

I have to face the facts. He's going to be in my face all the time. Veronica said it was good I finally found an outlet. From now on, if I have to deal with my feelings, I can just write them out of my system. "If our feelings start taking over again?"

"Honestly, Monty, I don't know. We can talk about them, and try to push them to the side. I guess we'll cross that bridge when we come to it. I'm sure that will happen at some point. We just have to try to make it *not* happen. So, can we try to be friends?" he asked, extending his hand.

She took it and they shook on it. "Yeah, we're going to be together, so why not try to make the best of it?"

"Can I hug you?" he asked sweetly. "Or is that against the rules?"

She draped her arms around him. "I think that's safe — as long as we have clothes on."

At dinner she sat between Justin and Jeane. How she ended up there she'd never know.

"So, Justin said you're working on a policy book for the school? How did you end up with that job?" Jeane asked.

Wow, she's nosy. "My friend, Veronica, is a teacher there. Actually, she was Callie's art teacher this past year."

"Veronica as in Veronica VonStross?" Pete asked.

"Yeah."

"I didn't realize Roni was there, too. I just knew about Maggie."

Kristy smacked his shoulder. "I told you this like a month ago."

"We all went to school together. Veronica, Kristy, another girl named Maggie, and I were all good friends from elementary through middle school. When we got to high school, we kind of went our separate ways." Devan explained to Jeane.

"Do you know her?" Jeane asked Kale.

"Kind of, she was in my art class. Is she still pretty extreme? I just can't see her as a teacher. I thought she'd end up fronting a death metal band or at a mortuary doing the makeup or something like that."

Devan laughed. "She was at the peak of her Goth stage when you knew her in school. She's slightly less intense now."

When the food arrived, everyone simmered down and ate like champions. The steak was moist and tender and the shrimp scampi was to die for. There were garlic rolls the size of Kale's hands, and the fruit was fresh and ripe.

Pete broke the silence, "Well, we have one day left with all of you, then we're on our own for a week. What would you all like to do tomorrow?"

Everyone started speaking at once.

"Wait — one at a time," Pete said, and laughed.

Jeane started, "I have meetings tomorrow with my uncle."

Justin piped up and said, "Oh, that's right. So do I."

Kale kicked Devan's foot under the table. "Ow!" she yelped and shot Kale a dirty look.

"That leaves us with the kids," Kale said, before taking another bite.

"Oh, no honey, we'll take the kids," Kristy's mom told him.

"Well, Kale, this is the land of your people, what do you recommend?" Pete asked.

Kale laughed at Pete. "The land of my people? Okay, I'll give you the grand tour."

Oh no!! I don't know if I'm up for that. I hope the tour doesn't include cliff diving or the cave. I'm definitely not prepared to take that emotional roller-coaster ride.

Kale looked at Devan and could see the concern written all over her face. He kicked her foot again to get her attention. "I was thinking about taking them to Happy Hookers for lunch tomorrow."

She smiled. That idea sounded great.

That night, Justin stayed out late again. After the kids went to bed, Devan called Veronica. "You know it's like 4 a.m. here, right?" Veronica whined.

"Oh, I forgot. I'll call you tomorrow."

"No, I'm up now. Talk to me."

Devan told her what had happened, and realized that Veronica was turning into her confidant. She didn't want to bombard Kristy right now, but she had to talk to someone.

"Hold on, my phone is beeping," Devan told her. She looked down at her phone and saw she had 5 new messages.

KALE: Are you still up?

KALE: Is Justin there?

JUSTIN: Staying out a bit longer.

KALE: Are the kids asleep?

KALE: Where should we go tomorrow?

"Dear Lord, Kale texted me four times and Justin once," Devan told her.
"So, what's it like to have two guys lusting after you?" Veronica teased.
"Oh, stop. I've kept you up long enough. Go to bed. I'll text you tomorrow. Thank you for listening."
"Yeah, yeah! Go call lover boy." Veronica laughed and hung up.
Devan texted Kale:

DEVAN: Yes awake. No, he said he's staying out longer. Yes, kids are asleep ... and I don't know."

Kale responded immediately, like he'd been waiting impatiently for her to answer.

KALE: Meet me out on the balcony.

What? That doesn't make any sense, Devan thought.

DEVAN: Kale, they don't connect.

KALE: They're only a foot apart. Go out there please.

She opened the sliding glass door and saw him leaning on his railing.
"See, one foot." He started to climb across to hers.
"No, Kale. What are you doing?"

He was over on her balcony in 30 seconds. "You realize my legs are like four feet long, right?"

"I don't care if you're nine feet tall, that was dangerous."

He sat down on the balcony's cement floor and dangled his bare feet over the edge. Devan sat down next to him and put her feet through the bars as well. "Oops—" she said as her flip-flop fell off of her foot.

"Hey!" someone yelled up. She retracted her feet and began laughing.

Kale thought it was hilarious. "Only you, Monty."

She took her other flip-flop off and put her feet back out. It was dark, but a few lights twinkled across the way. They could hear the tide rolling in as waves crashed onto the shore.

"Peaceful isn't it?" he asked while slowly raising his arm to put around her shoulders. Devan automatically scooted a little closer when Kale's hand rested on her shoulder.

"Where should we go tomorrow?" he asked.

"I like the idea of seeing Moshi again."

"Yeah, I do too, but I haven't seen him since—" he didn't finish his sentence.

"Since when?" she asked, looking over at him.

"It's not important." He looked down at his feet.

"Kale."

"Since I took your dad to lunch there," he murmured.

"Oh." *Why did I have to pry?*

There was silence for a little while, as they both stared out at the dark sky.

"I was hoping to make the transition from not speaking to being friends a lot less awkward," Kale said and laughed.

"Did your parents know we weren't talking?"

"No. Yours?"

"Nope, no one knew other than—"

"Kristy and Pete," they said at the same time.

"Let's do something special for them!" he said, getting up.

"Like what?"

"Set your alarm for six and meet me in front of the hotel." He kissed her head and climbed back over to his balcony. "Night, Monty!"

Chapter 33

Kale was waiting for Devan in front of the hotel, holding a coffee in each hand. He handed her one when she walked up.

"Mmm, thank you."

"Follow me," he said and walked down the road. Just past the hotel was a lava field where people had used coral pieces and white or light colored stone to write out messages.

"Get a handful," he said scooping up the coral pieces. "Okay, now I'll write 'Kristy + Pete' and you put 'Forever!' under it"

He's unbelievable. She smiled as she positioned the stones. "Kale, this is a cute idea. They'll love it."

He climbed down and looked at their creation proudly. "Perfect! Our first stop will be here."

"Then?" Devan asked, nervous about what he'd say.

"I'm thinking maybe Noelani and Russo's. My uncle inherited some land a few miles down from the farm. Mom emailed me some pictures last year. They have coffee, guava, lemon, macadamia nut trees, and a whole bunch of other stuff."

"That sounds cool." She took a breath. *Okay, it's not going to be as bad as I thought.*

Their tour went over well. Pete and Kristy were elated with Kale and Devan's artwork. They even got out and took a lot of pictures with it.

They were able to try some of the fruits and nuts growing at the farm, but lunch was a bit of a letdown because Moshi wasn't there; he was in Japan visiting family. The food was still delicious though.

Much to Devan's relief, they didn't go cliff diving, but they did stop and watch as other people jumped.

"Okay, kids, last stop! Ole Blue — her real name is *Nani Mau Loa* which means forever beautiful."

Devan's heart sank. *Why? Why here? There are a million other places on this island and he had to pick this one,* she thought, glaring at Kale.

He explained the history and they all got in and swam around for a bit, enjoying the crystal clear water.

"What's back that way?" Pete asked.

"Oh, that's a cave, but we don't have the right equipment to go back there. It's not safe," Kale lied through his teeth.

He glanced at Devan and she gave him a weak smile.

He obviously can't bring himself to go back there, either. This is just as hard for him as it is for me.

Kale had promised his aunt and uncle that he'd bring his and Devan's family by to see them the next day. Naturally, Jeane and Justin couldn't make it, so Devan and Kale took the kids.

As the rental van turned onto a long gravel and sand driveway, Devan admired the lush greenery. Monkey pod trees lined the road, creating a canopy and providing a cool escape from the hot Pacific sun. They could see the orchard off in the distance.

The kids got excited when they saw a donkey and few other farm animals. Half of the farm was acres and acres of tall green and yellow California grasses that swayed with the light breeze.

When they got to the house, Noelani was outside tending to her hibiscus plants. There were also birds of paradise and plumeria plants everywhere in a vast variety of vibrant colors. It was a beautiful sight to see.

When they walked into the house, Kale's uncle asked him to come over, sit down and have coffee with him while Noelani and Devan watched the kids play with the animals.

"Listen, Kale Kai, now that my uncle has passed, you're the only relative we have left, aside from your father."

"Yes, I know that," Kale said and took a drink from his cup.

"All this land will be yours one day. Don't let corporate America take it away from you."

"What do you mean?"

"My uncle had been fighting with some big corporation that wanted the land so they could build another resort, as if there aren't enough of those already destroying our beautiful island."

"Well, they can't have it if it is yours. Right?"

"No, it is safe for now, but I've heard stories of people being shoved out of their homes. My uncle came from Italy in 1962 and bought all this land. You see that clearing over there? About a half mile to the left of that is a waterfall. Just past that is where your parents are going to build a house."

He pointed toward the open space behind the orchard. "That's for you and Devan."

"Uncle Russo, you mean Jeane," Kale corrected him.

"*No*, I mean Devan. One day," he said and winked.

I know the whole family is anti-Jeane but they'll just have to live with it like I do. "Okay, old man, you need to stop putting whiskey in your coffee this early in the day. Devan and I are just friends; that's how it has to be."

"You keep saying that, but everyone can see the truth. Come on, friends do *not* look at each other the way you two do. And you still do it after all these years. Hell, I saw you do it five minutes ago. You won't stay with that wretched Jeane woman for much longer. Mark my words, a storm is brewing — and it's going to get a lot more than windy." He set his cup down.

"Uncle Russo!"

"That's all I'm allowed to say." Russo folded his arms.

"Says who?" Kale demanded.

"Your aunt."

Noelani came up to the house. "Boy doesn't believe me, Lani."

"About what?" she asked, while grabbing coffee cups from the cupboard.

"The storm!" Russo shouted into the kitchen.

"Oh, shush. Devan's on my heels," she hissed at him. Not a moment later, Devan entered the house.

"Can I have that cup of coffee you were talking about?" Devan asked, closing the door behind her.

"Yes, dear. Cream or sugar?" Noelani asked, grabbing both.

"Just cream. Thank you."

"Hey, why don't you guys go check out the waterfall? We can watch the kids," Russo said and winked at Kale.

Kale shook his head in disbelief. He knew his aunt and uncle were just trying to get them alone together.

"Hey, sorry about that," Kale said as they were walking through the high grass.

"Did I miss something?"

"Russo and Lani watching the kids — they just wanted us to be alone, in hopes that—"

"Oh."

She decided to speed up so that she was leading him and the discussion wouldn't continue. He jogged after her. She turned back and saw him catching up, so she took off in a full sprint, and he started laughing.

She stopped when she got to the waterfall.

"What was that for?" he asked, sitting down and trying to catch a breath.

"To get your heart pumping fast," she replied with a giggle.

It always does that around you, he thought and looked over at her. Her black hair was falling out of a bun and her face was flushed from running, making her blue eyes pop. *She's beautiful.*

She lay down and started moving her arms and legs.

"What are you doing?"

"Making a grass angel. Come on, make one with me," she said and grabbed his arm, pulling him down to her level.

They stopped and stared at the clouds going by for a while before Devan spoke up. "Well, since you're coming back home, what're you going to be doing?"

"I'm still going to be drafting for Alistar, and Pete asked if I wanted to help out with football."

"That's cool. Are you going to?" she asked as she turned her head to look at him. She couldn't help but notice how perfect his profile was.

"I haven't given him an answer yet. We're coming back toward the end of the year, so football season will be over."

"Oh, you won't be back until then?" she asked, a little disappointed, and a little relieved.

"Well, we might come back for a few days in the fall to get the house ready, but there's nothing definite right now."

"You know, Kale, we'll help you get things ready ... well at least *I'll* help you. Now that you guys are moving back, I guess Justin will be spending even less time at home. I'm not used to having him around much anyway, so I guess it won't matter," she said with a sigh.

"Things never got better?"

She shook her head no. "You?"

"Same old, same old."

"Shhh! Do you hear that?" she asked rolling over toward him and putting her finger on his lips.

"No."

"You can't hear the tiniest of little violins playing a sad song for us?" she asked and laughed.

"Oh, stop it!" He grabbed her finger and tickled her side. Their eyes met and he stopped, but he didn't let her go. They lay there for a few minutes, wondering how they were going to keep their feelings to themselves when they lived near each other again.

Devan sat up and looked at the water cascading over the moss-covered rocks. "This really is a beautiful place. I'd like to come back one day."

Kale sat up and snuck his arm around her. "We will," he promised.

Devan jumped up. "Race ya back!" she yelled and started running. He, of course, easily passed her. After a minute, he looked back but he didn't see her.

"Devan?" he yelled.

He saw a hand reach up out of the grass a few hundred feet behind him. "Yeah, I'm here!" he heard her shout.

He ran to where she was and saw she was sitting there holding her left foot. "What happened?"

"Um, I tripped and I think I might have sprained my ankle."

He bent down and said, "Let me see."

He felt around on her ankle. It didn't seem to be broken, but it was already swelling. "Let me help you up." She held on to his arm and hopped along as they started walking back. Without warning, he scooped her up in his arms.

"I could've made it back," she said looking into his big green eyes.

"We have another mile to walk. I want to make it back before it gets dark," he said and laughed.

She really didn't mind being carried in his big strong arms, not in the least.

"Russo, look what's coming up the hill," Noelani said and pointed. "Looks like our plan worked."

Kale brought Devan into the house and sat her down on the couch. "Can I get some ice?" he asked.

"What happened?" Russo asked, opening up the freezer door.

"I tripped," Devan said, embarrassed.

"Well, I thought it worked," Noelani whispered to Russo.

Noelani and Russo offered to keep the kids for the night so it would be easier for Kale to take Devan to the hospital. When they got there, Devan was taken back for an X-ray. They waited for the results for about two hours. She was in a lot of pain, so the nurse gave her some Ibuprofen for the swelling and hydrocodone for the pain.

By the time the doctor came in, Devan was higher than a kite. Kale tried his hardest not to laugh at her while listening to the ER doctor's instructions. After that, he wheeled her out to the van and put her gently on the second row of seats where she could lie down.

It was a 20-minute drive back to the hotel, and she slept the whole time. She woke up long enough to walk to the elevator with Kale's assistance. She leaned against the wall and stared at him, eyes glossed over, as they rode up to their floor.

Kale kept asking if she was okay. She would nod her head and smile at him. When they got to the room, he helped her to the bed and asked if he could get her anything. She asked that he brew some of the coffee sitting on the microwave stand. When he brought her a cup, she drank the whole thing and sobered up a bit.

Kale was sitting on the chair next to the bed trying to find something that interested them both on TV when she looked over at him, studying all of his features. His amazing dark tousled curls rested on his broad shoulders. *I want those strong arms wrapped around me. I need his hands running all over my body.* She sighed heavily, getting his attention.

He felt her eyes looking right through him to his soul.

She didn't look away. *His skin looks so bronze and warm; it's just begging to be touched. The olive tank top he's wearing really brings out the green in his eyes.*

"You all right?" he asked.

She still didn't drop her stare. She was mesmerized by his full lips and wanted to devour them. "I'm kind of hot. I think I'll change."

She got up and opened a drawer on the mahogany Yorkshire dresser. She pulled out a fawn chemise slip and slid out of her pants. She glanced over at him; he wasn't paying her the slightest bit of attention.

She continued undressing. She pulled her shirt off and threw it on the table next to him. His head turned her way, and she was still staring at him. He swallowed hard as he saw her unfasten her bra, letting it drop to the floor. She stepped into the slip and pulled it up.

As she walked over to the bed, he sat up straight and tried desperately to keep his eyes on the television. She fluffed up the pillows and lay down, then let out another long sigh.

He daringly looked over at her and asked, "Can I get you something?"

She looked at him with come hither eyes. He inhaled deeply. *What's happening? We just had a discussion — a painful discussion — about doing whatever it takes to just be friends.* He bit his lip trying to prevent an erection. He was unsuccessful.

"If you don't need anything, I'm going to go ahead and leave so you can get some sleep." He stood up and walked over to the door.

"No! Don't leave," she pleaded.

"Monty, you need to rest."

He went over the bed and bent down to kiss her forehead. She grabbed the front of his shirt. "I said, *don't* leave."

He could see the hunger in her eyes and didn't know if he had the strength to deny her. *Her plump lips just demand to be kissed. No, this behavior is* not *acceptable.*

"Devan," his voice was stern and hard, but she didn't loosen her grip on his shirt. His eyes shot daggers at her, and he demanded "Let me go!"

"I'll *never* let you go!" With her free hand she grabbed the back of his head and pulled his lips down to hers. Before he knew what was happening, his shirt was on the floor, her hands were in his hair and their tongues were intertwined.

She pulled him on top of her and reached for his belt buckle. He moved to give her room to complete the maneuver. She pushed him off her and onto his back, then unfastened the belt and pulled it off.

Instead of setting it to the side, she looped it around his wrists and jerked it tight. She then lifted his hands above his head and looped the belt over the headboard, pulling it even tighter.

When he was rendered completely helpless, Devan had full control. She yanked his shorts and boxers off, leaving him completely naked and subject to her deepest desires. She climbed on top of him, and he groaned. She slowly pulled off her slip, revealing her perfectly shaped breasts.

He was trying not to breathe so heavily, but he couldn't help it. She looked him dead in the eyes and licked her lips very slowly.

"Do you have any idea what you do to me?" he asked.

A wicked grin spread across her face and she answered him with her own question. "Do you have any idea what I'm about to do to you?"

Just then, the hotel door flew open, and Justin was standing in the doorway...

To be continued...

About the Author

Mindy Ford grew up in the suburbs of Summit County in Ohio where she started writing at a young age. Aloha Paradise is her first published book. She resides in Northwest Ohio where her imagination fuels her life.

Find the author online:

https://www.facebook.com/Mindy-Ford-338479953156955

https://www.instagram.com/author_mf13/

https://twitter.com/mingysue

Contact the author: Mindyford.writer@gmail.com

www.ingramcontent.com/pod-product-compliance
Lightning Source LLC
Chambersburg PA
CBHW020402120726
47904CB00002B/670